So that was Emily Robb

The problem of how to meet her was solved. He watched until she reached her car—an old Tempo, 1990, maybe—then he shut the door. It didn't do anything to shut out her indignation.

People reacted differently to a blank slate. Some rushed to please, some got angry, some got scared. He'd been up all night and had reached the point of not fully trusting his impressions, but it was clear her efforts to please weren't for his benefit. Daniel's, he supposed. Or maybe the community's.

Hard to know what to think about her. Flustered, emotional, a little on the schoolmarmish side. At least, that was what she presented. For some reason he kind of liked her. But that didn't have to be a complication.

He yawned and rubbed sandpapery eyes. His files were downloaded, passwords set up, contacts alerted. Time for coffee and a shower. Then he'd go exploring.

Caron Todd has created evocative and compelling characters who could be your over-the-fence neighbors. You'll want to get to know them.

Dear Reader,

Emily Moore and her mother, Julia, walked unplanned into *The House on Creek Road* (Harlequin Superromance #1159) as Elizabeth Robb's kind and accommodating cousin and uncommunicative aunt. Before Liz's story was finished I knew I wanted the two women to have one of their own, one that would give Emily an adventure far from her safe and cozy Three Creeks home.

That happens soon after Matthew Rutherford comes to town. Trying to figure out who he really is takes Emily to the wild and isolated country north of the fifty-third parallel. The trip tests her assumptions about herself and her family. Before she goes home she has a choice to make. With all she's learned, will it be different from the choices she's made before?

A number of people were kind enough to help with research. Jim Parres, who's writing a book about his grandfather and the gold mine at Snow Lake, and freelance writer Marc Jackson took time to give detailed answers to my questions about Manitoba gold. My father, Jim Shilliday, a former pilot and close observer of nature, answered a stream of e-mails about floatplanes and rural life. I've changed some facts to suit the needs of the story, but my thanks to all of them for helping bring it authenticity. (By the way, there really is a little place at Overflowing River where you can get the best butter tarts ever!) Thanks also to Laura Shin for the questions and comments that made the story stronger.

Hearing from readers is always a pleasure. I can be reached at ctodd@prairie.ca or c/o Harlequin Enterprises, 225 Duncan Mill Road, Don Mills, Ontario M3B 3K9, Canada.

Caron Todd

THE WINTER ROAD
Caron Todd

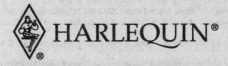

TORONTO • NEW YORK • LONDON
AMSTERDAM • PARIS • SYDNEY • HAMBURG
STOCKHOLM • ATHENS • TOKYO • MILAN • MADRID
PRAGUE • WARSAW • BUDAPEST • AUCKLAND

ISBN 0-373-71304-5

THE WINTER ROAD

Copyright © 2005 by Caron Hart.

This edition published by arrangement with Harlequin Books S.A.

® and TM are trademarks of the publisher. Trademarks indicated with
® are registered in the United States Patent and Trademark Office, the
Canadian Trade Marks Office and in other countries.

www.eHarlequin.com

Printed in U.S.A.

Books by Caron Todd

To my parents, whose appreciation of books and respect
for language—its poetry and its rules—helped
me find this very enjoyable path.

CHAPTER ONE

THE MORE Emily thought about Daniel missing the wedding, the more concerned she became. Nearly everyone from in and around Three Creeks had gone, whether or not they were formally invited, and he had certainly been invited.

She sank her hands to the bottom of the sink, feeling under the bubbles for any last breakfast dishes, then pulled the plug, wrung out the dishcloth and spread it over the rim of the sink to dry.

"Mom? I'm going to run into town to check on Daniel."

Julia sat at the kitchen table behind a stack of cookbooks, shoulders bent, graying hair twisted into a tidy roll just above her neck. She pressed one finger under the line she'd been reading and looked up, not quite at Emily, but beside her. "On Daniel?"

"In case he's fallen or something."

"Not him."

Emily wasn't sure if that was an expression of confidence or disappointment. She had never been able to figure out what her mother and Daniel thought of each other. "He's immune to trouble, is he?"

Julia had already gone back to her book. She rarely cooked, but she liked reading recipes.

"I'll drop in on Grandma, too. See how she's doing after all the excitement. I won't be long."

This time her mother gave an absent nod.

As soon as Emily took her keys and purse from the hutch cupboard, the cat appeared from under the table, nearly tripping her on her way to the door. It was a stray that had adopted them that spring, establishing itself first on their driveway, then their front step and, finally, at their feet, wherever their feet happened to be. So far they hadn't given it a name. It faced a tough decision when she opened the door, but decided to stay with Julia.

Emily stepped outside. Right away, perspiration prickled on her forehead. It was a still, quiet day, the heat too much even for the squirrels and goldfinches she usually heard. There had to be a hundred trees in the yard, with millions of leaves, but not one rustled. Not until Hamish emerged from under the caragana hedge. He stretched one leg behind him, then the other, and his tail gave a token wave.

"Good morning, old man." She bent to stroke the border collie's white-streaked face. "Don't worry, in a few months it will snow. Won't it be nice to have the cold to complain about?"

She emptied stale water and drowned flies from his dish and refilled it. "There. All set. You're in charge, Hamish." His tail wagged harder.

DANIEL LIVED on the north edge of Three Creeks, a few miles from Emily and Julia's farm. His house stood on the last of five elm-lined streets that branched off the town's main road and ended one block later in a field of mixed clover. It wasn't his family's original property. That was long gone, the trees and yard bulldozed when the provincial highway first went through and the house torn down years later, when it was widened.

The Rutherfords had moved away then, scattering across the country. Daniel had spent most of his adulthood moving from place to place, first in the Army and then the RCMP. No one had expected him to come back, but one day a sign had appeared on the community bulletin board—Daniel Rutherford: Security Consultant—and there he was, home for good.

All of that had happened before Emily was born. It was one of the stories she heard whenever her relatives were in the mood for reminiscing. As far as she was concerned, Daniel had always been in Three Creeks, as much a part of her world as her grandparents and her aunts and uncles.

She pulled up outside his house, a cozy story and a half—cozy except for the security bars on the basement windows. The driveway was empty.

He didn't usually park in the garage, but she decided to check. Protecting his car's finish from the sun wasn't an issue. He'd been driving the same sky blue '77 Cutlass for as long as she'd known him and it had done all the fading it was going to do.

The doors were locked. She leaned close to the window and shielded her eyes so she could make out the shapes inside. No car and, as far as she could see, no Daniel.

"I'm surprised you're out and about today, Emily." The soft voice startled her. An older woman wearing long sleeves and a wide-brimmed straw hat had come out of the neighboring house. "Don't you need a bit of slothful time?"

"I slept until nine, Mrs. Bowen. How much more slothful could I get?"

"A hammock comes to mind. How is your dear mother this morning?"

"Craving solitude."

Mrs. Bowen gave an understanding smile. "What a lovely day it was yesterday. Perfect for a wedding. It did my heart good to see you and Liz and Susannah together again."

"Mine, too." Emily's cousins hadn't been home at the same time since high school. After fifteen years in Vancouver Liz had recently moved back, but Susannah never would. Paleontologists had to live where there were fossils to dig.

"Liz and Jack are off, are they?"

"Somewhere over the Atlantic by now."

"And you're visiting already! You won't find Daniel home. He hasn't been around for the better part of a week."

That couldn't be right. She'd spoken to him a week ago, and he hadn't mentioned a trip then. "Did he say anything to you about going out of town?"

"Not a word, but he never does. Are you worried that something may have happened to him? He's a very self-reliant man, dear."

But in his seventies, Emily thought, and gone without explanation.

"I'll be right back." Mrs. Bowen disappeared into her house and returned a few minutes later, flushed from hurrying. "He leaves a spare key with me. I suppose we could take a peek inside."

After ringing the bell twice, then knocking, she unlocked Daniel's side door and opened it a few inches. Hot, stuffy air reached Emily's nose.

"Hello? Daniel?" It was a tentative call. Mrs. Bowen hardly raised her voice, as if even that would be an intrusion. They went up the steps from the landing into the kitchen.

"Oh, his plants! Look at them!" Mrs. Bowen pushed a half-full coffee mug out of the way and began carrying drooping begonias, philodendrons and violets to the sink. "What was he thinking, leaving them like this?"

Now Emily was even more worried. She quickly checked the main floor and the two small bedrooms under the eaves. Upstairs and down, dust had settled on surfaces, but there was no sign of Daniel and nothing to suggest he had run into any kind of problem.

"Some milk and fruit in the fridge were going off, and there was moldy bread in the box," Mrs. Bowen said when Emily returned to the kitchen. "I've got rid of those and watered the plants. You know, Daniel usually is quite responsible about them when he's away. He rigs trays of water so they can drink as much as they need. He must have been in a hurry this time."

She paused when Emily opened the basement door. "His cameras and so on are down there, all that police paraphernalia of his."

"I won't touch anything." She flicked on the light. A staircase with narrow steps and steep risers came into view. It was hardly better than a ladder. If Daniel had fallen anywhere, this would be the most likely place, but there was no huddled shape at the foot of the stairs. She sidestepped down, keeping one hand on the rail and the other on the wall.

Rows of metal shelves filled the room. They were stacked with sealed cardboard boxes, coiled wires and stainless steel equipment Emily didn't recognize. All she knew was it helped ranchers guard against poachers and small businesses ward off the occasional thief. She tried a door in the middle of one wall. It was locked.

Mrs. Bowen's voice came from the head of the stairs. "That must be the furnace room. At least that's where my furnace and water heater are, but they're not walled off like that."

"Why would he lock the furnace room door?" Emily felt over the top of the frame for a key. It didn't seem likely that an ex-Mountie who ran a security business would stash a key so close to the lock it opened, and of course, he hadn't. She rattled the knob. "Daniel?"

"He's not in there. I really think he's gone off the way he does sometimes. You worry too much about people, dear."

Emily started back upstairs. She didn't think she worried too much. Just a sensible amount, about sensible things…her grandmother's health and her mother's absent-mindedness. And now Daniel's unexplained absence.

The telephone sat on a recessed ledge near the

kitchen table. She opened the yellow pages and made a series of calls. The RCMP in Pine Point told her a '77 Cutlass hadn't been involved in any accidents. Daniel hadn't been admitted to the local hospital, or any of the hospitals in Winnipeg.

"I don't know what else you can do, Emily."

"There's still the garden to check."

They went out together, Mrs. Bowen unlocking the gate and recounting all the times her neighbor had disappeared for a day or two, or even a week, and returned without explanation. If you didn't have ties at home, why not travel whenever the urge hit you?

She broke off when they rounded the corner.

The soil was cracked and gray. Lettuce leaves wilted, tissue-paper dry against the ground. Tomato plants drooped despite the wire frames around them. Green beans shriveled on the stem. Muttering that it was too late now, and what was wrong with her not to have thought of it before, Mrs. Bowen hurried to the back of the house and began uncoiling a green hose from a metal bracket.

Daniel loved his garden. Digging in it, choosing seeds, watching daffodils come up in May and roses open in June, harvesting vegetables at exactly the right moment. If that wasn't a tie, Emily didn't know what was.

EMILY PARKED OUTSIDE the general store and post office. It was a Saturday morning, so the store was full of people getting groceries, picking up mail and helping themselves to fifty-cent cups of coffee at the lunch counter. Everyone stopped to comment on Liz and Jack's wedding and Emily began to wonder if she would ever reach Mrs. Marsh, who worked slowly and calmly, her ashtray and cigarette at her side. She belonged to the same generation as Mrs. Bowen, but seemed to want to disprove it. Her hair, a deep rust-red, was cut short, with bangs brushed flat against her forehead and a sculpted point of gelled hair in front of each ear.

When Emily finally had her turn at the counter, buying a bunch of bananas to be polite, Mrs. Marsh said, "Didn't think you'd be out this morning. No rest for the wicked, eh?"

"This from a woman who works seven days a week."

"Got me there."

"I wanted to ask you about Daniel Rutherford's mail—"

"You can ask, but I can't answer."

Emily paused, then tried again. "He seems to be away—at least he wasn't at the wedding yesterday and he isn't home right now. I wondered if he made arrangements with you to hold his mail or forward it somewhere."

Mrs. Marsh picked up her cigarette. She took a deep, appreciative drag, then inhaled the surrounding smoke for good measure. Smoking wasn't allowed in enclosed public places anymore—a sign staring right at them said so—but no one liked to mention that to the postmistress. "I'm not supposed to discuss customers' mail. Can't walk without banging into a rule these days." She went to the post office section of the counter. "Couple of things came for you and your mom yesterday. The hydro bill and another one of those book catalogs."

Emily put the mail in the bag with the bananas. "Is there anything the rules will let you tell me?"

"I guess you heard John Ramsey's coming to visit."

"No, I didn't." She considered leaving it at that, but ended up asking, "When is he expected?"

"Don't know exactly. In a couple of weeks. Going to take a little trip, like you did last time?"

"That was an in-service for people working in school libraries."

"Can't hope for that now, eh? Not in the summer."

Emily smiled. "I don't want to avoid John. I'll be glad to see him."

She thanked Mrs. Marsh for the mail and the bananas and went out into the hot sunlight, glad to get the door between her and the curiosity she felt coming from her neighbors. It wasn't a lie. After all this time she would be glad to see John, if they happened to run into each other.

Halfway down the road was the Legion Hall. Inside, five of Daniel's friends sat at a table with a pitcher of Guinness in front of them and mugs at varying degrees of emptiness in hand. They waved her over, mentioned how good the food had been at the wedding and told her how pretty she'd looked in her bridesmaid's dress. None of them had any idea where Daniel had gone.

"He does what he wants, Emily. Things like weddings and gardens don't stop him."

"Even if it's Liz's wedding?"

"Even if it's his own."

They all laughed at that. Five tolerant smiles came her way, along with a pat on the arm that felt more like a dismissive pat on an anxious child's head.

WHERE THE CREEK ROAD CURVED and narrowed, becoming Robbs' Road, Emily slowed the car. Manitoba maples and purple clover filled the ditches and hidden by trees on her right, one of the three creeks flowed. The road wasn't much of a barrier between woodland and water. Deer and rabbits went across to drink; sometimes at night she saw foxes and raccoons. She often lurched the last mile home, starting and stopping, weaving around toads and garter snakes.

Yesterday had been tough on them, with all the cars crunching along from town for the reception. Most wedding dinners were held in the church basement or at the hotel in Pine Point, but Liz had wanted to celebrate at their grandmother's place. It was the house their great-great-grandparents had built, where she and Jack had met, and where she had finally made peace with the ghosts of her first, short marriage.

When they came back in the fall, Jack would move in with Liz and Eleanor. They had already started working on the house, replacing windows, reshingling the roof and repainting inside and out. With so much work taken off her hands and someone to talk to whenever she wanted company, Eleanor had begun to look healthier and more rested.

It had been a hectic week, though, and today her fatigue was apparent. Emily found her at the kitchen table, shelling peas. The dogs, Bella and Dora, watched intently, as if every hard green kernel hitting the bowl was a slice of roast beef.

"On your own today?" Emily took a handful of pods and began to snap them open. The rest of the family had gone to the lake, a half-hour's drive away.

"A cool kitchen sounded better to me than a hot beach."

"To Mom, too."

"And you?"

"I don't mind a chance to catch my breath." Since the beginning of June she'd been going full tilt, helping with wedding plans at home, Field Day and Awards Day at school and doing inventory for the library. She'd closed it the previous week, around the time dress fittings and dainty making had mutated from cousinly togetherness to near panic.

She reached for more pea pods and began to tell her grandmother about her concern for Daniel.

"There couldn't have been anyone missing," Eleanor said at first. "The church was bursting." She looked out the window as if trying to visualize the crowd of guests. "Come to think of it, I didn't speak to Daniel at all yesterday. He must have been here. He left a gift."

Emily had seen the package on the gift table, too. Even without his signature on the card she would have recognized the sometimes ornate, always measured letters that reminded her of his age when nothing else did. "Maybe someone dropped it off for him."

"Wouldn't that suggest he made plans to be away?"

"I suppose it would. Am I fussing?"

"You?"

Emily laughed. "That's the thing about worrying. It's hard to know when it's reasonable."

"I do understand. What woman wouldn't? Learned or instinct, we tend to take care of people. School's out, my dear. We've finally got Elizabeth and Jack married and on their way. Isn't it time to relax and enjoy the summer?"

"Mrs. Bowen mentioned a hammock."

"What a good idea. Get yourself a hammock and a pile of books and don't budge for a month. Who knows, maybe your mother will notice the dust and take care of it herself!"

Emily couldn't help smiling at the thought of her mother minding dust that settled anywhere but on her books.

"Don't forget," Eleanor went on, "tea tomorrow afternoon." Because of the reception and a barbecue planned for later in the week the family wasn't getting together for the usual Sunday dinner.

"I'm looking forward to it."

"It's only you and your mother, and Susannah and Edith and me. I've already told Julia that, but remind her, won't you, Emily?"

"I don't think she'll come, Grandma."

"No, I don't suppose she will."

THE COOKBOOKS WERE put away. Julia sat at the kitchen table, this time bent over one of her book catalogs. Emily could see she wasn't reading it. Her neck and shoulders looked tight and her arms were pressed to her sides, elbows digging in.

"You said you wouldn't be long."

"I'm sorry, Mom." She put the bananas in the fruit basket, the hydro bill on the hutch and the new catalog on the table.

Her mother ignored it. "If you don't mean 'not long' you shouldn't say 'not long.'"

"I meant it at the time. Did you worry?"

"I didn't know I'd have to make lunch. I waited."

Emily went to the fridge and took out jars of mayonnaise, mustard and pickles, a tomato and their share of the leftover wedding ham.

"Then you still didn't come. So I had a sandwich."

"You did?" She put everything but the ham back. "You're ahead of the game. I haven't eaten yet."

"I don't know why you call it a game."

"Come on, Mom. You do so. It's an expression."

"An odd one."

Emily cut a slice of ham, then leaned against the counter while she ate it. "Daniel wasn't home."

"You see?"

"I sure do. You said he didn't fall."

"And he didn't."

"Nobody knows where he is, though. Everybody says he likes to follow his inclinations, and if that means a missed wedding or a dried-up garden, so be it."

Julia looked at Emily's feet. "His garden dried up?"

That small reaction was more effective than all the reassurance from Daniel's friends. "It's strange, isn't it? And his house plants are half dead. Mrs. Bowen said that's not like him."

Julia picked up a pencil and leaned closer to her catalog, her brief interest withdrawn. Emily watched her drift further away, pencil eraser to her lip, finger following the text. Every now and then she marked a title with a star. That meant interested, but not sure. Her library was huge and always growing. Fiction and nonfiction, painstakingly organized, filled floor-to-ceiling shelves on every wall of the living room.

When her mother began circling titles—the next step toward a decision—with the air of someone who was alone in the room, Emily put away the meat and washed the knife, then went outside again. This time the cat followed.

They crossed the crisp, brown lawn and the road, went down one side of the ditch, then up the other and through a narrow band of trees to the creek.

It was low this year. If the heat continued it might dry up completely. The water still bubbled along, though, over smooth, round stones. Emily took off her sandals and waded in, the warm water ankle-deep and cool against her skin.

The cat was still with her. It trotted along the bank, pouncing at rustling sounds, then rushing to catch up. Ahead of it, a red-winged blackbird flitted from grass tip to grass tip. Emily listened to the bird's piping song and wished for a breeze to cool her head, hot under heavy hair.

"The thing is," she said to the cat, "not turning up at the wedding, without a word, is odd."

She had run into Daniel at the post office the day she'd closed the library for the summer, around the time Mrs. Bowen had said he'd left. He'd told her then that he had a speech prepared for the reception. "A few impromptu words," he'd said, and his eye had flickered in what would have been a wink if he was the kind of person who winked.

At his house she had only looked for him, not for explanations. Now she remembered the coffee cup on the counter, half full with a swirl of murky cream on top, and the sour milk and moldy bread Mrs. Bowen found. Daniel wouldn't go on an impulsive holiday leaving unwashed dishes and food to spoil.

It hurt a bit that everyone had dismissed her uneasiness about Daniel's welfare. She had seen that happen to other women—legitimate concerns waved away because they'd reached a certain age without marrying, unspoken needs and fluctuating hormones blamed for their apparent fussing. She was only thirty-two, though, and half the time her relatives treated her as if she was fifteen. Was it the same in the city, or was it only in small places like this that it took marriage to make someone real in other people's eyes?

Everyone is a pair now, except for Grandma and Mom and me. The thought had never occurred to her before. That was the trouble with weddings, with red-letter days in general. They disturbed the contented flow of things.

Tomorrow, after lunch since it was Sunday, she would ask Mrs. Bowen to let her into Daniel's house again. If she could find his address book she could contact some of his relatives. With any luck one of them would know where he'd gone.

THE AIRBUS GOT INTO Pearson International from the Bahamas at eight in the morning. At the start of business hours, he picked up a couple of white, no-wrinkle shirts, replenished his supply of batteries—laptop, cell phone and camera—and made arrangements to pick up a car that evening. By noon he was at a lunch meeting, looking out at the SkyDome and wishing there was time to see a Blue Jays game.

The subject on the minds of everyone around the table was the recent discovery of a crash site in northern Manitoba. In 1979 a bush plane had disappeared between Flin Flon and Winnipeg. The plane, a deHavilland Beaver, and the pilot, a D-Day vet and ex-cop by the name of Frank Carruthers, were both considered absolutely reliable. Carruthers had done his preflight check, studied the weather charts, filed his flight plan, then taken off and was never seen again.

Last month a group on a fly-in fishing trip had found the plane's remains tangled in some dead trees on a lakeshore. What concerned the people in this room was that its cargo—fifteen gold bars—was gone.

Fifteen bars identified by a refiner's stamp and number, each weighing a thousand ounces. It was more than the mine usually sent out at once. A series of blizzards and a bad flu season had caused the cancellation of a couple of planned flights. Somewhere out there, in the muskeg or underbrush or transformed into gleaming ankle bracelets, was nearly seven million dollars' worth of gold.

He opened the map he'd bought at the airport. Most of Manitoba's population was concentrated in a band along the south of the province. The central and northern areas looked almost empty. Lakes, rivers, forests, bogs, tundra. It was easy to see how even something as large as a plane could go unfound for so long.

"Same arrangement as usual," said the woman at the head of the table. "Expenses and ten percent of what you recover."

"My partner is already in place." He refolded the map, leaving it open to show the area northwest of Winnipeg. "We'll do what we can."

CHAPTER TWO

AFTER THE SUN SET, he could hardly stay awake. Driving alone in the dark down a nearly straight, nearly abandoned highway felt almost like crawling into bed. The dotted yellow line disappearing under the car every microsecond didn't help at all.

He turned off the air conditioner and rolled the windows down. Fresh air felt better, even warm, humid fresh air. It smelled like hay. Hay made him think of farmers. Farmers made him think of farmers' daughters. That took him right back to where he had started the day.

Not happy.

He should be happy. The information he needed was waiting for him. The dark corners and unanswered questions connected with the job didn't bother him. Not even the remote chance of success bothered him. Long odds made things interesting; the potential payoff made them worthwhile. His problem was with the personal aspects of what he had agreed to do. If he was going to start getting fastidious about things like that he'd have to look for a new line of work.

The headlights picked out a sign on the side of the highway. Three Creeks.

Getting to his destination always gave him a shot of adrenaline. He felt alert again. The clock on the dash said one-twenty.

He slowed the car and turned onto the gravel road.

THE MORNING BEGAN with an argument over Eleanor's invitation to tea. Julia didn't want to go, not even if it was just the five women, not even if her mother particularly wanted her to be there.

"All they do is sit around and talk." She poured herself a glass of juice, took a piece of toast and jam from the plate in the middle of the table and opened a cookbook.

"It won't be long, Mom. An hour."

"You go. I'll make dinner."

"You will?" Those words never failed to make Emily's neck muscles tighten. The tension wasn't reasonable. From time to time she came home from work to find dinner simmering or roasting, the table set, the house standing. "Something cold would be fine."

Julia didn't answer. One minute they were having a conversation and the next, they weren't. Drawbridge up, moat flooded. Emily was never sure when the barrier was erected, before her mother heard or before she was expected to respond to an unwelcome idea. It couldn't be involuntary, not all the time.

"Did you know John's coming for a visit?"

The drawbridge eased open. "Who?"

"John Ramsey."

Julia turned a whole sheaf of pages and landed in the pasta section. "Never liked him much."

"I didn't know that."

"Pasta primavera. I have peas. I have tomatoes."

Emily waited, wondering if her mother would say more about John. They had dated all through grade eleven and twelve. She'd never expressed an opinion about him then.

"Why didn't you like him, Mom?"

"Who?"

"John Ramsey."

Julia went to the cupboard. "It should be fettuccine. We never have fettuccine."

"Mom?"

"You need those wider noodles to hold the sauce."

It didn't matter if her mother hadn't liked John, or why. He'd moved to the city and Emily had stayed home. If he'd wanted to take over his parents' farm they'd probably be married now.

Julia was on her knees, buried up to her waist in the cupboard. Emily could hear containers being moved back and forth. Boxes began to appear on the floor.

"When I go to town after lunch I'll get fettuccine."

"There's no need to go to town."

"I'm going anyway, back to Daniel's."

"Get some of that bread, then, the square white bread." Julia didn't like the taste or texture, but she liked the way the sides lined up straight for sandwiches.

While her mother put the boxes back in the cupboard, Emily began to tackle the housework that had piled up during the week. As she was finishing the laundry and about to start making lunch, her cousin Martin called.

"Grandma told me you were asking about Daniel. You can stop worrying."

"He's back?"

"Looks like it. I went through town late last night, saw the light on over his door."

The uneasiness that had clung to her all of yesterday still didn't let go. "You're sure it wasn't one of his neighbors?"

"I'm sure. His Christmas lights were on, too."

The thought of those bright colors sparkling through a hot July night made Emily smile. A couple of winters ago Daniel had decided he'd had his fill of climbing ladders. Now he left the lights attached to the eaves all year.

"Have you heard the other news?" Martin asked.

"News? No." She assumed he meant local news, family news. "What happened?"

"You're seeing Mom and Sue later, right? I'll let them tell you."

"Martin—"

But he had already hung up.

AN ALMOST NEW silver-gray Accord with Ontario plates sat in Daniel's driveway. He wouldn't have taken off without telling anyone just to buy a car, would he?

Emily rang the side door bell. She had raised her hand to ring a second time when the door opened. A stranger stood in front of her.

"Yes?"

He was tall, with a trim, hard build. In spite of the summer heat, he wore suit trousers and a dress shirt that looked formal even with the sleeves rolled up and the collar unbuttoned. He needed a shave, and he looked as if he'd missed at least three nights' sleep. It gave him a grainy, world-weary appearance that made her heart beat a little faster.

She stood straighter, her grade one teacher's daily admonition popping into her mind from wherever it had stayed dormant all these years. Shoulders back, chest out, tummy in. "I was hoping to see Daniel. Is he home?"

"I can give him a message."

It wasn't a very informative answer. The man didn't even smile. Emily felt as welcome as a door-to-door canvasser. "I'd like to talk to him myself. Is he here?"

Dark-gray eyes looked back at her. Did he really need to think it over? Daniel was either here or he wasn't. Her concern flooded back. "Has something happened to him?"

"He's been called away."

"He's all right, though?"

"He's fine."

Emily didn't want to play tug-of-war with the man over one simple piece of information. If his clothes weren't enough of a clue, his tone made it clear he was from the city. No one used to small-town life would sound so distant when company called, not even when that company dropped in without notice.

She used the firm expression that usually got children's attention when they were misbehaving and waited expectantly. Finally he added, "Daniel asked me to look after the place while he's gone. He should be back in about a week if you want to try again."

The door began to close.

She couldn't believe it. He'd been so cool through

the whole exchange, no more than polite. Not even polite. Stiff and distant and unhelpful, all with a sort of repressed energy that she found a little unnerving. "If you're talking to him, would you tell him I came by? Emily Moore—"

The door, half-shut, opened again. "Otherwise known as Robb?"

For a moment his eyes had some life to them. Why did he care if she was a Robb? "According to people around here." She smiled tentatively. "Not on any legal documents."

"My uncle mentioned you. I'm Matthew Rutherford."

A nephew! The name didn't ring a bell.

He leaned against the doorjamb. Maybe he was feeling more relaxed now that they were introduced. But if he was more relaxed, why was she still standing outside?

Daniel would be disappointed if his nephew didn't get a proper welcome. "I hope you'll enjoy your stay in Three Creeks. You've come a long way to watch the house. Not many nephews would be so generous!"

"I suppose it depends on the uncle."

"That's true. I'd do just about anything for Daniel, and we're not even related."

Her comment was met with a blank stare.

Emily sighed. She tried to catch it before it was out, but she was too late. "The last time I talked to him he was expecting to go to my cousin's wedding this past Friday. He must have changed his mind suddenly. Did he go to Ontario?"

"He didn't mention a wedding."

Another non-answer. Daniel wouldn't mind her knowing where he'd gone. She tried a subject the nephew might find less personal. "Have you met your neighbors yet?"

"You're the first person I've seen."

"Mrs. Bowen—" she pointed over her shoulder "—next door, is a dear friend of your uncle's. Once she knows you're here and alone—oh! Are you alone?"

As soon as she asked the question, something flashed between them. Awareness. She had forgotten about that sense of possibility. A pleasant, alert, tingly sort of feeling. It was a little rusty if it thought it should pop up now. There was no possibility with this unfriendly stranger.

"I'm here alone," he said.

"Then she's bound to be knocking at the door with salads and cookies and casseroles. She'll pack your fridge with enough food for a month."

The idea didn't seem to please him. This really was an uphill conversation. She wasn't going to give up, though. "Why don't you come for dinner at my place one evening soon?"

Again, the stare. It wasn't a complicated question. "Thanks, I'd love to," he could say. Or "Sorry, I won't have time."

He didn't choose either of those easy options. With traces of that disquieting awareness hovering, he stood in the doorway, apparently evaluating the invitation. She could picture him at the table, slowly and silently chewing and swallowing with that same look in his eyes. And she could picture herself getting very annoyed if he did.

"Daniel won't want you to sit and look at the walls while you're here. Now and then you'll need to get out of this boiling hot house and have a proper home-cooked meal."

The watchfulness became mild interest. His head tilted to one side. "Do you think a home-cooked meal is beyond me?"

Was he being curious or challenging? "Well, no...but there's nothing like a home-cooked meal eaten in the shade of a big old maple tree."

"That sounds appealing."

The maple tree had clinched it. She should have known food wouldn't be a draw. As far as she could see he didn't have an ounce of body fat anywhere.

"Good." She thought of her mother, still recovering from the wedding crowd. How long should she wait? He was only here for a week—it wasn't meant to be a farewell dinner. "Come tomorrow? Around six?"

His expression was less stern now. Was he thawing? Was it because she was about to leave?

She smiled, and hoped it didn't look as wooden as it felt. One dinner, and her duty to Daniel would be done.

SO THAT WAS Emily Robb. The problem of how to meet her was solved. He watched until she reached her car— an old Tempo, 1990, maybe—then he shut the door. It didn't do anything to shut out her indignation.

People reacted differently to a blank slate. Some rushed to please, some got angry, some scared. He'd been up all night and had reached the point of not fully trusting his impressions but it was clear her efforts to please weren't for his benefit. Daniel's, he supposed. Or maybe the community's.

He went up to the kitchen, ran the tap until the water was cold and filled a glass. From the window over the sink he could see the street. Her car was gone.

Hard to know what to think about her. Flustered, emotional, a little on the schoolmarmish side. At least that was what she presented. And why not? That's what she was. A small-town, high-school-educated teaching assistant. Flustered schoolmarms usually got his back up. Not this one. For some reason, he kind of liked her.

It didn't have to be a complication.

He yawned and rubbed sandpapery eyes. His files were downloaded, passwords set up, contacts alerted. Time for coffee and a shower. Then he'd go exploring.

BELLA AND Dora took the trouble to leave the shade of the lilac bushes as Emily's car approached, and three figures on the veranda waved. Aunt Edith and Susannah had already arrived.

As soon as Emily stepped onto the porch her grandmother handed her a cup of tea. "No luck with your mother?"

"Sorry, Grandma. I guess she needs a little more time to herself. She's fine, though. Reading recipes and ordering books, as usual."

"Just as if Susannah and Alex and Winston and Lucy weren't visiting," Edith said, smiling over her tea.

Eleanor frowned. "Really, Edith."

"I'm not criticizing her. I'm only saying what she's doing. That's allowed, isn't it?"

Susannah said, "Aunt Julia and I had a good visit at the reception." She looked content in a Muskoka chair, her long dark hair pulled back in its usual French braid, her feet up, and one hand resting on her very noticeable stomach. She and her husband Alex were expecting their first child in September.

"You've grown over the past couple of days, Sue."

"Must be all the somersaults. He's flinging himself every which way." She had told Emily they were sure the baby was a boy. Something about heart-rate and needles swinging over pulse points and deep-down instinct. They weren't acting like scientists at all.

"If only Liz hadn't left for her honeymoon yet," Aunt Edith said to Eleanor. "Wouldn't it be lovely to have the three girls here with us?"

"We did, all week—"

"Barely long enough to tease." Edith helped herself to a cookie. "You won't believe what happened yesterday, Emily. In broad daylight. Here, in Three Creeks."

This must be the news Martin had promised.

It seemed Eleanor had already heard. "The first thing Jack did when he moved into the Ramsey place was install better locks. He advised me to do the same." She looked at Edith pointedly. "And to use them."

"Someone broke into your house, Aunt Edith?"

"Well, not exactly broke—"

"The doors weren't locked," Susannah explained.

"Someone went in without our permission, though.

Corporal Reed says that's still called break and enter."
Edith was becoming more animated with every word.

"When we got back from the lake yesterday evening—oh, and it was a lovely day, Emily, you should have come—the door was open, the house was full of flies and bees, the cat—who knows perfectly well she's not allowed in—was comfortable as can be on the sofa and refusing to budge, and everything in your uncle's desk, all his bills and receipts and bank statements, were pulled out of place."

"Aunt Edith!"

"Pulled out of place," she repeated with satisfaction.

"They didn't take anything," Susannah added. "Dad thought they must have been looking for credit card receipts or checks they could use."

"Such nasty people. They were long gone by the time we got home. A pity, with Will and Alex ready to take them on. They've gone to town to buy dead bolts."

Emily looked at her grandmother. "I thought we'd be able to move into the long, lazy part of summer now that the wedding's over. When do you suppose that will happen?"

Susannah stretched. "Right now. Every moment from now until the first contraction is going to be peaceful."

"And not a single moment afterward, my girl," Edith said. "Never again."

A look of irritation crossed Susannah's face. Emily decided it was a good time to jump in with her news. She rarely heard anything first, so she tried to draw it out.

"A stranger has come to town."

Three curious faces turned her way.

"A handsome stranger?" Susannah asked, in a Twenty Questions voice.

"I suppose you could say handsome."

"We are talking about a handsome man?"

"Definitely a man." No need to think about that. In spite of his overall coldness, Matthew Rutherford had radiated more masculine energy than Emily had ever experienced from a single source. "Just standing in the doorway doing nothing he made Daniel's house feel smaller."

Three sets of eyebrows twitched.

"You know how men can be," Emily said quickly. "So…" Her voice trailed off.

"Yes, indeed," Edith said.

"But what was this handsome, virile stranger doing in Daniel's house?" Susannah asked.

Emily explained who he was, concluding that he had agreed to come to dinner the next day. Eleanor and Edith went back and forth listing Rutherfords and birth dates and agreed they didn't know a Matthew.

Susannah held out her cup for more tea. "Tell me, Em, what was that inflection I heard in your voice just now?"

"I heard it, too," Aunt Edith said. "Is he anything like his uncle? I think I remember Daniel being a very attractive man when he was younger."

"He still is," Eleanor protested.

"You can stop matchmaking, all of you. This nephew is only here for a week. Anyway, he hardly spoke to me. He seems used to being in charge, not answering to anyone. He sort of guards information." That was exactly what he did. As if it was his own personal treasure. "I couldn't even find out where Daniel went, or why. Whenever I asked him a direct question he ignored me!"

"I'll ask him. He can't ignore a woman who's about to give birth."

"I'm not so sure about that."

"Then I'll ask him," Eleanor said. "He can't ignore an octogenarian. Can he?"

"Wait until you meet him, Grandma. Then you'll see."

Edith passed around the cookie plate. "He doesn't sound like a very nice man. Of course, the Rutherfords were always like that. Standoffish."

"It's more that they're slow to warm to a person," Eleanor said. "They're good in a pinch, though."

That was a perfect description of Daniel. Emily wasn't sure it applied to the nephew, not with that analytical look in his eye. By the time he'd finished evaluating the pros and cons of getting involved the pinch would be over.

The conversation turned to the problem of feeding a rather large man when temperatures were so high. Now that she had promised a proper home-cooked meal, Emily would have to provide something more impressive than the sandwiches she and her mother usually ate on hot summer evenings. When she left her grandmother's, she had a jar of pickled mixed vegetables in one hand, a bag of frozen potato scones in the other and a promise of a green bean salad from her aunt.

"And do lock your door whenever you leave the house," Aunt Edith said. "With people driving so fast these days we're not as far from the city as we used to be. Who knows how many troublemakers are around?"

CHAPTER THREE

EMILY HAD ALWAYS LOCKED the door at night, so talk of troublemakers and break-ins didn't disturb her sleep. The thought of Matthew Rutherford did, though. It was the suit, she decided, while getting dressed the next morning. Who wore a suit to drive all the way from Ontario?

It was the attitude that went with the suit, too. Leaving her standing on the step while he looked her up and down appraisingly—as if she was the stranger! If she'd thought of it earlier she would have invited her whole family for dinner. Let him appraise them. See how he liked being appraised right back by a room full of Robb men.

She took an empty ice cream pail from the pantry and went outside to pick berries for dessert. She had just the thing in mind, something she'd seen once in a magazine—five or six layers of meringue with whipped cream in between and fresh fruit on top. Simple, but special.

Hamish and the cat followed her along the driveway. The dog stopped once, head raised, looking into the woods across the road. A few years ago he would have bounded after whatever he sensed there, but now he turned and continued down the path to the garden. As soon as they reached soil he stretched out, flattening himself against the cool dirt.

The cat stayed close to Emily. When she stood still to pick a few berries it sat down, and when she moved more than a few steps it jumped up and trotted after her.

"You do know you're not behaving like a cat," she told it. "Cats don't follow people. Cats play hard to get. Maybe we should call you Rover."

It stared, nose twitching.

"You don't like Rover? I don't blame you. It's not respectful. I apologize."

Its gaze intensified.

"All right, then, if you want to talk, tell me what you think about this nephew Daniel never mentioned. Am I being harsh? He's male and from the city, after all. How chummy can I expect him to be?"

The cat rubbed against her. She scratched behind its ear and it immediately threw itself on the ground, offering its belly for her attention, purring as soon as she touched it. When she got back to work it gave a protesting meow.

"Sorry. One day soon you can come on the porch with me. I'll read and scratch your tummy."

She hadn't been out to pick for days, except for snacking, and most of the berries hovered between perfectly ripe and overripe. When she cupped a hand under them whole clumps of dark red fruit dropped in.

Instead of concentrating on avoiding spiders and worms, her mind kept going back to Matthew Rutherford. In particular, back to the suggestion of hard muscles under a crisp white shirt. How could she be preoccupied by something so superficial? There was nothing attractive about a man who wasn't kind.

Maybe it didn't have much to do with attraction. It could be the challenge of defrosting that cold face of his. Once or twice yesterday it had shown a hint of warming. Did he ever laugh? She'd like to see that. And manners. Manners would be nice.

She looked down at the cat, rubbing against her legs again. "I'm asking too much, aren't I? A pretty tablecloth won't make him behave."

EMILY SQUEEZED PAST her pacing mother and began washing berries. "Something wrong, Mom?"

Julia gathered speed. After a few trips from the sink to the window and back, she said, "There's another early book."

"How early?"

"From Egypt."

She must mean from the time of the Pharaohs. An unexpected picture of Cleopatra curled up reading came to Emily's mind.

"*Sinuhe,* it's called. The originals are on papyrus. Fragments of papyrus."

"It'll be hard to get your hands on any of those."

Her mother didn't smile. "Only museums can have the originals. Old papyrus needs special conditions or it will crumble. It'll crumble, anyway." Doubtfully, she repeated, "*Sinuhe.* I don't even know how to pronounce it."

"We'll have to go to the library so you can look it up."

"When?"

Emily wasn't sure. She had promised to help with her grandmother's garden and housework while Liz was away. "Soon. Tomorrow, maybe, or the next day?"

"Tomorrow." Julia gave a determined nod. She'd never learned to drive. It didn't usually bother her because she rarely wanted to go anywhere. She picked up her new book catalog and left the room. Something heavy, no doubt the *Encyclopedia of Ancient and Medieval History,* thudded onto the coffee table.

The rest of the day went too quickly. Emily finished washing berries, fried chicken to serve cold, picked up beer in case the nephew liked it, defrosted a quiche she'd made during cooler weather, piped rounds of meringue onto cookie sheets, whipped the cream and prepared salads.

With an hour to go before dinner she dragged the picnic table into the shade of the maples, as promised, angling it so no matter where the nephew sat he would be able to see the perennial garden, where sweet-smelling daylilies and clumps of bright yellow heliopsis were coming into their prime.

It was an ordinary, weathered picnic table, more than weathered, really—in a few years it would be sinking into the ground, its very own compost pile—but with a bit of care it looked beautiful. Her mother's Irish linen cloth on top, a bowl of deep pink roses from the Henry Kelsey climber in the middle, sparkling glass and silverware, and the Wedgwood china her father had given her mother as a birthday present the year before he died. There was something about linen and bone china outdoors, with grass underfoot and branches overhead. No one, regardless of his personal deficiencies, could look at this table with anything but approval.

Hamish got up and gave himself a shake just before

Emily heard tires in the driveway. The nephew was early, or she was late. She smoothed her hair and pulled at her dress, fanning it against her skin, then went to greet her guest.

He stood beside his car with his back to her, looking at the house. Today he had dressed more casually, but city casual, in lightweight khakis and a shirt that looked so soft she wondered if it was made of silk. She wished she'd had time to shower.

"Matthew. You found us."

He turned, and in that moment her mental image of him, tended overnight, dissolved. The coldness that had surprised her yesterday, and that awful evaluating expression, were gone. He'd shaved, and he looked rested. Approachable.

Her body started humming about possibility again. She told it to give up. He was here for one week—less than that now—he had shown no interest in her, and he had been pleasant for all of thirty seconds since they met.

"Mrs. Bowen told me it was the house with all the trees around it," he said. "Luckily, she added it was the third house with all the trees around it."

"My aunt and uncle and my grandmother are the ones before us. You see why they call it Robbs' Road."

"Your very own road. The Robbs must be big fish."

"Little fish, but there's a big school of us."

He held out a plastic-wrapped rectangle. "This was in my uncle's freezer. Can you make use of it?"

It was a pumpkin loaf, like the ones Jack pressed on her when his crop outstripped consumer demand. Since his first harvest everyone he knew had received more loaves, pies and muffins than their appreciation for pumpkin could accommodate. "Lovely. We'll have it with tea after dinner."

Hamish hadn't barked when Matthew arrived, but he kept skulking with his low-to-the-ground herding posture, circling from Emily to the newcomer and back.

"It's all right, Hamish. Matthew is invited."

"Is he a good watchdog?"

"He doesn't get much testing. If he likes people he lets them do whatever they want." She gave the dog a reassuring pat. "He growls at the cat all the time. I hope he can do it with people. My aunt and uncle's house was broken into the other day."

Matthew's voice changed. "Anything taken?"

"Not that they could see. Things like that hardly ever happen around here."

"You're worried?"

She looked at him curiously. His manner wasn't protective, but it ranged in that direction. Short, to-the-point questions, a sudden return to yesterday's hardness. She found she didn't mind it when it wasn't aimed at her.

"Not really. There's nothing to take. No fabulous gems. No Group of Seven paintings."

"That's not what most thieves are looking for—so I hear, anyway. Your laptop or your DVD player will do nicely."

"We don't have those, either."

He smiled as if he thought she was joking. "I really have come to the backwoods, then. Next thing you'll tell me you don't have a telephone or the Internet."

"We do have a telephone."

"No Internet? Really? Are you Amish?"

Emily smiled. "Wouldn't the phone disqualify me?" It was good to see him feeling a little out of his element. Not quite so in charge. "Daniel doesn't have an Internet connection, either. If that bothers you the library in Pine Point has computers for the public to use." She started toward the house. "Why don't you come in and meet my mother?"

They walked side-by-side up the driveway. She caught a glimpse of the cat peering from behind an oak. The animals were behaving as if they had never seen a visitor. 'Never' was stretching it, but she hadn't introduced anyone to Julia for a very long time. She wondered if it would be a good idea to prepare Matthew and, if so, how much to say.

"Maybe I should mention…my mother isn't comfortable with new people. Right now I think all her sociability has been used up by my cousin's wedding. Don't worry if she ignores you. It isn't personal."

"Is there anything I can do, or not do, to help her feel more at ease?"

Emily shook her head, but said, "It helps if you don't stare at her." She touched his arm. "Thank you."

"For?"

"For asking." She led the way up the cement steps and pulled open the door to the kitchen. Her mother waited by the stove, standing almost at attention. She shifted when they came in, then stilled, her body more rigid than before.

"This is Matthew, Mom. Daniel's nephew. Matthew, my mother, Julia Moore."

Julia's eyes flashed his way, then settled on a patch of air near him. Her voice loud from nervousness, she said, "You look like Daniel."

"If that's so, I'm lucky. Uncle Daniel is considered the height of Rutherford evolution."

Julia smiled at the wall.

She likes him, Emily thought, then quickly told herself there was no need to be pleased.

It was even hotter in the kitchen than it was outside. "I'm sorry to disappear, but I really need to get out of these work clothes. Mom, could you fix us all something to drink?" She turned to Matthew. "There's lemonade or iced tea. I picked up some beer, but it might not be very cold yet."

"Lemonade sounds great."

Emily left the two of them getting in each other's way beside the fridge and nipped into the bathroom for a quick wash. There she came face-to-face with her reflection.

Oh, no. She'd greeted him like this? Stood beside his car chatting and feeling like a hostess, like this?

Not all her hair had frizzed into an auburn puffball. Sweat flattened some of it to her forehead. Her chin was smeared with icing sugar where she'd scratched a mosquito bite, and raspberry juice and flecks of meringue dotted her dress. And she had thought he wasn't polite.

At this stage, brushing would only make matters worse. She flattened the puffy sides of her hair and fastened it behind her ears with bobby pins, then scrubbed her face and neck and dabbed concealer on the bite. There. All the way from grubby to almost clean in less than a minute.

Matthew and her mother were still in the kitchen. Emily sprinted up the stairs to her room, leaned against the door to make sure it clicked shut, then pulled off her dress and threw it on the bed. She stood in her underwear with a feeling she'd never had before, a complete and blank-headed uncertainty about her clothes. She'd never understood how women could frantically claim they had nothing to wear. Now she did. She had nothing to wear for a home-cooked meal with Matthew Rutherford.

She took a flashlight from her desk and went into the closet. It was tucked under the eaves, large but unlit, like a cave. The ceiling sloped steeply so that dresses and slacks fit at one end, blouses in the middle, and nothing but pairs of shoes at the other end.

The jackets, skirts and slacks she wore to work would be too hot and too businesslike, her jeans and shorts too casual. Her supply of flowered, plaid or paisley sundresses, comfortable and cool to wear over coordinating T-shirts, were as shapeless as sacks. Why hadn't she noticed that before?

One of the dresses was a solid blue, almost the color of gentians. She tried it without a shirt underneath. It looked dressier that way, but still casual and summery. She buckled on low-heeled sandals—the only pair that had never seen garden soil—and hurried back downstairs.

WHILE MS. ROBB made herself presentable and her mother behaved as if he didn't exist, Matthew took a good look around the kitchen. There was nothing worth noting. It wasn't impoverished, or up-to-date, or luxurious.

As far as he'd been able to tell that went for all the properties owned by the Robbs. The relatives who had just got married—the children's author and the computer whiz pumpkin grower—were giving the original homestead a new lease on life, but it had obviously been moldering away as you'd expect of a house over a hundred years old.

He wandered into the living room, an action that got Mrs. Moore's attention. Was there something she didn't want him to see?

Ah, the books.

He went to the shelves for a closer look. They were mostly hardcover, some very old and a bit bedraggled—first editions? He could feel Mrs. Moore behind him, emanating silent protest.

"Treasure Island." He pulled it from its place and opened it to check the copyright date. Reprinted 1931. Probably not valuable—he didn't know enough about that to be sure. "I must have read this three times when I was a kid." He smiled over his shoulder. "You, too?"

"I haven't read it." Her voice and posture were stiff.

"You should. You won't be able to put it down."

"One day." She almost snatched it from him, then examined it carefully, checking for injury. He moved along and chose another book, small, with a faded, wine-colored cover. This time she rescued it before he got it open.

He turned at a sound on the stairs. There was Ms. Robb, clean and tidy and unduly alert, looking quickly from him to her mother and back. He got it. Don't touch the books.

"This could be a lending library." He smiled, trying to put them both at ease. "You two must own a copy of every book in the world."

"It's my mother's collection. She's getting there."

"I don't want every book. Just the main ones."

"The main ones?" he asked.

"The ones that changed things."

"How do you decide?"

She slipped the books he'd handled back into place, making sure they were lined up with the others, then left the room without another word.

He raised his eyebrows at her daughter. "Don't touch?"

"It isn't the end of the world if you do."

But it was. The mother seemed every bit as obsessive as he'd been told. The daughter, an anxious caregiver. He felt a moment of sympathy, but got rid of it. Objectivity was going to be difficult. He needed time to get used to how gentle she seemed, how soft.

"You must have chosen that dress to go with your eyes."

The comment startled her. It startled him, too.

"I chose it because of the sale tag."

"A lucky chance, then."

His voice was acting on its own, sounding almost intimate. He went to the kitchen, expecting physical distance to bring emotional distance with it. "Can I help with dinner?"

She followed, bustling around, and loaded him with serving dishes to carry outside. Every couple of minutes she threw him puzzled glances, and he found himself wanting to tell her that everything would be all right.

BY THE TIME they sat under the maple trees, Julia on one side of the picnic table, Matthew on the other and Emily on the very end of her mother's side in an attempt to sit beside both, or neither, she was upset with herself for judging him so quickly the day before. After all, he had just finished a long, hot drive, and some kind of problem in his family had brought him here.

He was different today. Relaxed, friendly to her mother, helpful with dinner…and then there was that moment in the living room. She still felt a catch in her chest remembering the way he'd looked at her when he commented on her dress. Her eyes were not the color of gentians, she knew very well they weren't, but she felt less embarrassed now about the mess she'd been in when he arrived.

He hadn't volunteered any more information about himself, though. Not where he was from or what work he did or where Daniel had gone. Most people would have covered all that in the first few minutes. Then it would have been easy to move to more personal things, like whether visiting Three Creeks alone meant there was no woman in his life and where he belonged on the Rutherford family tree. Her only clue to that was his Ontario license plate.

She waited until all the food had been passed around once. "Matthew, do you belong with the Toronto batch of Rutherfords, or the London batch, or the one that's scattered around the Ottawa valley?"

"I grew up in Ottawa."

His voice was nice when he wasn't being guarded. Deep, but quiet and warm, not loud like Uncle Will's. "Right in the city? I've never been there."

"You've never been to the capital?"

"Is that awful? I've never seen the Parliament Buildings or the tulips in spring." The longest trip she'd taken was to Alberta with her mother to visit Susannah. "We should travel more, shouldn't we, Mom? Maybe one day we could go to Europe, like Liz and Jack."

"There's no need to go to Europe," Julia said flatly.

"Well, not a need—"

"You sit for hours. It's bad for your legs."

"Liz is the cousin who just got married?" Matthew asked.

Emily turned to him, glad to avoid getting into details about blood clots. "They'll be spending two months exploring the ruins of British castles."

"That's an unusual honeymoon."

"Jack has been surprising us since he first moved here. Right, Mom?"

Julia didn't answer, so Emily kept going. "All the farmers in this area plant grain, but Jack put in blueberries and pumpkins, then Christmas trees. Everybody thought he was crazy. You have to wait ten years to harvest them."

"Lots of people must do it."

"If they can afford to wait."

"And Jack can?"

Emily nodded. "We all thought he'd go bankrupt. Then we found out he'd already made his fortune with computers."

"An actual fortune, or just a nest egg?"

"A fortune." She offered Matthew another potato scone. "My other cousin, Susannah, had an even odder honeymoon. She and Alex went to the Gobi Desert to dig for dinosaurs."

"Adventurous."

She smiled at her mother. "Doesn't Europe sound tame after that? If we went, you could visit museums and see real papyrus fragments."

"Behind glass."

"Or we could go to Ireland." One line of Robbs had come from Waterford. "I wonder if they have tours of the crystal factory. You'd like that."

Julia perked up. She began to talk about the history of crystal, how it was made and whether the lead content was dangerous. She went on to list books she owned that were connected to Ireland in any way. Matthew listened intently, and when she switched to the botany lesson she gave whenever she was feeling comfortable and had half a chance, he showed an interest in the bark, leaf shapes and insect hazards of every kind of tree in the yard.

Emily handed him the plate of cold fried chicken. "You didn't mention yesterday where Daniel's gone."

"Didn't I?" With murmured thanks, he took the plate. "This is great chicken. Tender, crisp, not greasy."

"Almost good for you."

"Did Edith make it?" Julia asked.

"No, Mom, I did, this morning." Her mother knew that. She'd been researching Egypt in the next room, complaining about the danger of fat droplets reaching her books.

"But the bean salad, that's Edith's."

Emily moved the chicken to the other side of the table and passed Matthew the tossed greens. "For him to miss the wedding I'm afraid it must have been something serious."

"There was a health emergency in the family."

"Oh, dear. I'm sorry."

"An aunt. He wanted to be with her."

Any aunt of Daniel's must be ancient. "I'm still surprised you came all this way to watch the house. Mrs. Bowen would have been happy to keep an eye on the place."

"You're collecting information, aren't you?"

She couldn't tell if he minded. "Isn't it more of an exchange?"

"I'll bet everyone's waiting at the coffee shop to hear what you find out."

"Of course not!"

Julia said, "Three Creeks doesn't have a coffee shop."

Matthew looked amused at that. "I guess it is a long way to come to house-sit—"

"There's the counter at the post office," Julia went on. "People get coffee there. And gossip."

Matthew smiled at Emily, as if her mother had made his case. "We were planning a visit anyway. I'm researching our family history."

"You don't seem like a family history buff."

"No glasses?"

"Not old enough and…not female enough."

"You'll have to come to a genealogy meeting sometime."

"Are you trying to tell me genealogy meetings are full of athletic men in the prime of life?" She had said what she was thinking without realizing how flirtatious it would sound. Maybe not such a bad thing. He was looking at her again the way he had in the living room.

Julia reached for the quiche. "My husband was interested in genealogy." She cut a thin slice and paid attention to lifting it without losing a crumb. "He liked reading the births written in my mother's Bible. He liked the way my family uses the same names over and over."

It was the longest speech Emily had ever heard her mother make about her father. She didn't know anything about his relatives. "Is there a Moore family Bible?"

"This looks like Edith's quiche."

"No, Mom, it's mine. Remember? I stocked the freezer with them in the spring, for hot days like this."

"It's sure good, whoever made it," Matthew said. "Emily, would you be able to show me around sometime?"

"Around Three Creeks?"

"Around this farm. It could stand in for the Rutherford homestead, couldn't it? Give me a sense of the way things were for my family—if you and your mother don't mind."

"I'd be glad to, but there isn't much to see."

"Would tomorrow work for you? After lunch?"

Julia said, "She's busy tomorrow."

"Tomorrow afternoon would be fine, Matthew." More than fine. Her grudging sense of duty had disappeared. She wanted to spend time with him.

She stood up, gathering plates. "I'll get dessert." No

doubt her mother would find it necessary to remind them Jack had baked the pumpkin loaf, but there was no way she could give anyone else credit for the raspberry meringue torte.

MATTHEW DIDN'T STAY LONG after dinner. He helped with the dishes and then Emily walked him to his car. Croaking sounds came from all around them.

"Isn't it supposed to be quiet in the country?"

"The creek is full of frogs and toads. They make quite a racket in the evening. And then when you're trying to fall asleep there's the crickets and the whip-poor-will."

He stood beside the car door, but didn't move to open it. "I've never heard a whip-poor-will. Never heard of one, either."

"It's a bird. A plain, clumsy brown bird that whistles its name. At night, unfortunately. You probably won't hear it in town."

"I guess that's a good thing. Thank you for dinner, Emily. It was a terrific meal. A group effort, I take it."

She made a small sound of protest. "My grandmother and my aunt donated a couple of things. Not as much as my mother wanted you to think." What her purpose had been, Emily didn't know. "Thank you for being so nice to her."

"Nice?"

"Not everyone is. She makes some people uncomfortable."

"I can see she has her own style. That's good, isn't it? A little variety? I enjoyed meeting her."

He seemed to mean it.

"You'll have to let me know if there's anywhere else you'd like to go while you're here—for your family history, I mean. There's a pioneer museum in Pine Point that might be helpful."

"I'd appreciate that."

Matthew smiled and got into the car. Emily waited while he backed out of the driveway, and waved when he started toward the creek road. She spent most of the walk back to the house wondering why there had been no warmth in his eyes when he had smiled so kindly.

CHAPTER FOUR

ALL JULIA WANTED to do in Pine Point was get to the *Encyclopedia Britannica.* She agreed grudgingly to stop for a midmorning ice cream cone, then refused to have one and stood silently while Emily tried to enjoy her single scoop of maple walnut in a waffle cone.

"Done?" she said, as Emily took the last bite.

"You know, you could be a little more cooperative. I'm not going to stand beside you groaning while you read ten pages of fine print about obscure Egyptian publications—"

"Publications isn't the right word. There wouldn't have been actual publishers."

Unsure whether fondness or exasperation was her dominant emotion, Emily started for the library, barely listening as her mother explained about pharaohs and government ministers and clerks who knew how to write hieroglyphics. As soon as they stepped inside the building, Julia stopped talking and headed unswervingly for the reference section. Emily wandered off to find paperbacks suitable for long afternoons stretched out in the relative coolness of the porch.

When she had a pile of books, enough that she could

discard any that didn't catch her interest when she settled down to read, she made her way to the checkout desk, past book carts in the aisle, people reading in chairs and a toddler half-asleep on the floor. The winding route took her almost to the door of the adjoining computer room. Feeling a pleasant little jolt, she stopped. Matthew was there, intent on the screen of a microfilm reader.

She stood watching him, enjoying the focused stillness of his body. Most of the people she knew were solidly one way—of course they had variations in their personalities— but she could say without hesitation that Aunt Edith fussed and Liz dreamed and Martin teased.

Matthew seemed different. Cold and distant on one hand; warm and kind on the other. Analytical, with an air of professionalism, but physically strong, not bookish. In spite of the suit that had annoyed her for no good reason, she couldn't picture him doing desk work.

He was a puzzle. Maybe that was why Hamish didn't trust him. Yesterday he'd lowered his head whenever Matthew had spoken to him and kept his tail still. The dog had met people he didn't like before, very nice people. He wasn't that keen on Aunt Edith. It made Emily wonder, though. Two days, and two versions of Matthew. Why assume the one she liked was more real than the one she didn't?

JULIA PILED the reference books she'd borrowed from the library onto the kitchen table. She shuffled through them a few times, rearranging them, then placed her catalogs and several sharpened pencils beside them.

"I'll just put my books away upstairs, Mom. Then I'm going out to the garden." Emily wanted to pick radishes and green onion to add to the leftover fried chicken sandwiches she planned to make for lunch.

There wasn't much time before Matthew came, but she ended up staying outside longer to deal with some weeds. She had ignored them for the past few weeks, in the name of nice fingernails for the wedding. The cat sat next to her and watched as she pulled plantain and pineapple weed from between the carrots, sometimes batting a paw at a trailing root.

"That's it," Emily said softly. "Kill that root! You're such a hunter. Oh, dear." She'd got a baby carrot by mistake. She rubbed it clean and ate it in two bites, then picked more, thinning the row. "We'll take some to Mom. There's nothing like baby carrots to cheer a person up."

"Talking to the cat now?"

Emily jumped. Martin stood at the edge of the garden, his truck parked behind him. "You startled me!" She got up, brushing dirt from her knees.

He climbed through the rails of the fence and stepped over the rhubarb to reach her. Every time she saw him he looked more strained. He and Liz's brother, Tom, were working toward organic certification. It would be a few more years before they got there and in the meantime they were using grain profits to feed cattle they couldn't sell. Given the date, she thought she knew why he'd come.

"Is your mom still excited about her thief?"

He grinned. "Oh, yeah, it was the best thief ever. You're keeping your door locked, right?"

"I always do, Martin."

"Like right now?"

"Well, no…but I'm here, close by, and Mom's in the house."

"You didn't see me come. The dog didn't bark. You should lock it during the day, too, Em, even if you're home." Changing pace abruptly, he smiled and patted the cloud of hair above her head. "You've got your Albert Einstein look goin' on."

Emily pushed his hand away. "Quit it, you."

"Except you're prettier and not quite as smart."

"Thanks for clarifying."

Martin's tense smile faded. He shifted from one foot to the other and looked out at the road. "We were hoping this wasn't going to happen again. We haven't got the end-of-June check yet."

"That's all right."

"Not really." He glanced her way. "It's just the buildup of expenses. You and Aunt Julia shouldn't get the short end of the stick, but if we don't pay for feed they won't give us any more—"

"It really is all right."

"We might be moving a few heifers in the next week or two. Can you wait till then?"

"Of course, Martin. On one condition—"

He perked up at the mention of a condition. "Sure. Whatever you say."

"No more hair jokes."

"Aw, Em…"

"I know it's tough, but that's the deal."

He gave her a quick kiss on the head, which under

the circumstances she thought probably qualified as a hair joke, and went to his truck with a wave over his shoulder. The engine revved and with a spray of gravel he roared away.

A WAIT OF A WEEK OR TWO wasn't worth mentioning to her mother, not today, when she was just starting to settle down about the book from Egypt.

Emily hurried through lunch, then showered and braided her wet hair the way Susannah did, making sure every piece was well secured. Her Einstein look? Martin made it sound like a regular thing.

She came out of the bathroom feeling refreshed and polished, ready for company, and found her mother balanced on tiptoe on a chair, stretching to wash the highest bookshelf. Well away from potential drops of water, stacks of books blocked the path to the kitchen.

When she was safely on the floor Emily said, "I thought you'd be diving right into your library books. Did you forget Matthew's coming?"

The cloth dipped vigorously in and out of a bucket of water.

"Mom—"

"I didn't forget." Julia climbed back up on the chair.

Emily tilted her head to see which books were piled on the floor. Prehistory and ancient history. Under a book about cave paintings were a few about the origins of the universe. Those moved back and forth regularly, from the very first spots on the shelf to a much later shelf devoted to modern science. Julia wanted her collection to run seamlessly from the beginning of all things to the present moment in time. The fact that the present moment kept changing complicated her plans. What Emily found endearing was that right near the end, included with all the books in the world that her mother thought were important, were the children's books Liz had written and illustrated.

A bit of a mess didn't matter. Emily wanted to help Matthew with his research, not impress him with her spotless house. It would be easier to remember that if he didn't have such an air of spotlessness himself.

"Here he is." She felt a lift when she saw his car, another when he stepped out of it.

Hamish got to him before she did and circled him warily. Matthew wore khakis again and another button-up shirt, a more casual cotton blend, as if he was noticing how people dressed in Three Creeks. Maybe by the time he left he'd be wearing jeans and a T-shirt.

"Another hot day," he said.

"And in spite of it, my mother's climbing up and down scrubbing book shelves."

"Will it disturb her if we look around?"

"If you imagine a boundary around the books on the floor and don't cross it, we'll be fine." They walked to the kitchen door. "Our house was built a generation later than the Rutherford place. I'm not sure how a tour will help."

"I thought I'd soak up atmosphere."

"You mean the overall creaky floor, crooked walls, cobwebs in the corners kind of atmosphere?"

He smiled. "If that's what you've got, that's what I want."

Emily began in the living room, pointing out the characteristic lumber used at the turn of the twentieth century, three-inch strips of tongue-and-groove British Columbia fir, applied vertically up to a chair rail and then horizontally. Julia continued to clean, ignoring them.

"My great-great-grandfather gave parcels of land to his children when they married, so there's the original place, where my grandmother lives now, and a number of houses built for his children, like this one. My cousin Tom and his wife Pam built their own place." She smiled. "Pam didn't want to soak up anybody else's atmosphere."

"The houses have changed hands by inheritance?"

"Sometimes. My grandfather bought this place for my parents from his sister—"

She stopped. Matthew had stepped over Julia's barricade of books and was examining the shelves. After one startled glance, Julia stared at the book she was holding as if she had discovered mold on its cover.

He tapped the backboard. "That's not the original wall, is it? It's not tongue-and-groove like the rest of the room."

It was the one thing Emily had asked—that he respect her mother's territory. "My dad built it out a few inches. He didn't think the books should rest against an exterior wall."

"Temperature differences, condensation?"

"You never know."

"He did a nice job." Matthew ran his hand along one of the shelves, feeling the tight joins where boards met boards, apparently unaware of the disapproval around him. "Beautiful work."

Stiffly, Julia said, "My husband liked carpentry."

"I can tell. Did he put the shelves up in stages as your library grew?"

"All at once."

"He had an idea you'd want a whole room full, did he? The wood's dried out. He must have done this a long time ago."

"In the fall of 1980. After harvest."

"It's a big job for one person to take care of a library of this size."

"You can't let the books get dusty," Julia said. She still frowned at the one she was holding, but she had relaxed. "You have to give them air. You have to think of an organization that makes sense, so you can find what you want."

She began telling Matthew about *Sinuhe,* everything she had learned at the library that morning. That it came from Egypt's Middle Kingdom—1940 to 1640 BC—and that Sinuhe was the name of a clerk or scribe who worked in a palace. He ran away during a time of conflict and spent his life in exile until his king pardoned him. It was pieced together from papyrus fragments and carvings on limestone, and it was the reason she was cleaning—to make room for a section of books about and from Egypt.

When she ran out of facts she fell silent. Matthew rejoined Emily outside the circle of books.

"I wasn't supposed to do that, was I?" he said quietly, as if he had just remembered.

"No, you weren't."

"I'm sorry. Your place is so different from where I grew up. My parents liked the minimalist look."

She opened a door at the front of the house. "This is our only minimalist room. It's supposed to be for company."

There was no bed, no furniture at all. Only rows of plastic containers piled on top of one another. "I call it the Robb-Moore Archives," she said lightly. "At first my mother kept everything in cardboard boxes, but I put my foot down. Too much of a fire hazard."

Matthew read one label out loud. "'School reports, Emily Moore, grade 1-12.' It's nice that your mom wants to keep things like that."

"Until you know she wants to keep everything. Wedding invitations, birth announcements, obituaries, sales receipts, newspaper clippings, livestock papers…"

His gaze deepened into something she was afraid might be sympathy so she quickly added, "Which is great. If someone in your family had done this you could have found all the information you wanted in a day."

She backed out of the room and led Matthew to the second floor. When they reached the landing he looked at a trapdoor overhead.

"An attic?"

"Not a usable one. It's rafters and cobwebs and the odd chipmunk."

He reached up, easily touching the door. "Could I take a look?"

"There's nothing to see. The last time I opened it a whole load of dust and little bits of gray insulation poured down." She wasn't going to clean that up again.

Her mother's room was on the left, with the door

shut, and hers was on the right, overlooking the front yard. As soon as she saw her twin bed, so childish under the window, she wished they had stayed downstairs.

Matthew took in the bed, the photos of horses and dogs, the books and the dolls and teddy bears left out because they had too much personality to be shut away. "Cozy."

"But not very helpful for your family history."

"It is. Really. I've never been in a big old prairie house." He knocked on the wall. "When I was a kid I always thought old houses had secret rooms."

"Hang on." Emily pushed her bed to one side. Behind it was a small door held shut by a block of wood. She turned the block on its nail and the door swung open. "It doesn't qualify as a room, and it isn't a secret. It's just so we can access the space under the half-roof."

Matthew knelt beside her and peered in. "Great place for hide and seek."

"My father was firm about that." It was one of the few things Emily remembered about him, he'd warned her so often. "He told me I'd crash right through to the room below."

"Scary thought."

"I hid things, though. Notes to Susannah and Liz. Or Halloween candy once. That was a mistake. A whole family of chipmunks moved in that time."

Matthew laughed, and she immediately wanted it to happen again. It made his face so warm and open.

"Mind if I take a closer look?"

"It'll be dusty."

Brushing past her, he leaned deeper into the crawl

space. It was a long time since she'd been so close to a man who wasn't a relative. How did her body know? There was quite a divide between its point of view and her own. It was always tingling and softening and perking up when he was around. She couldn't seem to impress on it how short a week was, and how quickly it was passing, or the fact that she didn't know anything about him, not even if she liked him.

No, she knew that much. The question was whether she *should* like him.

As his head and shoulders came back into the light his knee knocked against hers. She edged away. He was out of place in her room, with her old teddy bears staring from the shelf. Through the warm air grate in the floor she could hear her mother working. What she was feeling didn't belong here. John had called it her nun's cell.

She stood up quickly. "You wanted to see outside? The barn, you said? The outbuildings?"

"If you don't mind." He went around to the other side of the bed and pushed it back into place.

BETWEEN THE TIME he stuck his head under the roof and pulled it back out, something had changed Emily's mood. Did thinking about her father upset her? Or was she worried about having someone snoop around the house?

As helpfully distancing as the name was he hadn't been able to think of her as Ms. Robb for very long. Only until the third or fourth time her mother had asked which relative had made the quiche or the salad or the chicken and she'd looked as if one word of appreciation would go a long way. Then she'd become Emily in his mind.

He followed her downstairs and out the kitchen door. The dog, back in the shade of the hedge, gave him another baleful stare. No growling or biting so far. That was good.

The yard was like a forest. It looked as if long ago someone had felled just enough trees to make room for a house and left the rest. Emily and her mother barely kept up with it. A closer inspection was confirming yesterday's first impression. Inside and out, there was no sign of big spending—except for the books and not even those if the collecting was spread over the years.

No gems, no Group of Seven paintings, she'd said. It was the kind of joke people might make when they were covering something. He didn't think that was the case here. Liars usually gave themselves away with tics and avoidance gestures or expressions so blankly innocent alarm bells went off. Emily had been five or six when the gold had disappeared. Not involved, obviously. That didn't mean she wasn't drawn in later. He had to remember that.

THE OUTBUILDINGS WERE all well past their prime, with moss on their shingles and scampering sounds overhead. There was a single-car garage to check, a pump house, a henhouse, a storehouse, a granary and a barn.

"I suppose all this would have been typical of the Rutherford place." Emily was still looking for connections to Matthew's family history. He had been quiet since they'd come outside and she wondered if he was losing interest in the tour. "Working farms have updated their buildings."

"This isn't a working farm?"

"Not since my father died. Martin and Tom—two of my cousins—use the land for grazing."

Matthew swung the storehouse door back and forth. "No lock. You don't care if your friendly neighborhood thief comes in?"

"He'd be welcome to anything he found in here."

She led him between moldy saddles and dusty buckets and out the back door into a meadow. One step, and they were knee-high in prairie grasses. Here and there were spots of color—deep-yellow black-eyed Susans and pale-yellow buttercups, orange tiger lilies and purple Russian thistles. Beyond the meadow were poplar woods dotted with darker green oak and spruce.

"Do you mind a walk? There's a spot I'd like to show you."

"Good. I was hoping to see the woods."

"We can take a roundabout path to the place we're going, or a shortcut through a marshy area." As soon as she mentioned the marsh she knew she didn't want to go that way. "It wouldn't be wet now and the woods on the other side are beautiful, almost all oaks and elms."

"Whatever you prefer is fine with me."

She smiled. "You're easy to get along with."

"Always."

She chose the longer way. He was full of questions

as they went. How big was the farm, had they sold any parcels of land, were any other buildings found on the property? Emily couldn't remember anyone being so interested in her home.

Cattle traveling in single file had worn a narrow path through the bush. They followed it to a more densely wooded area, mostly thin poplars too close together, with an undergrowth of highbush cranberry and hazelnut. Not far off, they heard water bubbling.

"The three creeks?"

"One of them. The biggest one."

The woods thinned again and they entered a small clearing where daisies grew almost as thickly as grass. Large, smooth rocks—lichen-spattered granite—rose out of the ground at the edge of the creek.

"It's beautiful, Emily. From the road you'd never know it was like this."

"Your uncle taught me to fish here. That's why I wanted to show it to you."

Matthew climbed onto the stones. "It looks too shallow for that."

"You can get jackfish or suckers in the spring, when the water's high."

"Suckers. Yum."

She laughed. "And then in the winter Daniel played hockey with us here—with Sue and Liz and me. Three Creeks can be such a guy-ish place. Daniel is different."

Matthew cocked an eyebrow. "Not guy-ish?"

They both smiled at the thought.

"He made time for us when we were kids, not just

for the boys. He helped us if our horses weren't behaving or had a problem with their hooves, he knew more about making snow forts than anybody. He taught us how to whistle."

"Sounds like a father. Or an uncle."

"Maybe not." Daniel was never like the other grown-ups. "When we were little, he used to give us coffee. No one else let us have coffee. And while we drank it—hating it—he'd tell us stories about his Army days or about chasing criminals. He always called them 'dumb clucks.'"

Matthew smiled at that.

"So if I seemed…impatient or anything when we met it was because I was afraid something had happened to him. I didn't think he'd voluntarily miss Liz's wedding."

"You weren't impatient—or anything. He'll be sorry to hear he worried you."

"Don't tell him."

She climbed up beside Matthew on the rocks, then stepped onto the next stone and sat down, her feet dangling above the water. Remembering the purpose of the afternoon, she began to tell him what she knew of the first settlers' arrival, how the Robbs, the Rutherfords and five other families had traveled from Ontario by train and oxcart, and at the end of a long and difficult journey had found an untouched forest where they could hunt, with creeks that provided fish to eat and fresh water to drink.

She stopped when she noticed how intently he was watching her. "Matthew?"

"Hmm?"

Had he heard anything she'd said? "You're staring. Past eye color, past freckles, right down to DNA."

"Sorry. I guess I zoned out. Maybe it's the drive." He gave a quick, unconvincing smile. "Car lag."

It wasn't the drive. "You must be worried about your aunt. Or great-aunt, I suppose. Has Daniel called to let you know how she's doing?"

"Not yet."

"I wouldn't mind talking to him—"

Matthew wasn't listening. He lifted his hand to brush her cheek. "What a very nice woman you are."

Oh boy.

She stood, casually she hoped, and moved off the rocks. Funny what one touch could do. All those questions about time and character vanished.

She patted the bark of the tree closest to her. "This is a poplar. Good for firewood, not so good for building, because it tends to twist. Do you have poplars in Ontario?" Silly question. Of course they did.

"Aspens."

"Oh, right, trembling aspens. I love that name. My mother told me it comes from the way the leaves are attached. There's something unusual about the stem that makes them shake and flutter in the breeze."

He had the most intense eyes. They had been intense at Daniel's the first day, especially when he heard her name. They had been intense yesterday while he stood with *Treasure Island* in his hand. They were intense now, in a way that confused her. She couldn't tell if he was flirting with her or putting her under a microscope, and if he was putting her under a microscope she had no idea why.

"My cousins and I used to climb these poplars on windy days. We'd pretend we were up in the rigging of a tall ship out on the ocean. Cartier's ship, usually, or pirates off Newfoundland's coast. The tops of the trees swayed so much you could just about get seasick." She was talking quickly, and a lot. Chances were her attempt at a casual retreat hadn't fooled him.

"Sounds like fun. The girl cousins, I suppose?"

"Susannah and Liz."

"Daniel told me about the three of you. They both left and you stayed. No wanderlust?"

"They had good reasons to leave. I didn't."

"Did you have reasons to stay?"

"Why would I need reasons? I live in a beautiful place with clean air and clean water. We produce most of our own food. We know exactly what's in it and on it. I love my job, I love my family, and they love me."

"It sounds perfect."

"It is."

"Except for the archives?"

"That's a little thing." She patted the poplar again, encouraging him to focus, the way she did with six-year-old boys in the library.

"So," she said, her voice sounding too much like a teacher's, "the woods at the Rutherford place would have been exactly like this. My grandmother might have pictures. I'll call her later today and ask."

He kept looking at her, evaluating, adding and subtracting, amused, and then he allowed his attention to be redirected to the trees around them. She could see that unlike the six-year-old boys in the library, he was only humoring her.

CHAPTER FIVE

THE BELL OVER the door jingled when Matthew went into the post office the next morning. The place had just opened but there were already a number of customers inside and, if he wasn't mistaken, half of them were Robbs. Four men, two older and two younger, visibly related, clumped together at the far end of the grocery counter drinking coffee from takeout cups, visiting as if they were in one of their own kitchens. They noted his arrival, then ignored him.

A woman with her back to the door sorted mail. She smoked while she worked, keeping two fingers busy with the cigarette and managing envelopes and flyers with the other three.

"Good morning," Matthew said.

The hand came up, telling him he would have to wait. From a distance she looked young, with one of those unnaturally red hair colors. Up close, her neck and hands and the way she stood gave a more realistic idea of her age. Late sixties, he guessed. This must be Virginia Marsh. Born in Three Creeks, widowed at thirty. Bought the store in '72 and finished paying off the mortgage just twelve years later.

While he waited he half listened to the conversation by the coffeemaker. One of the older men was saying something about looking on the bright side. His voice became louder as he made his point, confident and nostalgic.

"When I ran my farm, I was my own boss. Decided what to do and when, worked out in the sun and fresh air. That's worth something!"

"That's exactly what we were telling the bank manager," one of the younger men said. "Weren't we, Tom?"

"Oh, yeah. 'But the fresh air!' we said. 'That alone's got to be worth another fifty grand.'"

These must be the cousins who used the Moore farm for grazing. Matthew didn't hear the rest. The postmistress had turned to look him up and down with a frankness he found disconcerting in someone older than his mother.

She smiled through a haze of smoke. "You must be Matthew Rutherford."

The Robb conversation paused.

"That's right. I'm taking care of my uncle's place for the week."

"He's not back?"

"Not yet. He's staying with a sick relative."

"Funny kind of visit. You come here, he goes away."

Matthew smiled. "I've always had that effect on my uncle."

She winked. "You and me both. Sad, but true."

"I came by to see if he has any mail. He wants me to pick it up if he does." He handed her his Ontario driver's license.

She peered at the photo and then at his face. "Spitting image. Close enough, anyway." She passed it back to him. "Now, technically, Daniel needs to ask me himself. But I've seen your ID. I'll make an exception."

"Thank you."

"If he gets any mail, that is."

Matthew nearly laughed. He got the feeling she'd gladly keep him going all morning. "I'll check again another day."

He went in search of meals in a can. While he tried to choose between ravioli stuffed with ground beef or ravioli stuffed with cheese, the bell over the door rang and another customer came in, going straight to the grocery section.

Early twenties, T-shirt, designer denim. No one in the store greeted him, so Matthew assumed he was a stranger, too. A black Mustang was visible through the windows at the front of the building. He couldn't see the plates.

But he did see Emily. She had parked on the other side of the road by the railway allowance, a wide flower-filled strip of meadow. He watched her hurry across to the store, hardly checking for traffic.

She looked hot and tired, as if she'd been working outside. She gave him a quick smile, but went to the counter in the no-man's land between the grocery store section and the post office section without saying hello.

"Look at all of you!" she called to the men by the coffeemaker. "I've weeded Grandma's whole garden already this morning and you're here doing nothing."

"Not nothing, sweetheart. I'm visiting with my fellow man."

"You're excluded from the criticism, Uncle Winston, because you're on holiday."

He gave a little bow of thanks. "But busy nevertheless. I want to talk to everybody one more time before Lucy and I go home. Will's helping me."

"Martin and I are working," Tom said. "Hard. We're waiting for the parcel delivery guy."

Martin nodded. "It's very stressful. And all this caffeine isn't helping."

"We're going to show Alex how to change a combine bearing." Tom checked his watch. "Soon as it gets here."

The customer in the designer jeans went to the counter with a loaf of bread and a jar of peanut butter. As if no lighthearted chatting was going on around him he said, "I thought you weren't supposed to smoke in public buildings."

Nobody responded. The Robb men continued to sip their coffee and Emily stared at a basket of licorice cigars beside the cash register. Mrs. Marsh rang the man's purchases through and dropped them into a brown paper bag—jar on top of bread, Matthew noticed. That was a bit of nonverbal communication he would have paid attention to, but the customer seemed to feel a real need to make his point.

"There's a sign. Right in front of you. No smoking."

Mrs. Marsh slapped his change onto the counter. "I know there's a sign. Who do you think stuck it there?"

"Well, then—"

"Well, then?" she repeated, her anger clearly increasing. Anybody would think it was the worst thing he'd said yet.

"I'm just saying—"

"More than you should. Honestly! I won't have somebody I don't even know coming into my store and telling me what I can or cannot do. When a woman can't stand in her own building without some young—"

The man picked up his grocery bag and hurried outside. Mrs. Marsh, still looking flushed and ready to do battle, watched him go.

"You may have scared away our only tourist for the year," Emily said mildly.

"No, no. There'll be others. There's a honeymoon couple in town right now."

"Someone chose Three Creeks for their honeymoon? Don't tell Aunt Edith."

Mrs. Marsh gave a snort. "This isn't their destination. But they stopped for a bit, that's the point, they turned in off the highway. It was the name of the place, she told me. Poetic. They've decided to stay a while."

"But we don't have a hotel."

"They put up a tent somewhere. Not my idea of romantic. They're on a road trip. They want to go all the way to Churchill. See the polar bears. I told them they won't get to Churchill driving, but they were in too good a mood to care about that sort of detail. Silly with it."

Matthew put his tins on the counter. "Why can't they get to Churchill?"

"Because nobody ever made a road up there. It's all

lakes and muskeg. There's a train track and planes flying in and out, but that's it."

"You could go by boat," Will said. "Right up the Churchill River. But you'd have rapids to contend with and you'd have to watch out for whales."

Matthew made eye contact with the group for the first time. "Whales?"

"Belugas. They feed at the mouth of the river."

"Not that most of us ever get up there to see them." Mrs. Marsh hardly looked at Matthew's cans while she rang them through the cash register. He wondered if she was going by memory or making up the prices as she went along. "You want something, Emily?"

"Just the mail—ours and Grandma's, if there is any."

"Not today. I suppose you're all waiting to hear from Jack and Liz. That'll take a while, postcards from Europe. Next summer, maybe."

Matthew put his bag under one arm. "Emily, I was going to ask you—" The conversation at the coffeemaker stopped again. He lowered his voice. "—if you'd be free tomorrow morning to help me in Pine Point. I'd like to find the museum you mentioned and take a good look around."

Emily smiled with enough pleasure to stimulate guilt. "I'd be happy to go with you. I won't have a lot of time, though. I'm helping my grandmother with her housework in the afternoon. Would you mind if my mother came, too? She always enjoys the museum."

"Of course." They started walking to the door, but Matthew stopped when one of the older Robbs—Will—called his name and waved him back in, telling him to take a minute for coffee.

Emily leaned close to say something. Matthew's body responded to the proximity, to the faint smells of shampoo and sunscreen and sweat, and he missed the first half of her sentence.

"…your line of Rutherfords has been doing since they left town."

He got the gist. "Then I hope there's a really big pot of coffee."

She smiled again. He'd never met anyone who smiled as often and as warmly as she did. "See you tomorrow, Matthew."

"Pick you up at nine-thirty?"

She nodded, backing out the door.

EMILY KNEW Matthew didn't really need her help with the museum—he had found the library on his own and he didn't seem like a person who needed company— but she was glad he'd asked her to go along.

She made a pot of tea and arranged toasted cucumber sandwiches and a few muffins on a plate, then tried to find room for the food without disturbing her mother's work area. Julia had started the day by cleaning another section of shelves, but now she was trying to narrow down the list of Egyptian books that interested her. Seeing her eager posture and wondering if Martin's estimate of a week or two was optimistic, Emily decided she would have to tell her about the rent check.

"I'm afraid there's going to be a wrinkle in your plans, Mom. Martin says he and Tom can't pay the rent yet."

There was no response. Sometimes Emily wondered if her mother even knew that money was a required element in the quest for food and shelter. A small life insurance check came each month, but there wouldn't be anything from the school division until fall.

"We'll be fine," she added, in case reassurance was needed. "He hopes it'll be a short delay. If it isn't we have lots of the beef they gave us and the garden's coming up well. But you'd better not order any more books for now."

Julia's hand, peeling paper from a muffin, paused. When the peeling resumed, it was with tight, precise movements. Emily wondered how a hand could look so annoyed.

"I can show you the last bank statement."

"I won't order anything."

"Thank you."

"Until when?"

"Until they give us a check. Or until school starts."

For barely a second, her mother's startled eyes met hers. Emily smiled encouragingly. "I'm sure it won't be that long."

MATTHEW REACHED for the telephone, punching in a number from memory. He could have made the call his first day in Three Creeks. Should have. For some reason he'd been putting it off.

"Hey. Yeah, it's me. Can you run some checks?… Well, I dunno, what do you want? Cigars? Silk stockings?" He smiled at the response. "Sure, I'll go that far. Ale or lager?… Thanks. I'll fax you a list right now."

He pressed the send button, then replaced the receiver and watched the paper inch through the machine. Names, addresses, birth dates. It was half the family, which made him feel both guilty and incompetent. They were all connected, however tenuously, to the downed aircraft. By acquaintance with its pilot, by age, by financial need.

Julia and Emily. William and Winston. Martin, Thomas and another cousin, Brian. The new member of the family, Jack McKinnon, apparent fortune-holder. Alexander Blake, another Robb in-law. Matthew wasn't sure why he'd included him. The guy had a high profile—he was always talking about dinosaurs on TV, going on expensive digs. And last, Virginia Marsh, the lady with the quickly paid-off mortgage.

He entered a second number and got an answering machine. After the beep, he explained what he wanted, concluding, "I'm out of town right now, but you've got my e-mail address. Whatever information you can give me, just so I have an idea what makes a book a good investment. As soon as you can, that'd be great. Thanks."

He went up to the kitchen and stood at the window eating a cinnamon bun from a batch Mrs. Bowen had brought over that morning. After three cups of syrupy coffee at the post office, Will Robb had wanted to move the party back to Daniel's house, where there were chairs to sit on. Only his brother Winston's determination to stay where he could greet old friends had stopped him.

Houses around here seemed to be no more than semiprivate. The doorbell rang at least twice a day because someone from down the road or across town or from miles away wanted to welcome Daniel's nephew. Everyone who came by expected to be invited in. They expected to be given a snack. And they took the opportunity to look around, as if they thought he might have redecorated or something.

Which was exactly what he needed to do.

He washed off the sticky cinnamon sugar and went to the desk in the living room. He found red and blue pens, and paper—just the usual letter-size sheets, but he taped several pieces together on the wall over the desk to make one large writing surface. There was a family Bible in the downstairs bedroom, like the one Julia had mentioned her husband reading. He checked the front pages. In various handwriting, with various inks, there was a record of Rutherford births, marriages and deaths.

He printed them onto the paper on the wall, drawing boxes around names, then lines that connected them horizontally and vertically. There were a lot of early deaths in the old days. Young women whose names were often followed by those of infants. Men who were hardly more than boys from 1914 to 1918 and then again from 1939 to 1945.

When the chart was done he piled genealogy books and family photo albums on the desk under it. It looked productive enough for a few days' research.

EMILY FOUND HER MOTHER upstairs, digging around in her bedroom closet.

"Ready?" They had been invited to Aunt Edith's for

tea that afternoon. It was five days since the wedding, more than enough time, Edith had insisted, for Julia to recuperate and show interest in her niece.

Julia backed out of the closet empty-handed, clothes clinging to her, pulling at her hair. She batted them out of her way, frustrated, and ran her hands over her head before starting downstairs. "I'm not going."

"Susannah's hoping to see you."

"I don't want to go." Her voice became louder and flatter. "I go and I go and I go." In the kitchen she began sorting through her library books, banging them on the table as if they made her angry, too.

"But you don't go."

"You don't see everything. She calls it tea but it might be lemonade. Nitter, natter, chitchat."

"Mom, that's mean—"

"It's a waste of time."

"It isn't a waste of time, because when you go you make Aunt Edith feel good."

Julia snorted. "When she leaves me alone she makes me feel good."

Emily leaned against the counter, suddenly tired. "Is this about the book? Because we don't have money to buy a copy right now?"

Her mother looked offended. She pulled a chair back, dragging all four legs hard across the floor, and plopped herself into it. She stared at the table and Emily stared at the floor and neither one of them spoke for several minutes.

Quietly, as if it was an explanation, Julia said, "I don't want to go to Edith's."

"I picked up on that." Emily pushed away from the counter. "It's all right. They'll understand."

They wouldn't, really. Emily wasn't sure she did, either.

AUNT EDITH HAD brought out a trunk of baby clothes: doll-size nighties with ties at the back and a band of pastel embroidery across the front, snowy-white undershirts, footed sleepers and tiny ribboned dresses. Most of them were piled on Susannah's lap, but Edith caressed one, a rose-pink dress.

"Sorry I'm late. I've come alone, I'm afraid."

"And we're very glad to have you." Edith looked closely at her niece. "Oh, dear. Had a tiff, did you? Not over this little tea party, I hope. Am I imagining it, or is your mother more of a hermit every day?"

"Of course she isn't," Susannah said. "Aunt Julia needs room, that's all. But, Em, tell her I'm going to drop in on her one of these days."

Edith held up the pink dress. "Remember this, Emily?"

"I don't think so. It looks too big for a kitten. Sue must have outgrown it before I was born."

"Come to think of it, she wore it to your mother's wedding. With white tights and pink satin slippers. She was my only girl, so I've kept it all these years hoping one day to see a granddaughter wear it."

When Edith turned away to rest the dress in the trunk, Emily spoke in her cousin's ear. "Is your mom still hoping you'll move back home?"

"Alex has been out on Dad's tractor every day. It's given her hope."

"What are you two whispering about?" Edith sounded pleased. "You always did that. Always planning something. Conspiring in a corner and the next thing we'd know the poor dogs were hitched to a toboggan and up-ending you into the ditch! Think of that, Susannah. Your child will be alone. Who will she plan and scheme with?"

"I've seen a baby or two in Drumheller."

"Not family. Not little ones she can disappear into the woods with and do whatever you did all day, no television dictating to you."

Emily put an arm around her aunt. "It's a bad old world, isn't it? Too many miles between everybody."

"I suppose I'm being awful."

"No, Mom," Susannah said quickly. "I wish we lived closer to home, too. But we'll be here for a long time yet. Alex wants to stay for the Fair."

Edith perked up. "Lovely! Oh, he'll enjoy it. The tractor pull, especially, don't you think? You know, Susannah, Alex is growing on me, he really is. He's so enthusiastic. So easy to entertain."

The Fair was a month away. Emily tried to hide her pleasure at the thought Sue might stay that long. Liz had told her the family's opinions and wants could be overwhelming at times.

"Aunt Edith, would it be all right if I invited Matthew to the barbecue?" Edith and Will had organized one last family get-together before Liz's parents flew back to White Rock.

"Daniel's nephew? Certainly! I should have thought of it myself. Will ran into him at the post office this morning—well, you know about that, Emily. He said they had a such a good gossip after you left. I don't know what you were talking about the other day. According to Will, Matthew is very nice. You'd think he grew up here."

"They have nice men in other parts of the world, too, Mom."

Edith flushed. "You know that isn't what I meant." She scooped the heap of baby clothes into the trunk and closed the lid. "Speaking of nice men, Emily, did you know John Ramsey's coming home?"

"I heard. In a couple of weeks, for a visit."

"Did you hear the whole story?"

"Mom, don't."

"She's going to hear sooner or later. Later wouldn't be good, would it? If she walked into the grocery store and saw them shopping, how would she feel then?"

"I guess he isn't coming alone," Emily said.

"He's bringing a woman. Someone said it's his fiancée."

"We broke up when we were eighteen, Aunt Edith."

"It seems like yesterday, doesn't it?"

"It seems like a hundred years ago."

"Brave girl." Edith squeezed Emily's hand. "I'll get some snacks ready while you two visit." She avoided looking at her daughter. "Dear Susannah is always hungry."

Susannah waited until she was gone. "You look upset, Em. I hope it isn't all that talk about John."

"It isn't John at all. Mom's in a bit of a state and I don't know why. You and Aunt Edith seem to be feeling some tension, too."

"We're both doing what we do, that's all."

Emily smiled. It didn't take much to get Aunt Edith and Susannah going. "Your poor mom."

"Poor Mom!"

"She really does miss you."

"Isn't it her job to get over it?"

"Ouch. Something tells me eighteen years from now you'll think back to this moment."

"But my baby will already live in the badlands. He'll have no reason to move away." There was a touch of sadness in Susannah's smile. Her voice changed, putting the subject away. "Now tell me about Matthew Rutherford."

"What about him?"

"He's been here four days and you've seen him every one of them."

"Accidentally today."

"A happy accident?"

Emily smiled and nodded. "He's so easy to talk to, Sue, so interested in what I've got to say, even when it's boring. Yesterday we walked along talking and the next thing I knew an hour had gone by."

"That sounds nice. Be careful, though."

"Of?"

"I don't know." Susannah seemed to be choosing her words. "I guess I mean, in case his interest gets the better of you."

"Are you seeing a big bad wolf, Sue? I'm kind of old to worry about that."

"Not a wolf, and not a little girl in the woods. But you're usually the listener around here. I don't want you to mistake his listening for—"

"For genuine interest in me?" Emily had to interrupt. Susannah's suggestion stung.

"I'm putting this badly."

Emily couldn't believe she had almost snapped at her swollen-footed, seven-and-a-half-month pregnant cousin. "I'll keep it in mind. But I'm all grown up. I can handle being hurt, and if Matthew wants to lead me down the garden path while he's here I wouldn't be unwilling."

Susannah looked surprised, maybe even just this side of shocked. That was the trouble with being the youngest.

"You've been hurt a couple of times."

"Who hasn't? Both times I had a choice and I didn't choose the guy. Anyway, it isn't an issue with Matthew. He'll be gone soon." She was aware of a sinking feeling as she said it. "In the meantime, what's wrong with enjoying his company? He's different. Surprising. I was planning to make raspberry jam this week. I like making jam, but hanging around with Matthew is better."

The afternoon was all downhill after that. Uncle Will, Martin and Alex came back from changing the bearing on the combine in time to hear the end of the conversation and of course the teasing began right on schedule.

Not from Alex. He just checked his wife's feet and went into the house for some cooling peppermint lotion, but Martin went on about seizing the opportunity, the day and the bull by the horns until Susannah told him, firmly, to shut up. They spent the next half hour making him feel better while Emily tried to batten down her unreasonable envy that Susannah not only had a gorgeous man in her life, but a gorgeous man who liked to rub her tired feet.

CHAPTER SIX

MATTHEW PUT ASIDE the file he'd been reading and answered the telephone. "Hey. What have you got?"

He listened. No arrests, no aliases. A couple of speeding tickets, one driving under the limit.

"The paleontologist? What about him?... On a regular basis? Good to know. Talk to you later."

He checked his watch. Time for a quick breakfast and a shower before picking up Emily.

THE CAT PREFERRED dealing with the world at foot level, but this morning it let Emily pick it up and hold it in her arms. She didn't often try because it seemed to think the use of claws was a necessity that far off the ground.

"Today's going to be very busy." She rubbed under its chin. "Pine Point in the morning, vacuuming for Grandma in the afternoon. I don't know when I'm going to read that pile of library books."

She grimaced at a sharp jab and quickly set the cat down. "That's what we should call you. Dagger. All right, let's find you some breakfast."

The cat leapt to the steps and waited for her to open

the door, then trotted to the cupboard where the pet food was kept. Emily's mother was at the table paging through a cookbook. Billowing steam filled the air above the stove.

"Mom, the kettle."

Julia looked up, unfocused and blinking. "Oh!" She hurried to switch off the stove, gasping as she touched the handle and moved the kettle to a cold burner.

Emily shook dry food into a dish on the floor, spilling half of it when the cat pushed its way in before she was done. By the time she'd swept and put the broom away her mother still hadn't budged from the stove or poured the boiled water into the teapot.

"Are you sure you won't come to Pine Point this morning? Some fresh air and sunshine would do you good."

"Do you damage, too."

So that was how things were going to be.

Movement outside the front window caught Emily's eye. Hamish had pulled himself up and was walking stiffly toward the driveway.

"That must be Matthew now."

"All of a sudden it's always Matthew."

"I thought you liked him."

"I like him once a week."

Emily smiled. "Things will get back to normal in a few days." Her mother looked so dejected. "Hamish misses you."

Julia half turned. "He does?"

"You've hardly left the house except for the wedding. Why don't you pick some lettuce before the heat makes any more of it go to seed? Then you could spend time with him."

"I didn't know he missed me." The thought quickly took root. Julia collected her hat, gloves and garden trug and went outside, calling for the dog.

Emily followed as far as the step. "Do you have a key to let yourself back in? I should lock the door."

Hamish looked almost sprightly greeting Julia. The two of them headed off, giving no sign they had heard Emily's voice.

She tried to pull the storm door shut. As usual its edges had expanded in the humidity, and it stuck. She kept pulling until she heard it click into place. Looking locked would have to do.

WHILE HAMISH FOLLOWED Julia into the garden, his tail wagging gently, Emily settled into the passenger seat of Matthew's car. It had the cleanest interior she'd ever seen, especially so soon after a long drive. Usually she could tell something about people from the inside of their cars—like whether they ate fast food while driving or what kind of dog they had. She supposed she could tell that Matthew was neat.

"Your mother doesn't want to come with us?"

"I couldn't persuade her. A quiet morning is probably best for her, anyway."

His hand rested on the gearshift. "You said you're going to your grandmother's this afternoon. Is a quiet morning best for you?"

The thoughtful tone touched her. "A morning in town is best for me." She handed him a small manila envelope. "My grandmother had a few pictures you might be able to use. She doesn't think Daniel has the same ones."

Matthew thanked her and promised to return the photographs after making copies, but he didn't open the envelope. When he reached over the seat to put it in the back she saw past the unfastened first button of his shirt to a shadowed collarbone and the rise of chest muscle. She turned to look out the window instead, at the sprawling caragana bushes and the weeds sprouting at the edge of the driveway.

"I'd better get busy or this place will be a jungle."

He did up his seat belt again and backed out to the road. "Don't you have someone to help you?"

"Sometimes Uncle Will or one of my cousins comes by to cut grass or prune branches."

The car moved along Robbs' Road, slowly at first and then gathering speed.

"Careful, Matthew."

He touched the brakes lightly, almost bringing the car to a stop. "Of what? I don't see anything."

She pointed at the road ahead, at small, dark, nearly motionless blobs. "Toads. And frogs."

He looked at her in disbelief. "You're joking, right?"

"Well, you don't want to squish them, do you?"

"How about flies and grasshoppers? Should I be careful of those, too?"

She smiled. "I do have a soft spot for grasshoppers. There's a book at school I always read to the grade ones. The main character is a grasshopper. An endearing grasshopper."

"I must have missed that one." Matthew let the car

ease forward. He steered left first, then back to the center of the road, where he paused while a bigger toad hopped out of the way. He angled left again, then right. "Do we do this all the way to Pine Point?"

"Just on this stretch of road, because of the creek."

"I can avoid them with the front tires, Emily, but I have no idea what the back ones are doing."

"You're trying. That's the main thing."

After a quick, puzzled glance in her direction he kept his eyes on the road. "If you need help with the yard, aren't there teenagers looking for after-school work, or retired farmers who want a part-time job?"

"A hired man, you mean? That involves wages, Matthew."

They were on the creek road now, headed toward town.

"You know, despite being from the city, and a big, eastern city at that, you're just as—how shall I put this?—just as inquisitive as anyone from around here."

A quick, sheepish smile relaxed his face. "I'm only a couple of generations away from Three Creeks, remember."

Two whole lifetimes. Long enough to make him a different kind of person. She didn't want him to fit a more familiar pattern.

Although if he did, it might help her deal with him sensibly, until he went back to Ottawa. This morning she hadn't been sensible at all. They weren't going on a date. She was only helping him get a better feel for his family history. Even so, she had spent almost an hour in front of her mirror, holding up outfit after outfit, thinking of the response he'd had to the blue dress.

Finally she had pulled on her next least unbecoming sundress, one with muted white flowers on a creamy yellow background, straps that buttoned over the shoulder and no waistline at all. After some deliberation she'd added a bracelet, an inexpensive circle of small plastic daisies. She'd taken it off and put it on three times before leaving her room. Silly. Pointless. She touched the bracelet. Kind of fun, though.

WHEN THEY REACHED the highway he accelerated to slightly over the speed limit. As far as he could tell, that was all right with her. He still wasn't sure if she'd been pulling his leg about the toads.

She was quiet for the first five miles, fingering her bracelet and looking out the window at scenery she must have seen a thousand times. Worrying about field mice trying to cross the road, maybe.

Traffic was light. A few tractors chugged along, half on the shoulder, hauling machinery that did who knew what. Heading away from the city and Pine Point, toward the lakes, he supposed, were camper trailers, SUV's pulling speed boats, and cars with canoes clamped on their roofs.

"Everybody but us and a few farmers is on holiday."

She looked at him with mild surprise. "I'm on holiday. Aren't you?"

"I mean everybody else is goofing off."

"I knew it! You don't like genealogy."

"Well, I don't love it."

"You're doing it for your parents?"

"More for Daniel." It was almost true. He could see she approved.

"We could go to the beach one of these days, if you like. There's one nearby that city people don't know about. Even a couple of generations ago your relatives would have gone. That makes it research, doesn't it?"

A day at the beach with Emily. A simple, ordinary day. It was tempting. But not a good idea. Not after the way they'd reacted to each other by the creek.

"Emily, I wanted to ask you about the man Mrs. Marsh chased away yesterday. The one you called a tourist."

"Only because I've never seen him before. We don't really get tourists. Just people stopping in on the way somewhere else."

"You're sure you don't know him? Do you recognize everyone who lives around town?"

She looked as if he'd asked whether she recognized everyone in her house. "In the whole municipality, probably. Although I haven't met those honeymooners Mrs. Marsh told us about. Maybe they've left. Why?"

"New people must move to the area."

"Sure. But they need things. Food, gas, doctor's appointments. They don't stay invisible long."

"What about bird-watchers or campers…people who hang around a while, make friends?" This wasn't coming off as small talk. His questions were puzzling her.

"Sometimes people come looking for lady's slippers or morels."

"Lady's slippers?"

"A kind of orchid."

"Orchids, here?" And Will had talked about whales.

"You see? There's no reason for me to leave. We have

everything." She smiled. "We just don't tell anybody. It would get too crowded."

The drive to Pine Point took twenty minutes, another thirty seconds to find the museum. He paid the admission—two dollars each—and began strolling through the exhibits. He tried to pay attention to each one—an 1890 dentist's chair, a 1905 schoolroom, a 1920s hospital ward—but he had seen the same kind of thing in museums since he was a kid. It didn't take long for him to make a circuit of the building. Soon they were out on the sidewalk again.

"Ready for lunch?"

She gave him that schoolteacher look of hers. "We haven't earned lunch. You didn't find out anything about your family and I wasn't any help."

"You were a big help. I couldn't have found the museum without you."

"You could have found it if I'd blindfolded you and spun you in circles before you left Three Creeks. I thought you'd want to spend hours here."

"You don't have hours, though. I'll come back on my own another time. Now, will you help me find a typical Pine Point lunch?"

"In the 1880s there was no such thing as a typical Pine Point lunch, not unless your forbears hunted ducks here."

She was trying not to smile. Most of the time, smiling or not, her face had a low-key sparkle, warm and amused. She probably looked at everybody like that.

"How about the bakery?" she suggested. "It's close by, and they make great cheeseburgers. Their own buns, fresh every day, local grass-fed beef, homemade pickles."

"Sounds good."

They left the car in front of the museum and walked, staying in the shade of the boulevard trees. The buildings they passed—small stores, the post office, the courthouse, the town hall—were made of rose-colored brick or gray-white limestone that she said came from the local quarry.

He could feel himself slowing down, his pace and his thoughts. You couldn't walk along a street like this and stay in high gear. Emily had that effect on him, too. When he was with her he didn't want to hurry anywhere, especially not away.

"I thought Pine Point would be more…" He stopped, unsure what he meant.

"Piney? And pointy?"

He laughed. "Yeah. A frontier outpost. But it's an old-fashioned, pretty town. Reminds me of Stratford."

"That's one of my dream vacations—to stay for a week and go to the theatres every day."

"Then you could wander down to the river and feed the swans. You'd enjoy that. They glide up to the shore, all stately and dignified, then grab whatever food they can get."

"Sometimes whole flocks of swans come over Three Creeks in the fall. I've seen them in my uncle's field, grazing. A hundred birds, maybe two hundred."

"You have a competitive streak."

Her cheeks went pink. "I don't."

"There's nothing wrong with it."

"There isn't, but I don't."

"Okay." If that was what she wanted to believe. "So your mother won't travel at all and you won't travel without her?"

"I don't like to leave her alone too long."

"Why? She's a little on the eccentric side, but she's not a child." He had spoken without thinking, something he almost never did. It was a mistake. Emily withdrew, surprise and irritation easy to read. He went on, anyway. "If for some reason she doesn't do well on her own, what about the rest of the family? After all, there are so many Robbs in Three Creeks they've got their own road."

After half a block she still hadn't replied. He'd have to be more careful. Chasing her away wasn't the idea.

IF IT HAD BEEN a longer walk she might have tried to explain, but they had reached the bakery. Emily led Matthew inside, handed him a tray and took one for herself. The girl behind the lunch counter was from Three Creeks.

"Hi, Miss Robb!"

"Bren, I didn't know you were working here."

"It's my first summer job! Just flipping burgers." She grinned. "But they pay me!"

"Good for you." It was hard to believe someone who used to come to circle time in the library was old enough to work with hot grills.

Bren took their orders and relayed them to the cook, then poured coffee and ice water and put a number on each tray. "I hear your aunt and uncle's was one of the places broken into the other day."

"One of the places?"

"Oh, yeah, didn't you know? There was a whole bunch of break-ins, all the same, a mess made of desks and papers, but nothing taken, not as far as anybody could see, anyway."

"That's exactly what my aunt said."

Bren leaned as close as the serving counter allowed. "Couple of Mounties were in yesterday and I heard them talking when I took their trays. They were saying something about an identity theft ring. Creepy, eh?"

"What a horrible thought." Emily opened her purse, but Matthew got ahead of her and paid for both lunches. Bren promised to bring their food as soon as it was ready.

They carried their trays to a table by the window where they sat in uneasy silence, Matthew's comments still between them. She could understand him thinking it was odd that she lived at home and was so protective of her mother. He wasn't the only one with that opinion.

She'd made the choice when she was thirteen. There'd been a dance at school, so she'd come home late. Even before she'd opened the door she could smell smoke. The curtains over the stove were on fire, the wall and ceiling scorched. She'd called to her mother and run for water and baking soda, afraid of what might happen if she used the wrong one. Julia had wandered in from the living room talking about a copy of *Beowulf*. She was excited because it had the translation and the original Old English side by side, with a glossary showing how to pronounce the words.

Emily had doused the flames and turned off the burners, all on high, and accepted the truth that the kids at school already knew. Her mother was different. Not the way Wayne said it with a sneer and a knowing look at his friends, but clearly, Julia needed help. She lived partly in the world Emily occupied, but mostly somewhere beside it. She couldn't be left there on her own for long.

"My relatives are happy to look in on my mother if I need to go somewhere," Emily said. "I don't like asking too many favors."

"I shouldn't have said anything. No one can look at someone else's life from the outside and know what they should do." Matthew stirred milk into his coffee, tasted it and added more. "You were quiet in the car. At the museum, too. Is this trip all right with you? I dropped onto your doorstep and haven't stopped monopolizing your time since."

"I dropped onto your doorstep. Daniel's, anyway."

"And right away became annoyed with me."

"No, not at all."

Amusement softened his face. "Yes, absolutely. Do you want to tell me why?"

Emily decided to avoid words like *grim, rude* and *unwelcoming.* "It wasn't anything major. You weren't very communicative. That's all."

Bren swept up to their table with two plates of cheeseburgers, then rushed away to deal with a line forming at the counter. When she was gone, Matthew said, "I suppose I approach people I don't know with a certain amount of caution. You're more accepting of strangers than I am. I've appreciated that, but it isn't really a good idea."

"You're not a stranger. You're Daniel's nephew."

"Are all his relations welcome in your house?"

"Of course."

"Even the black sheep?"

Was he finally going to tell her something about himself? No list of indiscretions came tumbling out. He continued eating his cheeseburger, making the occasional approving sound.

"Daniel never mentioned any black sheep," she said.

"Every family has at least one."

"Not mine." She smiled as a thought struck her. "Aunt Edith might say Alex qualifies, for keeping Sue in Alberta."

"The paleontologists? I've heard about the selfish wedding in the badlands, with only the hoodoos for witnesses. It's not like your cousin, apparently, and the guy, this Alex, has obviously changed her for the worse."

"You've met my Aunt Edith?"

"She came by last night with a cake."

"And told you her life history."

"Not just hers."

"That isn't fair! All I know is your name. I don't even know what work you do."

"It bothers you, doesn't it? Not to know all about me, the way you know about everybody else in town."

"It doesn't *bother* me. I'm just interested." She waited, giving him a chance to fill her in, but again he didn't. Maybe his job embarrassed him. It might, if it involved doing something cut-throat, like hostile take-overs. She could see him being ruthless enough for that, but nice enough to mind.

"I'm not used to all this secrecy, Matthew. I'm going to guess your exact connection to Daniel if it's the last thing I do."

"Oh, good. A game. I always win games."

"Not this one."

"Not that you're competitive."

She ignored him. "Let's see…are you the nephew who loves motorcycles and always goes to the rally in Sturgis?"

"Nope."

"The one whose grade eleven science project went all the way to the provincial exhibit and got a commendation from the Canadian Space Agency?"

He shook his head, then popped the last bite of his lunch into his mouth. He took a sip of coffee and sat back with a satisfied air. "Good burger."

"Don't tell me you're the one who presses flowers?"

"I can honestly say I've never pressed a single flower. It's possible I've never picked one, either."

"Not even dandelions?"

"Maybe those. Long, long ago."

So he had never picked flowers for anyone but his mother. Of course, people in the city couldn't help themselves to flowers. They bought expensive bouquets from a florist. Emily had never been given a florist's bouquet. They were strictly for weddings and funerals.

"Which of Daniel's siblings is your dad? Is he older or younger?"

"Daniel's actually my great-uncle."

That widened the field considerably. And it didn't answer her question.

Matthew pushed back his chair. "If you're helping your grandmother this afternoon we'd better get you home."

JUST BEFORE THEY REACHED the Three Creeks sign an impulse struck her. "Turn here!"

He didn't ask why. He checked the rearview mirror, braked and took a left-hand turn from the highway onto a dirt track. The car's bumper dipped down and nosed upward, into potholes and out.

"You can pull over now."

"Over? There's no over." Matthew parked where they were, right in the middle of the path.

Emily met him on his side of the car and led him through grass grown high and gone to seed. It reached under her skirt, tickling her bare legs. She put her foot on the bottom strand of a barbed wire fence and lifted the top so he could squeeze through, then gathered her skirt so it wouldn't catch when he held the wires apart for her.

"Why are we trespassing in a wheat field?"

"It's barley."

"Well then, why are we trespassing in a barley field?"

She turned to smile at him. "You'll see." She kept walking between the rows of grain, expecting him to follow. At a grove of bur oaks she stopped, her eagerness fading. There was nothing to see but trees and barley.

"I'm sorry, Matthew. It was here somewhere."

"The Rutherford place?"

She nodded. "My grandmother said it was a huge yard site. I thought there'd be more left for you to see." Stones from a foundation, traces of a fence, a covered well.

"I'm glad you brought me, Emily. Even if there's nothing left. If I'm going for glimpses, why not a glimpse of this?"

It was the first time she had seen him show real interest in his family. It made her feel closer to him. "You're standing right where your great-great-grandfather stood."

"Is that so? And how would you know that?"

"It's the nature of trees. People stand under them."

He nearly laughed. "Very scientific."

"He'd be out here working, getting hot, and he'd come into the shade of these trees to cool off. He'd take out a jar of water—"

"A jar?"

"They drank from sealer jars." She kept going from where she'd left off. "So he'd take his jar of water and his lunch box and sit under these trees. His son would have been working with him, learning the ropes. While his dad rested, he would have tried to catch gophers."

Matthew pulled at the knees of his trousers and sat at the base of one of the oaks. Emily joined him, staying an arm's length away, her legs folded under her and her skirt tucked around them.

"Think we'll get ticks?" he asked.

"Not in July."

They sat in silence, but this time it wasn't uncomfortable. She liked his ability to be calmly quiet, not searching for small talk, not needing to hear himself all the time. Even so, he tended to fill the space, his presence big and solid and, at the moment, reassuring.

"How long has it been just you and your mother?"

Back to her again. He never wanted to focus on himself. "Forever. My dad died when I was eight."

"That's very young to lose a father."

"I barely remember him. It's been hard on my mother, at least I think it has. She doesn't connect with many people."

"What happened?"

"To my father? Oh, you know." As long ago as it was and as little as it had ever seemed to have to do with her, she didn't like going over it. "It was an accident. There's no shortage of accidents on a farm."

"And your mother turned to her book collection?"

"That started before. My grandparents gave her some boxes of books from their attic when she was still in high school. I remember her reading to my father." It was a comforting picture, the two of them sitting by the Franklin stove on a winter evening, her mother's voice going on and on, pages turning. "She hardly ever reads anymore."

"I noticed she talks about her books, but not so much about what's in them."

"That's because she wants to start at the beginning."

"Start reading at the beginning? You're kidding."

"I'm not. She wants to get all the books that matter, then read from the start."

Matthew leaned back, resting his head against the tree trunk. "So she doesn't collect because of the monetary value. She's seeing the books as a sort of map of civilization. When she's done collecting she'll follow the route."

He understood. How could he? No one else did. Emily felt as if she had fallen in love with him, right in that instant. She kept her eyes on her sandalled feet, dusty from walking through the field. She was alone too much, if gratitude felt like love.

"Most people don't see that. Aunt Edith thinks they're dust catchers."

"I suppose they are. Dust catchers *and* a map of human thought."

Emily smiled. "She'll never be done collecting, though. She goes sideways, too."

"What do you mean, sideways?"

"After she got all the books from the Enlightenment that she thought were most important, she decided she needed music from that time, too, and art prints. The same thing happened for the Renaissance, for every period of time."

"Amazing."

"It gets frustrating for her. I mean, she can't own a cave-painting. And a poster doesn't capture the scale and mood and texture."

"She'll need a couple of extra lifetimes for all she wants to learn."

"If she does want to learn. I'm never sure if that's really the point. Maybe she just wants the map."

Matthew had listened intently. His face, in leaf-shaped shadow, looked so touchable she tucked her hands under her knees to make sure they behaved themselves.

She hadn't kissed a man in years. Who could she

kiss? Everyone around Three Creeks was her cousin or married or eighty or fifteen.

She closed her eyes in an effort to stop seeing the picture that came to mind, herself sinking backward into tall grass, him coming after. Right away, she opened them. Eyes closed made it worse. Eyes closed she felt his weight against her.

"Are you all right, Emily?" He sounded concerned. "I should take you home. You've had a lot of sun."

She could explain why she'd closed her eyes. Or show him. How would he react if she wrapped her arms around him, pressed against him, touched his mouth? Something besides good sense stopped her from finding out, something she sensed from him.

He helped her to her feet. "Should I take you to your aunt's house? Heatstroke isn't something to fool around with and your mother, if you don't mind me saying so, doesn't seem like the first-aid type."

"I don't have heatstroke, Matthew. All I need is a glass of water and a fan."

"A fan would suit you. The folded paper kind. You're an old-fashioned woman."

"I'm not old-fashioned."

"Hmm. Delusions. Another sign of heatstroke." He was smiling, but he kept one arm around her all the way back to the car, and she didn't try to step away.

When they reached her house she said, "I nearly forgot! Aunt Edith and Uncle Will are having a barbecue tomorrow evening. I wondered if you'd like to go. There'll be lots of untinned food. And trees to eat it under."

"That sounds great."

"You'll come?" She wished she didn't feel so pleased. "Why don't you drop by here earlier? Around four? You could help me pick berries—that's my contribution to the meal. We can all walk over together."

"See you at four, then."

He backed out to the road and drove away—slowly, she was glad to see, and with a reassuring zigzag motion.

She walked up the driveway, humming, and only noticed the tune when she reached the door. "Have Yourself a Merry Little Christmas." It wasn't even a song she liked, but she smiled, thinking of snowflakes and cocoa and Matthew.

THE TELEPHONE WAS RINGING when Matthew got back to the house. He hurried to pick up the kitchen extension.

"At last! I was beginning to think you'd found yourself a deserted island with white sands and your own personal bank. How's it going?"

The voice on the other end crackled. "Slowly. With bites."

"Bugs are bad?"

"They're thriving."

Matthew got juice from the fridge with his free hand. The cupboard was too far to reach, so he drank from the carton. "Where are you?"

"Just back from the crash site. The so-called crash site. That plane is in surprisingly good shape. Broken struts, damaged undercarriage, that's about it."

"Supports your theory," Matthew said.

"He beached it."

"Kind of risky on a rock shore."

"Frank never minded risks. Between the canopy from the living trees and the dead ones leaning over it nobody was ever going to see that wreck from the air." The voice faded. "You can't tell after so long if the trunks were broken or cut. What I will say is they're conveniently arranged over the fuselage."

"Did you get a look inside?"

Static cut off some of the reply. "…snowshoes in winter. Hatchet, snare wire, first-aid kit."

"What's that? You found the gear?"

"No, no. It's gone." The voice faded again, then came back. "I'm losing the signal. Have you been to the Moore place?"

"Couple of times. It's hard to get a good look around. The mother never leaves." Matthew held the phone away from his ear during a burst of static. When it ended, the busy signal took over.

He hung up the phone, dried his hands to make sure there was no condensation remaining from the juice carton and took the manila envelope Emily had given him into the living room. He spread out her grandmother's photographs on the desktop.

One showed a scruffy-looking bunch beside an ox-cart. Another, a house building bee. Grim-faced men in undershirts and sagging trousers looked at the camera as if their worst enemy was holding it. In the third, a hollow-eyed man stood behind a seated woman who held an armload of blankets he supposed contained a baby. The last was a threshing scene, interesting for the look at agricultural technology of the time. No names or dates were written on the backs. He had to take Eleanor Robb's word for it that these gray-faced people were Rutherfords and other early settlers.

He tucked them back in the envelope, then picked up the digital camera he'd left on the desk. He turned it on, switched to view mode and scrolled through the most recent shots.

The Moore house from a distance, with its hedges and forestlike yard. The dog, slow but observant, looking toward the faraway camera.

Mrs. Moore through the kitchen window, reading.

He touched the last image. Emily, in her garden picking raspberries. Emily who looked beautiful in blue and in yellow.

CHAPTER SEVEN

SHE WAS EXCITED, and she shouldn't be. It was like
drinking, getting a little tipsier with each glass. She felt
a little more…a little more what? Not in love. Not after five days. But a little more something each time she
saw him. Enticed. Attached. Lucky.

Even though he was different from everyone she
knew, puzzling and unreadable so much of the time, he
seemed right, right for her. She didn't believe in the idea
of one perfect mate. You could be compatible with any
number of people. It was more a matter of geography.
A compatible person who lived where you did. And
Matthew didn't.

So she shouldn't be excited.

"Mmm." An appreciative look came over his face,
shaded by the straw hat she had lent him. "You haven't
tasted raspberries until you've had one you picked
yourself."

"City people usually worry about the worms."

His chewing paused. "You're kidding."

"They're very little worms."

He swallowed deliberately and looked closely at a
second berry, peering inside the hollow where it had

been attached to the branch. It must have been bugless, because he popped it into his mouth, unconcerned.

A few berries later he paused, then pulled it open to expose a tiny, white, wriggling worm. "Is that the critter you meant?"

"That's it."

Matthew tossed the berry into the bushes. "I don't mind for myself. I'm thinking of the worm's welfare."

She wanted to kiss him for the unexpected silliness, the mock-serious face. Her heart beat faster, as if she was about to make a speech or parachute from a plane. She should do it. She should kiss him.

"You're staring." He tugged the brim of the straw hat she'd lent him. "You chose the hottest part of the day to go picking just so you could make me wear this ridiculous hat, didn't you?"

"It's an efficient hat. Keeps the sun and the mosquitoes off your neck." She squished one that had landed on his cheek, then quickly pulled her hand away. "If you tried to pick too early or too late in the day you'd get eaten alive."

"Living close to a creek has a downside." He reached past her to a clump of fruit. "So, I'll meet the whole school of Robbs this evening, will I?"

"All the Three Creeks group will be there, along with Susannah and Alex and Uncle Winston and Aunt Lucy."

"Except for the paleontologists, are they all farmers?"

"Tom's wife, Pam, is a teacher. Uncle Winston and Aunt Lucy are retired now, but when they lived here, they farmed."

"Winston was talking about that before you came into the post office the other day. He sounded nostalgic."

She smiled. "He does that. To listen to him now you'd think he never lost sleep over wheat prices or drought or wet years and rotting crops. He only remembers the good things." It made him nice to be around, but disconcerting. He thought everyone he had left behind was living a different life than they really were.

She glanced at Matthew, still eating a couple of berries from every handful he picked. "You probably have a university degree, accounting or business, something like that."

"It's no help to me today. I had no idea raspberry bushes had thorns." He held out a scratched arm for her to see. "Doesn't your aunt have her own berries? Mrs. Bowen does."

"Sure, everybody does. But this is what we do to each other. Give each other berries and zucchini and tomatoes—"

"And pumpkin loaves?"

"You've got it."

"I'm catching on. Must be genetic memory."

It was good to see him so relaxed. Every day he loosened up a little more. Three Creeks had that effect on people—that, or it sent them screaming for city lights.

He shook his ice cream pail, settling the berries. "Do we have enough?"

"We need more than enough. It's an unspoken rule of barbecues." She turned her back so she couldn't see him. Scratched and silly, he was more appealing than ever.

JULIA HAD SUDDENLY dug in her heels about the need to "get together and eat." The momentary change in Emily had startled Matthew. Her hands had stilled, her shoulders drooped, a look of exhaustion had touched her face. The next second she was back to normal, her expression soft with good humor, her voice warm while she reminded her mother that Winston and Lucy would be leaving the next day.

That point didn't seem to have any effect, so he had jumped in, telling Julia he wished she'd go to the barbecue for his sake, that for an outsider like him another familiar face in the crowd would be welcome.

The problem of being in a crowd was something she understood. So here they were at a family dinner where he didn't belong and where he had no real expectation of learning anything new. Julia was off by herself studying the flowers growing in a border along the driveway as if she was the first botanist in the South American rainforest, and Emily looked happy chatting with her pregnant cousin. Susannah. Would his clients be satisfied with his work for today? Journal entry: *Helped make Emily happy.*

He should have been done in Three Creeks by now. Close to done, at least. Ever since she'd come to Daniel's door he'd been operating on half power. Right then he'd started dancing around the issue instead of getting at it. He wasn't a tourist in the land of orchids and belugas. He had a job to do. A lucrative job, at that.

"Here they are!" Emily said. "Can you believe they drove here? Lazy things."

Two trucks turned into Will and Edith's driveway, the

second one riding the first's bumper. Passengers piled out and greeted each other as if they didn't cross paths nearly every day. They pulled at children, checked to see if faces were clean and teased whoever they weren't actually talking to, all at once.

Emily pointed out the people Matthew hadn't met. Eleanor, her grandmother. Brian, Susannah's oldest brother, and his family. Martin's wife, Pat, and their daughter, Nell. Tom's wife, Pam, and their three kids.

"Jennifer's the oldest, she's a real animal lover. Young Will's in the middle, hockey's his thing, no matter what the season. Anne is the littlest. She's quiet, except when she scolds people."

"I'll be sure to steer clear of her."

"You won't hear a peep from her this evening. You're a stranger, Matthew. Dangerous." She looked amused at the thought.

"Good for her. Not a bad example for you, Emily."

There were only twenty people, but they were noisy and energetic and the group felt bigger. Some resembled Emily, reddish and willowy, others were dark, like her mother. Robbs seemed to come in two varieties. Any new genes added to the mix must sink out of sight.

Emily began to lead him around the yard, introducing him face-to-face, going through the whole family again. As she did, her hand kept lighting on his arm, distracting him from attaching names to faces. He heard snippets of conversation, with Edith's voice rising above the others.

"I couldn't help but cry, to see the three of them side by side…"

"We should have gone organic at the beginning…."

"…standing together outside the church, no husbands, only Liz and Emily and Susannah with her tummy out to here, well, the tears just flowed."

"…love castle ruins. There'll be a book in it."

"…there with his handkerchief. Susannah has found herself a very kind man. Very brown, too—he's careless about the sun. A pity dinosaurs didn't deposit themselves in more temperate climates."

Emily stopped circulating when they got to Susannah.

"Before I'd even met Alex I used to imagine my children digging with me," she was saying to Pat. "Now it'll happen."

"Don't count on it. Nell thrives on being contrary."

Patting her stomach, Susannah looked at her husband. "He won't give us trouble, will he? This little guy?"

"No more than we gave our parents." He caught the end of her hair with his fingers, and she bent her head so her cheek touched his hand.

Matthew looked away from the intimate gesture. Emily didn't. She watched with a tender expression. He felt his own face soften in response. She had that effect on him, took away the hard edges he'd built up over time. Built up intentionally and for good purpose.

He'd be crazy to get involved with her. This was a woman who worried about hurting toads. He had to back up. Get the job done and get out.

EMILY WAS HAPPY to see Matthew fit in so well. He helped Tom and Alex keep an eye on the steaks, talked local history with Eleanor, agriculture with Uncle Will, pet care with Jennifer, and when Uncle Will and Aunt

Edith's dog brought him drool-covered sticks he threw them as if he enjoyed it.

After dinner the children went off by themselves and most of the adults moved closer to a few smudges that smoldered to keep mosquitoes away. Uncle Will always said his skin was too thick for them. He sat right where he was, with his back against the picnic table, wasps circling, the heels of his steel-toed boots digging into the grass.

The talk had gone around a few times from the wedding to the baby to bankers and back. The repetition was making Emily sleepy until Uncle Will mentioned a story he had seen in the newspaper a couple of weeks before.

"This guy's supposed to be flying gold out of Snow Lake and he never turns up. You must remember that happening, Mother. Didn't Daniel know the pilot?"

"They were good friends. It was very hard on him."

"I suppose a Mountie knows all kinds of people." Will looked around, including the rest of the group in the conversation. "There was a storm system in the area, but not toward Winnipeg, where he was headed. They figured he must have got caught up in it anyway. Didn't seem likely to me. I always thought he hightailed it to the Dominican Republic or some such place. But now they've found the plane."

"Way out nowhere," Tom said. "Some guys on a fly-in fishing trip found it."

"But get this—no body."

"And no gold."

Everyone but Emily had read the story. She'd hardly

looked at a newspaper for weeks. If she didn't get to an issue quickly, her mother had it clipped, filed and recycled.

"Who would it belong to now?" Martin asked. "I mean, if Tom and I found it could we keep it?"

"You won't be the only ones thinking about that," Uncle Will said. "Bet you the lodges will be offering gold-hunting packages. Never mind black bear and moose."

"It must still belong to the mine," Eleanor said. "So you just pay attention to your farm, Martin."

"Forget the farm." Pat laid a hand on her husband's chest. "Go find gold, sweetie. For me."

There were chuckles and whistles and a call of "None of that, missy!" Matthew didn't seem to be listening to any of it. He rubbed the dog's ears while its head rested on his knee, brown eyes fixed on gray ones.

Emily went to sit beside him. "How are you doing?"

"Great. Too full, and sleepy."

"Same here."

"Your mother didn't seem to mind the getting together and eating once she started."

"It's the difficulty of taking that step, getting from one thing to another, letting go of the house."

He nodded, his expression distant, as if his mind was half on something else.

"I hope you're not bored. Sometimes my family gets started on a story and they go on for hours."

"I'm enjoying it. What might have been, right?"

"Do you wish your family had stayed? They could have built another house, I suppose. They still had lots of land."

"Maybe we would've gone to school together."

"But then I wouldn't like you, because I'd remember you pulling my hair." She wasn't aware of moving closer until her arm pressed against his, sending quivery feelings all the way to her stomach. She quickly leaned away.

"Have you heard from Daniel yet?" Her voice was back to normal. Just friendly. "He must be coming home soon."

"He's going to be longer than he expected."

"I'm sorry." It meant his aunt wasn't getting better yet. "You must have things of your own to do. Will you continue taking care of the house?"

"For a while yet. Unless he asks me to join him."

Emily wondered how long "a while" would be. Not long enough.

"HEAR THAT? That's a whip-poor-will."

They were walking down the middle of Robbs' Road after dark, going home from the barbecue, Julia on one tire-hardened track, Emily on the other, and Matthew in the gravel on the side. The bird call was between a whistle and a hoot, clearly *whip-poor-will,* with the last syllable most strongly accented. It started slowly, lilting, and gathered speed until it lurched from note to note.

"That drunken-sounding racket?"

Emily laughed. She heard a puff of air escape from her mother—it was as close as Julia ever came to laughing. The bird's song had sped up to the point that the *poors* were almost tripping over the *wills.*

Matthew said, "It sounds pretty at first, but after a while you kind of want to shoot it, don't you?"

"No!"

"Oh, really?"

"Well…"

"Truthfully."

"Well, maybe throw something at it."

The singing ended as abruptly as it had begun. "It does that," she said, "and then it starts the cycle over. It must wear itself out. Or get a sore throat."

Partway up the driveway Matthew stopped. "Did you leave a lamp on?" Soft light glowed through the drawn curtains.

"I don't think so."

"The door's open a crack."

"Sometimes it opens after we shut it."

"You didn't lock it?"

"I did. It sticks, though. You think it's closed all the way and it isn't. Oh—" Then the lock wouldn't have turned.

"You two should head back to Will and Edith's place."

Neither of them moved. Matthew headed up the driveway. "At least get in the garage, out of sight." He opened the side door. Moonlight filtered in, showing vague shapes of tools and boxes. He felt around in the shadows. "It's clear. I'll call you after I check the house." He disappeared behind the hedge.

Emily had lived without a man in the house for too long to accept anyone trying to protect her. She told her mother to stay in the garage and went after him.

It was darker on the other side of the caraganas, the high sharp branches shading the moon's faint light. She heard something rustle, then saw a moving shape. He was in the elms. When she reached his side, his hand closed on her arm and he drew closer, lips to her ear. "Emily, listen. I want you to stay safe."

Something cool and damp touched her hand. Hamish's nose, sniffing. "There he is," she whispered. "Bad old dog. What have you been doing? Letting people in?" His tail waved against her leg. "Hamish isn't worried. The door's just popped open."

"If you're coming, stay behind me."

Matthew went up the steps and pushed the door open wider. He seemed to know which boards he could walk on without squeaking. Emily put her feet where his had been and didn't look up until they reached the living room.

A young man stood at the shelves, his back to them, a book in one hand. He looked as if he belonged there, as if he was choosing something to read. Then he turned, his eyes widening when he saw them in the doorway. He was younger than she'd thought, no more than fifteen. He looked from them to the front door, and his muscles bunched.

Matthew said, "Stay where you are."

He threw the book at them and ran. Before he was halfway across the room, Matthew got to him and pulled him to the floor. It was done so quickly, with so little resistance that it seemed almost gentle, but Emily heard the boy gasp in sudden pain. He didn't move. He didn't even twitch. She was relieved to see his eyelids blink, then lift.

Matthew looked at her, too calmly for the circumstances. "Got a rope?"

A rope. All she could think of was the string she used to tie parcels. Then she remembered the leash from Hamish's puppy days, when his herding instincts sent him onto the road every time Tom moved his cattle from one pasture to another. She found it at the back of the glory hole under the stairs.

"This all right?"

"Perfect." He tied the boy's hands behind his back, then ran the leash to his feet, and tied them. "Call the police, then keep an eye on the kid. Stay out of his way. Just watch."

Emily hurried to the phone in the kitchen and looked up the number of the RCMP detachment in Pine Point. While she waited for them to answer and then explained what had happened, she heard Matthew going from room to room.

"Emily?" Julia was outside the door, with Hamish and the cat. All three heads peered into the kitchen.

"It's okay, Mom. There's a burglar—at least I suppose he's a burglar—but it's okay."

Julia didn't move. Emily stood where she could see her mother and the boy. He didn't look any more dangerous than her nephews. No piercings, no tattoos, no odd hair dye or style designed to scare grown-ups.

"You're not hurt, are you? The rope isn't too tight?"

The side of his face pressed to the floor, he stared at her ankles.

"We need the police." Julia took a couple of steps into the kitchen. "For burglars, you need the police."

"I called them, Mom."

"Are they coming?"

"Right away, they said."

Matthew was back. "There's no one else in the house. Nothing disturbed. It looks like he started with the books."

Emily thought her mother was going to run into the living room. Instead, she sat in the chair by the window and stared outside.

"What did he do? What did he do to the books?"

"He only looked at them, Mom."

Matthew bent to untie the leash. "Get up."

The command was given quietly, but this time the boy hurried to obey. He shook out his arms and legs, winced, and rubbed his right hand.

"You're crazy, man. I didn't do nothin'."

In spite of the aggressive words, he didn't sound tough. Just scared. Given that he was standing uninvited in the living room, his claim of innocence was almost funny.

"Turn around. Hands on the wall." Matthew felt the front and back of the boy's shirt, under the waistband of his jeans, then down each leg.

"I don't got nothin'."

Nothing but a penknife, the blade folded shut, in one pocket and a wallet in the other.

"Sit."

He didn't move, so Matthew propelled him into a chair, then opened the wallet. "No driver's license, no health insurance, no student ID." There was only a red plastic card. "Rogers Video. You're Peter Wallis?"

He shook his head.

"You borrowed someone's wallet?"

"Don't I get a lawyer?"

"No doubt the police will advise you to do that."

The boy's expression flitted from puzzlement to fear to dawning bravado.

"Personally, I don't care if you talk to a lawyer. I don't care if you go to jail or pay a fine or walk out of here free as a bird. I want to know who you are, who sent you and what you were told to find." Matthew held up the red card. "Who is Peter Wallis?"

"I don't have to listen to you." He'd figured out he wasn't dealing with someone in authority.

Matthew gripped the boy's head and pushed it back so they looked eye to eye. "I asked you a question."

Emily had never heard Matthew sound so cold, or so threatening. The kid wet his lips and swallowed hard. "He's my dad."

"Did he send you?"

"No, no way. That's just his card. He signed up and they gave him a bunch. Don't tell him, okay? I won't come back, I promise."

Matthew let go of him and stepped back. "And what's your name, Mister Wallis?"

There was a second's hesitation. "Jason."

"Where's your transportation?"

Jason blinked, his lids fluttering quickly. "In the woods out back. I rode my bike."

"Motorcycle?"

"My bike," he repeated, emphasizing the word.

"A bicycle?"

He gave a curt nod. If Julia didn't look so shaken, Emily might have smiled. What kind of getaway could you make on a bicycle? You couldn't take much with you. Maybe he wasn't a thief at all. Maybe he was disturbed in some way—mixed up, or really and truly ill. Maybe all he'd wanted was a book to read and if they'd got home later they would have found him curled up and content.

"All right. You rode your bike from…"

"Miller's Crossing."

Matthew looked at Emily.

"It's about ten miles from here. Smaller than Three Creeks."

"A long ride. Who asked you to do that, Jason?"

"Nobody."

"You decided to ride your bike ten miles, go into any random locked house and, what, steal a book, then ride ten miles home?"

"I didn't figure it out too good."

"That's an understatement. How did you really get here?"

Jason's mouth opened, but before anything came out he closed it again.

"Don't you think the people who put you up to this deserve to take some blame?"

"There's no people."

Matthew's voice was quiet. "Did they scare you, Jason? First they offered you something nice. What did they give you? Or are they still holding it out of reach?"

Julia spoke up from her place by the window. "The police are here."

Matthew continued talking, almost soothingly. "But then they got demanding, didn't they? And you wondered what you'd got yourself into. You're right to be scared. You should be very careful." He leaned closer and spoke too quietly for Emily to hear. Jason shook his head. He spoke again and the boy's head moved more vehemently.

Matthew straightened and turned to Emily, his expression so remote it chilled her. "Holding up okay?"

"I'm fine."

"The police will want to look around and ask you some questions. I'll be checking outside." He grasped Jason's arm and pulled him out of the house. As soon as they left, Julia hurried to the living room.

The patrol car's headlights lit the driveway. Emily watched Matthew hand the boy over to two RCMP officers, then go to his car and take something from the glove compartment. A flashlight clicked on and he strode away. At first she could see the bobbing light, then nothing.

AN HOUR LATER Jason was still handcuffed in the back seat of the patrol car, and the officers had finished searching the house. They sat down with Emily and Julia and went point by point through the evening, concentrating on events from the moment Matthew had noticed the open door.

"Looks like Wallis used his knife to force the lock," one of them said. It was Corporal Reed, the same officer who had spoken to Aunt Edith.

"Do you think he's responsible for the other break-ins?" Emily asked.

"Can't say at this point."

"What happens to him now?"

"He's a minor. We'll check for priors, call his parents and likely release him into their custody."

"Tonight?"

"With a curfew and a Promise to Appear."

"A promise—"

"That means he and his parents agree he'll show up for fingerprinting when we tell them to, and for court next time it sits in Pine Point."

It was a lot of trust to put in the person who'd just broken into her home.

The corporal closed his notebook. "It seems clear Wallis was interrupted almost immediately after gaining entry, but I'd ask that you both take a good look at your belongings in the morning. Make a list of anything missing or damaged. We'll come back for it and let you know what's happening."

When the patrol car started down Robbs' Road Matthew reappeared, turning off the flashlight as he neared the house. Uncle Will arrived at the same time, concerned about the back and forth of the police vehicle. The two men did another check of the grounds and the outbuildings and made sure the locks on both doors still worked.

Emily turned down offers from both of them to stay the night. Will left first, promising to buy dead bolts as soon as the stores opened in the morning. He kissed Emily's cheek, gave his sister an awkward pat on the shoulder and said good-night.

Finally Emily walked with Matthew to his car. It felt much longer than hours since he'd arrived to pick berries. He had clowned around in a girlish hat and then he had threatened a teenage boy.

"Quite a day," she said.

"Think you'll sleep?"

"Sure. We were lucky, right? He didn't take anything or do any harm."

"Except to your feeling of security."

There was that. Locks didn't mean as much as she had thought they did. "How did you know how to stop him? Tackle him, I mean."

"All guys know how to do things like that."

"No, they don't."

"If they play football."

"Did Daniel teach you?"

"Emily, it's nothing. A male instinct."

They stood beside his car, neither making a move to go.

"I know I've already thanked you—it would have been an awful thing to deal with alone. I'm so glad you were here."

"So am I. Emily, the other day you said you and your mother have nothing of value. Are you still sure about that?"

"The silverware might be worth something. And we have a few pieces of jewelery that were passed down— a locket, a couple of brooches. But they're just garnets, amethysts."

"What about your mother's books? That's what the kid was looking at."

"I don't see how they could be valuable, if Mom could afford to buy them." Emily hesitated. "There are the ones that belonged to her great-grandparents."

"Having them appraised might not be a bad idea."

That was all she needed, another bill to pay. "Maybe one of these days."

"I could help. It's sort of what I do."

"You appraise books?"

"Things of value."

"I thought old men with those little—" she held two fingers up to her eye "—microscope things did that." She didn't like his expression. Amused tolerance.

"You need to get out more, Emily."

"Do you appraise things for museums?"

"For insurance companies."

She tried to react the way a person who got out more would. No surprise. Just a thoughtful nod. "I see."

"They need to know what an item is worth and what risks are attached to providing coverage."

It fit with some of his behavior, all that adding and subtracting she saw in his eyes. Not that he'd stopped to assess risk before dealing with Jason.

"I don't know how Mom would feel about someone looking that closely at her books."

"If she decides she's interested, let me know."

He leaned forward and for a second she thought he was going to kiss her. No such luck. He was only opening the car door.

CHAPTER EIGHT

BY NOON THE NEXT DAY Uncle Will had dealt with the doors. He installed a new garage light as well, one that would come on automatically if anyone approached. Looking pointedly at Hamish he told Emily the light would startle and discourage intruders, since the dog appeared to have retired.

After he put his tools away, he stayed for a glass of iced tea and a chat. He seemed to have something on his mind and not know how to get around to it. On his second glass of tea, he lowered his voice to a normal volume and asked, "How does your mom seem to you these days?"

Emily checked the living room. One by one, her mother was removing all the books that had been within Jason's reach and rubbing the covers with a cloth as if they were stained. She had already done the same thing early that morning.

"Let's go outside, Uncle Will."

She waited until they stood in the shade of the elms, far from the windows, before answering. "Mom's been unsettled lately, and the break-in hasn't helped, but she's all right, I think."

He nodded, not in agreement, but as if he was thinking. "She's always been more or less like this, even when we were kids."

"Easily bothered, you mean?"

"The whole business. Being persnickety about her things, testy if people got in her way or touched her stuff. But that was just Julia. Families call in doctors nowadays. We didn't then. If people were a bit funny, they were a bit funny."

Emily had heard this before. "Are you worried about her, Uncle Will?"

"No, no. Not worried. No more than usual." He looked deep into his glass, nearly empty again after a few good gulps. "I'm worried about you, Emily."

"Me!"

"It's not much of a life for you." His face colored. "I shouldn't say anything. It's none of my business. But then again, it is. You're my niece. She's my sister. You've grown up without a dad. So who's going to say it?"

Nobody, would be her preference. "I suppose it's Liz and Susannah who've brought this on. Weddings and babies."

"And this nephew of Daniel's."

"Uncle Will—"

"I heard Martin giving you the gears about him the other day."

"Martin does that. It doesn't mean anything."

"And I saw the way you looked at him at the barbecue."

She wasn't going to discuss her feelings about a man, whatever they might be, with her uncle. "I've been showing him around Three Creeks, that's all."

"*And* I saw the way he pitched in last night. Checking every door and window three times. Checking *you* more than once, I might add, fretting like a new mother."

"Uncle Will!"

"What I'm trying to say is, if you like this guy…single men are thin on the ground around here these days, Emily, and he was more than neighborly last night."

It was true. Matthew had been wonderful. Strong and capable. Not to mention a little frightening. "I'm not going to grasp onto a man just because he's around for a few days and I've turned thirty." She had actually crept a couple of years past that.

"Thirty," Will said disbelievingly. "Imagine that. Little Emily." The thought only distracted him for a moment. "Exactly. Thirty." He swished the remaining tea around the bottom of the glass. "We can keep an eye on your mom. Should have told you that a long time ago. Don't ignore your own chances like you did with John. You go where you want, sweetie."

She took his empty glass and gave him a hug. "This is where I want to be, Uncle Will."

ONE THING WAS SURE, that clueless kid wasn't working alone. Matthew had searched the woods close to the Moore house last night and again, more thoroughly, after the sun came up. Not finding an abandoned bicycle in acres of bush wasn't conclusive. More convincing was the kid's demeanor when he was pressed about it. He didn't get angry or frustrated. He got scared.

If Emily's radar was as good as she claimed the man in the black Mustang and the honeymooners Mrs.

Marsh had mentioned were the only strangers around. Since he hadn't managed to get the Mustang's license number, he could only check out the happy couple.

He was delayed by a visit from Corporal Reed, wandering around the house and asking questions about Daniel and the neighbors and the Robb family. He forced himself to relax and answer helpfully. When Reed left, Matthew began to search for a field that doubled as a honeymoon hotel.

He soon found a tent behind a grove of willows past the Three Creeks exit. A canoe was turned over beside it, but he didn't see a vehicle. He drove past the site, parked behind another strip of trees, then walked back. He made himself comfortable in the willows and waited.

Finally, an old Toyota Tercel came bumping across the field. A man and a woman, both thirtyish, got out. No cuddles or playful touches. They hardly looked at each other. Before they went into the tent he zoomed in and got close-ups. One of him, one of her, one of the license plate.

CORPORAL REED ACCEPTED a cup of tea and sat with Julia and Emily at the kitchen table. He'd already told them that Jason Willis had been released to his parents' custody, as expected. His first court date would be on Tuesday.

"You've checked your belongings?" he asked. "You're sure nothing is missing?"

"Not that we could see," Emily said. "Jason didn't even mess up the desk. That's what happened everywhere else, didn't it?"

The corporal tried to make eye contact with Julia. "The books are yours, ma'am, not your daughter's?"

Julia looked a little alarmed at being singled out.

"Do you keep a list of titles? Would you know if one or two were missing?"

"I'd know."

"I assume they're insured."

"Insured?"

"It's an extensive collection. You must have insured it against theft or fire."

Julia blinked at the table.

Emily said, "I don't think it occurred to either of us to insure the books."

Reed turned back to her. "Have you noticed anything unusual going on—out here in the country or in town? Vehicles parked where they shouldn't be, strangers loitering, even people you know who suddenly have a large amount of money to spend?"

She had been worried about Daniel, but his absence had been explained. The only people she knew who had been throwing money around were Liz and Jack. "People come in off the highway to get gas or snacks, especially in the summer. There's a lot of traffic up to the lakes."

Reed took his first sip of tea. "The hotels in Pine Point were full of Robb friends and family last week. For a wedding, I'm told. Any of those folks still in town?"

Emily stared, for a moment too surprised to answer. "Most of them are gone. Are you suggesting…"

"I'm trying to get all the facts, Ms. Moore. The man

who was with you last night—" The corporal consulted his notebook. "Matthew Rutherford. He's not local?"

"He's visiting, taking care of his uncle's house. Daniel Rutherford."

"I know Daniel. Taking care of the house, why?"

"Daniel's spending time with a sick relative."

"And he's been away how long?"

"I'm not sure. A couple of weeks."

"How long have you known his nephew?"

"About a week. Since he arrived in town."

"Any impressions?"

"I don't understand."

"Of what sort of person he is."

Emily looked at her teacup, wondering what to say. "Jason was caught in my house. He doesn't deny breaking in. Why are you asking about my relatives and friends?"

"It's routine, Ms. Moore. I'm trying to get the whole picture." The words were reassuring, but his tone wasn't.

"Matthew's a lot like his uncle." She was surprised to see her mother nodding in agreement. "He's a smart, capable, helpful person."

"Okay. That's all I need for now." Reed closed his book and stood up. His tone became less formal. "And how did you ladies sleep last night?"

"Not that well."

"People really feel uneasy when someone's managed to get into their home." He stood with one hand on the doorknob. "I see you've got a new lock. That's good. The old one wasn't accomplishing much, was it?"

Emily was beginning to feel as guilty as Jason. She decided to ask a few questions of her own. "Jason said he came by bicycle. All the way from Miller's Crossing."

"Right."

"If that's true it's hard to believe he's responsible for all the break-ins, isn't it? Because of the distance and because of how little he could expect to take away with him."

"That's still to be determined."

"But if he didn't break into the other houses, who did, and are they still around? And if he didn't ride his bike, how did he get here? He didn't have a driver's license in his wallet. And why was he reading a book? Standing in the middle of the room, taking his time. What did he want?"

The corporal's professional expression was back. "Those are good questions. You can be sure we're asking them as well, Ms. Moore."

He didn't tell her she worried too much. Just this once it would have been nice to hear.

ALMOST EVERY MEMBER of the family turned up that afternoon. Before catching his flight, Uncle Winston came, wanting to reassure his sister. Aunt Edith wanted to compare break-ins and Eleanor wanted to know Julia and Emily weren't still frightened. The cousins wanted to have coffee and talk about the crime rate and the children wanted to take turns being the thief and Matthew Rutherford and tackle each other in the living room. Julia soon took to her room.

After dinner, Matthew came. Emily was so pleased to see him she forgot to invite him in. The questions that had been flying around her mind all day quieted.

"How do you do that?" she asked.

"What am I doing?"

"You're making me feel safe."

His voice cooled. "I'm sorry if you haven't been feeling safe. Any reason, besides the obvious?"

She felt pushed away, the way she had the day they met.

"Emily?"

"I already mentioned it to Corporal Reed."

There was a flicker of a smile. "Mention it to me, too."

"Okay." She sat on the step so she wouldn't have to keep looking at the distant expression on his face. "I don't believe a kid on a bicycle rode ten miles several times to mess up some desks and look at a book. It's odd."

"People do odd things."

"I feel as if there's…somebody else." She shrugged. "Out there." The feeling was strong, but as soon as she put it into words it sounded irrational.

"Have you been cooped up all day? How about a walk?"

"If Mom will come. She's beside herself."

Matthew went into the kitchen. Emily heard him ask her mother if she was all right on her own. After a murmured response he was back, pulling the door shut behind him. The lock clicked into place.

"Road or meadow?" he asked.

"At this time of evening, road. We'll have a fighting chance with the bugs."

They walked along, swatting mosquitoes every few steps.

"Matthew, I'm sorry if I made you uncomfortable. The safety thing, I mean."

"Not uncomfortable—"

"You don't need to explain," she said quickly. "I didn't get enough sleep, and now I'm sounding clingy."

"You're sounding scared. A reasonable response to finding a stranger in your house."

She didn't understand him. First a don't-dare-need-me face, then kindness that invited more needing? It wasn't that she needed him, anyway. A few days didn't cancel out thirty-two years of not needing him. It was just that being with him felt good.

She gave him a coffee-party smile. "You know what surprised me almost as much as seeing Jason in the living room? Hearing that you work for an insurance company!"

The small-talk tone seemed to puzzle him. He glanced at her, frowning a little, then looked back at the road.

"I hope you're not the kind of insurance man who gives people trouble about their oil furnaces." Before he could answer she added, "No, I suppose not. You wouldn't be interested unless it was a really valuable furnace."

He ignored her attempt at a joke. "Is someone giving you trouble about your oil furnace?"

"All the time."

"Well, I'm not that kind of insurance man."

Emily turned and started back to the house. "Corporal Reed asked me about you today."

"Did he? He asked me about you, too."

"About me!"

"That's what the police do when they're investigating a crime. Ask around about everything."

"He mentioned insurance for Mom's books. I wondered…I know you're busy with your family history—"

"I have lots of time. And I offered."

"Once Mom has a chance to think it over she might be glad to have the books evaluated. Not right away. She's still rubbing Jason's fingerprints off everything."

Making stilted conversation was so uncomfortable. Talking without touching, wishing for comfort when he only wanted to give advice. It was a relief to reach the driveway. She offered him a cold drink and was glad when he said he couldn't stay.

AS DUSK APPROACHED Emily and Julia's uneasiness grew. Knowing someone had been in their house touching their things was unsettling. Their home wasn't their castle—it was a thin barrier of wood and glass that anyone could knock down if they had half a mind to do it.

Emily double checked the new dead bolts. They didn't have much choice but to leave most of the windows open with fans in front of them, even the ones at ground-floor level. She made sure they were all set low enough that no one could squeeze through, then fit them with broomsticks and pieces of wood cut to size so they couldn't be forced open any wider. It wasn't foolproof. She paced from room to room knowing that sounds from outside would frighten her and wondering what on earth she would do if she actually found someone cutting through a screen.

Finally she stretched out on the sofa with her pile of library books. She read until her eyes stung, then wished her mother good-night and went up to her room.

Even past midnight the day's heat was concentrated under the eaves. A small fan resting on the windowsill brought in air that was a few degrees cooler, and full of good smells, roses and willow and the summer's first cut hay.

A nightgown felt too vulnerable. She kept her clothes on and turned off the light, then lay down on top of the covers. In the kitchen, the kettle whistled. The cat, who had followed her upstairs, jumped from the dresser to the floor and padded away, going where the action was.

Emily didn't realize she had fallen asleep until a sound woke her. A faint thud. She lay still, listening, until the sound came again. From beneath her, from the living room.

Heart pounding, she eased to the side of the bed. Light came through the floor grill. Robbers didn't strike the same place twice, did they? She crouched by the grill. She could see the living room carpet, part of the sofa, and her mother's hand, holding a book.

No longer frightened, she hurried downstairs.

"Mom? Everything all right?"

A quick frown and a flurry of blinking. Julia was deep in concentration. Emily sat on the edge of an armchair in the corner of the room. One lamp shone a warm beam of light onto the floor in front of her mother. She was sorting books again.

Not just a few, either. 3:00 a.m. and she'd started a major reorganization. There was no point trying to help. Whatever had dissatisfied Julia about her collection, the solution was lined up in her brain and any distraction would send her back to the beginning of the never-ending task.

Emily eased further back into the chair. The movement brought another frown to her mother's face but her hands, shuffling books, didn't pause. She made a sound, a little slap of the tongue against the roof of her mouth. What had irritated her? She spread out some books again. It reminded Emily of a child's game of Go Fish. *Give me all your…*

Give me your what? Her mother's continual sorting and organizing suggested wanting something, looking for something. Was a book lost? A borrowed book kept too long? Julia was always reluctant to lend one out and mar her collection, however briefly. Or maybe it was about the books she could never have, like the ones on papyrus.

Emily nearly asked again what was wrong, but managed to keep quiet. She let her eyes close. Soon the sound of hard covers rasping over each other and the soft thump of books hitting the floor faded.

CHAPTER NINE

"WAKE UP, lazy bones."

Emily smiled before her eyes could open. "Sue?" She stretched. She wasn't in bed, she was curled into the armchair in the living room. Susannah stood in front of her.

"We've come for breakfast."

"Made it yet?"

"Grandma's checking your cupboards."

"We can't have that." Emily yawned and sat up straight. In spite of the chair she had slept deeply. She checked the floor. The books were put away.

In the kitchen she found her grandmother searching the fridge while Aunt Edith held open the door and chatted.

"They could stay," Edith was saying. "If they really wanted to, they could. The Science Museum in Winnipeg has skeletons of things dug up in Manitoba, doesn't it? A plesiosaur. A giant sloth. Now, I realize a sloth isn't a dinosaur, but it's very old and very big."

Julia sat at the table, ignoring the visitors, a cup of milky tea in hand. Like Emily, she was dressed in the same clothes she'd worn the night before. "I made tea. It's still hot."

"Thanks, Mom." Emily touched the pot, then peered inside. There was just enough for a cup, more warm than hot. She filled the kettle. "Grandma, Aunt Edith, why don't you sit by the fan?" She glanced at Susannah. "You, too. Keep those feet up."

She took a bowl of raspberries from the fridge and a bag of summer scones from the breadbox. "Can we call this breakfast?"

"We certainly can," Eleanor said.

Aunt Edith spooned berries into a dessert bowl and handed it to her mother-in-law. "It may be that we did too much for our children and it's made them selfish. Not you, Emily."

Emily winked at Susannah.

Although they'd already heard the details of the break-in and arrest, Eleanor and Edith wanted to hear about it again. Emily waited until the tea was ready, then told them about every thudding heartbeat, every glance and every tone of voice. When she was done they sat back, satisfied.

"Good in a pinch, like his uncle," Eleanor said. "Just as I thought."

"A very useful man," Edith agreed.

They went on about the useful Rutherford men for at least ten minutes. Emily began to feel as if she was being handed an assignment. She picked up the teapot and made the rounds, starting with her mother who sat looking at a catalog, hands over her ears, then her grandmother, her aunt and her cousin.

Susannah hadn't touched her cup. "I'm waiting for it to be iced tea."

"Poor girl," Edith said. "This heat is hard to take at

nearly eight months! Every morning I'm sure there's going to be a huge thunderstorm and every afternoon the clouds simply don't build. If it doesn't rain soon there won't be much of a crop left."

"Or much of a me," Susannah said.

"We should go to the lake. Would you like that? You could wade in up to your chin and stand there all afternoon. With a hat, of course, or your poor face will never recover! We should all go. Julia, you'd come, wouldn't you?"

Julia picked up her catalog and left the room.

"Oh, dear. Did I get between her and her plans?"

There was a short, stiff silence.

"Aunt Edith, try to remember it's not personal." Emily softened her words by dripping more tea into her aunt's already full cup. "I'd love to go to the lake." Much better than waiting inside a locked house for a thief to come along and test their dead bolts. "Does anyone mind if I invite Matthew? The other day going into town he was envious of people headed in that direction."

"Of course he should come," Edith said. "We'd all love to see him."

"Don't wait, though. If he wants to go, we'll join you later." It was a moment before Emily noticed what she'd said. She'd made it sound as if she would only go if Matthew did. He wouldn't like that at all.

SHE TRIED CALLING first, but got no answer. Twenty minutes later there was still a busy signal and again twenty minutes after that. She couldn't imagine Matthew having such a long conversation. She decided the telephone must be off the hook. So, only slightly un-comfortable about dropping in, she turned up unan-nounced again and wasn't surprised by Matthew's lack of enthusiasm when he opened the door.

"Emily." He looked and sounded neither pleased nor displeased. "Come in. I'll warn you, it's a sauna in here."

There was hardly room for both of them on the land-ing. She slipped past him and went up to the kitchen with him on her heels. The door to the basement was ajar. He pushed it shut as he went by.

"The plants," she said.

"What's that?"

"Daniel's plants are gone."

"Oh, those. They were half-dead when I got here. I tossed them." He reached into the fridge. "If you stay for more than a minute you'll need hydration. Water, juice, coffee?"

"Water, thanks." Best not to ask how the garden was doing. She hoped Daniel wasn't expecting his nephew to be out there with a hose each day.

"I've been sleeping in the basement," Matthew said, pouring two glasses of water. "It's too hot every-where else. I don't know why my uncle doesn't get an air conditioner."

"He doesn't like the noise."

"Is that why?" Matthew led the way into the living room, where a fan on the coffee table hummed steadily, moving from side to side. "You probably know him better than I do."

Away from the gentle air currents the desk was open,

with photographs spread out and folders stacked in a pile. Emily glanced at a basic family tree taped to the wall. Was that all he had accomplished? She could have given him most of those names herself.

"I do know him well. It makes me feel as if I know you and then—"

Matthew raised his eyebrows inquiringly, waiting for her to go on.

"Then I realize I don't at all."

He gave a quick smile. "Maybe a little."

"Not at all."

"I've upset you somehow. I didn't mean to do that."

"You didn't upset me."

"Emily, I may not know my uncle very well, but you're not difficult to read."

"Thanks."

"That wasn't meant to be an insult. I mean you're honest and—"

"Transparent." She tossed the word out, testing it. He didn't contradict her.

"Isn't that a good thing?" he asked.

"Simple and boring and—"

"No, no, no. Complex and fascinating." His eyes were sparkling now. Great. She wasn't trying to amuse him. He went on, "But I do value transparency. I know it isn't fair. It isn't a quality I have."

"All right. Since you value transparency, I'll admit I'm very slightly upset."

"Because?"

"Because you confuse me."

"How do I do that?"

"By not being transparent!" She waited, but he stayed as inscrutable as ever. "You must know how hot and cold you are, how you push and pull."

That made it sound as if they had a relationship. They didn't. He didn't owe her an explanation. Circumstances had brought him to Three Creeks and for some reason, while he was here, they continued to seek each other out.

"I wish I could be clear about what we're doing," she said. "That's all. We have moments when we seem to get close, and the next thing I know you've gone back to the way you were the day we met. A week ago today—can you believe it?"

"That's still on your mind?"

"Don't you know how…unwelcoming you were?"

"I didn't mean to be. I'd had a long trip."

"In a suit."

"What?"

"You wore a suit on a three-day drive."

"What's this, some kind of rural snobbery? Men in suits are—what? Untrustworthy? Weak?"

She thought of him standing in Daniel's doorway, the formal white shirt against tanned skin, energy palpable but held in check. "It's impractical."

"I had some meetings on the way here. The suit seemed like a good idea."

"You haven't had a three-day drive today. Or yesterday."

He raised his hands in a frustrated gesture. "Emily, I'm sorry. I was working when you got here—last week and today. It took me a few minutes to refocus. And yesterday we were all reeling from the break-in."

If he'd been reeling, he'd hidden it well. "That's all?"

"Of course that's all."

She took a breath. He really didn't seem to know how cold he'd been. "I didn't come to fight." She smiled apologetically. "I came to invite you to the lake."

"The quiet, secret one? It's an appealing idea. Is your mother going?"

"She hates the beach. It's right up there with thieves in the house."

"Then why don't we check the books instead? If it's all right with her."

"We're choosing between sand and surf or a hot house and dusty books? It's a tough one, Matthew." She got the feeling he would really rather appraise her mother's collection. "Books it is. And we'll have lunch."

"Don't prepare anything this time. I'll bring tins. What do you like, spaghetti or ravioli?"

"Why not both? We'll have a buffet."

He smiled, his warmth back. This time his pleasure was easy to read.

BEFORE MATTHEW ARRIVED Emily discussed with her mother the possibility of appraising the book collection as a first step toward insuring it. Julia didn't say much in response but when Matthew was ready to start her opinion of the project became clear. They dropped the idea and went to prepare lunch.

They each opened one tin and began heating the contents, while Julia paced nearby. These days agitation was always close to the surface.

She sighed. "I'll never be finished."

Emily looked up from the ravioli. "Finished?"

"Every time a new catalog comes there's something new. Newly published or newly found." Her voice was tight, with pressure behind the words. "Now there's this Herculaneum."

"I saw that in Saturday's paper," Matthew said.

"So now what? How many books will there be?"

Emily looked questioningly at Matthew. "I didn't see the article."

"It was about a huge library in a city near Pompeii—"

"Herculaneum," Julia said impatiently.

"It got caught by the volcano, too. Archeologists uncovered the library years ago, but the papyri inside were scorched absolutely black." He took some bowls from the cupboard and began spooning out the spaghetti. "Now there's a new technology that might make it possible to read them, in spite of the damage. People are excited, because who knows? Some of the ancient world's lost manuscripts could be there."

Julia nodded emphatically. "Important manuscripts."

"But why is it a problem, Mom?"

"The shelves. They're full."

Matthew handed her a bowl. "Why don't I build some more while I'm here? I can't do as nice a job as your husband did, but a bit of paint will hide the imperfections."

"What kind of imperfections?"

"I don't know, but there's bound to be some."

"The shelves can't slant. The books won't sit on slanting shelves."

"I wouldn't make them slant."

"And no rough patches on the wood."

"I'll sand it smooth."

"The edges need to meet. In the corners. No gaps."

"I can do that. I think."

With a long sigh of satisfaction, Julia picked up her spoon. "There's room on the staircase wall."

"I'm afraid more shelves will have to wait," Emily said. "Until fall, when I go back to work." The rent check, even if it came soon, wasn't intended for extras.

Julia muttered, "We don't have the money. That's what she told me."

"What if I got wood from the outbuildings?"

"That wouldn't be fair to you," Emily said. "You're busy with your family history."

"Not all that busy." He smiled. "I'd enjoy it. You know how I feel about genealogy."

EVEN IF Julia didn't want Matthew to assess her books, she didn't mind talking to him about them. Emily sat on the sidelines listening, wondering why her mother was so much more comfortable with him than with most people. Was it his voice? Most of the time he spoke quietly, and in spite of his reserve, with a warm tone that was easy on the ears. He listened calmly, too, without fidgeting or insisting on eye contact.

Soon Julia got on to one of her favorite times, the Enlightenment, and started pulling out books to show him.

"This is my Voltaire. Not a first edition. A nineteenth-century English translation." The book rested on her open hands. "It belonged to my father's father's mother. Do you know about Voltaire's mistress?"

"I don't know much at all about him," Matthew said.

"Gabrielle-Emilie de Breteuil, marquise du Châtelet. Born 1706. Died 1749. All she was supposed to do was get married. Be entertaining at court."

"What did she do instead?"

"She did those things. She also studied mathematics and physics, even though she had to build her own lab to do it. She translated Isaac Newton's work from Latin to French. Not word for word, accepting it all. She challenged one of his ideas. An eighteenth-century woman challenged Newton. Now they say she was right. She completed the book, then she died. Complications of childbirth."

"A first edition of that book would be valuable."

She nodded, her body tight with feeling. "Nobody wants to sell it. I looked. To have it, this woman's thoughts. From that time."

Julia never spoke so expressively, or at such length. If she could, why didn't she more often? Matthew's patience, his quietness must have given her time to sort out what she wanted to say, to say it with some expectation of being understood.

"Only to have them?" he asked. "You're talking as if the book is a box of ideas to keep. Rather than a resource for learning."

Julia smiled softly. Sheepishly, maybe. Pleased. She nodded. "That's it."

"A box of ideas?"

"That's it."

MATTHEW RINSED OUT his teacup. The two women were putting away lunch dishes, Emily as if she didn't mind where they went, Julia slowly and precisely, making sure the bowls were stacked in a perfect tower. While they were distracted by the task it might be a good time to bounce a few questions off them. Nothing subtle. He wanted to see how they reacted to some potentially sensitive ideas.

"Have you ever been up North, Julia?"

The bowls still had her attention. "What do you mean by 'north'?"

"Wherever that mystical area is that people are always talking about. Clear cold water, dancing lights in the night sky. Blueberries and bannock. Caribou. That North."

"I haven't."

"Virginia Marsh was talking about a couple on their honeymoon who want to drive up to Churchill. Only problem is they don't seem to be aware there aren't roads going that far. I guess if it was winter they'd be all right."

"Oh, the winter roads." Emily hung up her tea towel. "I've heard of those."

"My uncle told me about them," Matthew said. "A crew packs down snow, clears trees, waits for thick ice to form on the lakes. Then people can drive in places they'd sink into or drown in most of the year."

"It sounds dangerous."

"You've never ridden on one?"

She gave him a look, amused and maybe a little bit annoyed. "Are you mocking me, Matthew?"

"You're going to have to take a holiday, that's all

there is to it. Try something new, do something that surprises you. You know what you might like? Seeing the North by cat train."

He was almost sure Julia stiffened. Emily just looked curious. "What's a cat train?"

"I've only seen pictures. They're tractors fitted with caterpillar treads, pulling open sleds and boxcars on skis. They used winter roads, mostly carried freight, sometimes passengers. Picture a bunkhouse traveling five miles per hour at forty below."

"And that would be a holiday?"

"You could probably find out more about them from your mom. She has books about everything."

"I don't. I have a book about the invention of the steam engine. And one about the building of the CPR. Nothing about cat trains."

Matthew wondered if he was imagining a slight return of agitation. He couldn't bring himself to push her. "Think I should start looking for wood?"

She frowned. "Looking for it? Used wood?"

"That's what we agreed, isn't it? Used wood in good shape, or wood that's been stored under cover."

"All right." When he was nearly out the door she added, surprising him, "Thank you."

From the shade of the caraganas the dog glowered. The cat, friendlier, followed him to the garage. Its walls were exposed 2x4's crossed by 1x6 boards. The ceiling joists were exposed, too, and used for storage. No hiding places here. He read the date etched into the cement floor—1965. Poured long before the relevant time.

He moved on to the storehouse, a much older building. The floor was cracked and heaving. No attic or enclosed area here, but a non-weight-bearing dividing wall seemed to have been added later. There were more storage boxes than he could check in the time he had today.

The barn was next, through the door into the meadow where Emily had taken him walking. Open doors and empty stalls. Enclosed walls. He knocked here and there, listening for sounds that suggested something solid inside.

"Matthew?"

How had she done that? He hadn't heard a thing. "Emily. I didn't think you'd come out. Are you going to help me choose wood?"

"She'll never accept barn wood. No matter what you do, she'll swear she can smell manure."

"What about the planks on that little dividing wall in the storehouse? Can we take that down?"

"And evict the mice?"

He thought she was joking, but given her concern for toads the other day he couldn't be sure.

She smiled. "If there are mice in the wall I'm not sure I'd want the wood in the house. Otherwise, you're welcome to use it. It's so nice of you to do this, Matthew."

Nice. That was him, all right.

He nearly told her the whole story right then.

MATTHEW LEFT soon after she found him in the barn, promising to come back in the morning to start building. Emily took one of her library books to the screened porch and stretched out on an old canvas chaise that nearly touched the ground when she was in it. Bees attracted to the geraniums outside bumped against the screen from time to time and Hamish occasionally peered in at her before returning to the hedge. The cat sat on her stomach digging in its claws while she rubbed its ears. She only got up once, around six, to make sandwiches, and then she returned to her book.

Two-thirds of the way through, she let it drop onto the floor. Mosquitoes or thieves or anxious mother, she could not stay inside the walls of her house or the confines of her yard for another minute.

She called into the kitchen that she was going to take a walk, then started down Robbs' Road. The cat followed. They would really have to give it a name if it was going to stay. Maybe going upper-case would do.

"Hey, Cat!"

It looked at her, eyes alert, and leapt over a few patches of gravel to reach her side.

"Is that what they called you, whoever you lived with before? Simple, but descriptive."

When she reached her grandmother's house the cat bolted in the opposite direction, taking precautions with the dogs. Emily was surprised to see Eleanor sitting on the porch. She waved and hurried to join her.

"I thought you'd gone to the lake this time, Grandma."

"I'm glad I didn't. Look how long they've stayed. I saw Matthew go by. Did he spend the afternoon with you?"

"He's going to build more shelves for Mom."

"Goodness. There goes my hope that when she finally ran out of space she'd take up a different hobby. Visiting her old mother, for example." Eleanor smiled.

"Or collecting money. Imagine, neat little bundles of money all over the house!"

"Would you prefer she collected twenties or hundreds?"

"Good question. Both. Twenties for chocolate bars and hundreds for dresses."

They smiled fondly at each other.

"Something on your mind, my dear?"

There was, but Emily didn't want to worry her. "The berries are turning into jam on the branches. Summer's getting away on me."

"The day worrying about berries gives you circles under your eyes, I don't know what I'll do. Take you to the Pine Point hotel for a stiff drink, maybe."

Emily laughed. "Grandma."

"Did the thief frighten you? Are you worried about Julia?"

She was worried about Matthew. Matthew not answering simple questions, like what work he did or exactly how he was related to Daniel. Avoiding the details whenever she asked where Daniel was, or if she could call him somewhere. Leaning close to Jason Willis before turning him over to the police, saying something she couldn't hear. His manner had been so confiding. Or threatening. Either way, not right.

"I'm wondering if someone I know is being honest

with me. There are inconsistencies and I'm not sure what to make of them."

"That's an uncomfortable thing. I suppose we all keep something hidden. When we'd been married for fifty years your grandfather could still surprise me."

Emily nodded slowly. She had only started getting to know Matthew, so surprises and questions, even doubts, were to be expected.

"It's not your mother, is it? I know she's a bit of a mystery."

"Mom doesn't say who she is at all. So there's no lying going on there."

Eleanor looked concerned. "You think someone is out and out lying to you?" Before Emily could answer, she added, "Not Matthew? He's the only new person in town."

"There are some things about him that don't add up."

"He strikes me as a complicated man. You don't come to understand someone like him in a week or two."

"Maybe that's all it is." She smiled. "I wish you'd seen him with Mom today. He really connects with her. It made me wonder about her and my father. How she—" Emily stopped. She didn't want to hurt her grandmother.

"How your mother, being the way she is with people, managed to find a man to love her?"

Emily nodded.

Eleanor thought for a minute. "Each had something

the other needed, I suppose. That might not sound romantic, but they suited each other very well."

"They met here?"

"That's right. We hired him to help on the farm. Very nice young fellow—well, not all that young. He was in his thirties. He didn't seem to have much formal education. Not that he wasn't a smart man. He was, anybody could see that talking to him. Maybe he just didn't have the patience for it."

Emily said, "And that was why he noticed Mom. Because she liked books." People had told her that before.

"He usually joined us for dinner, and he had a nice way with your mother, so sometimes I encouraged him to stay a while. They'd sit here, where we are now, and he'd tease her into reading to him."

It was hard to imagine her mother responding to teasing, unless it was to wander away. She must have liked him from the start.

"Not that she was much of a reader, out loud," Eleanor added. "But your dad would sit back watching her with a look on his face as if any book she read was the most engaging thing he had ever heard. And I think she got to like it. She always read to him, all those years they had together." Eleanor stopped, then said with a note of sadness, "Well, it wasn't so many years, was it?"

"People say he brought her out of herself."

"It often seemed the other way around to me. Your father was willing to join her in her world from time to time."

"Getting married is a big step from reading aloud."

"He was clever about that. Once when we were on a picnic, Julia spent the whole time telling him about the grass they were sitting on—which was the timothy hay and which the fescue, and which insects preferred which species. How the grass held the soil together and protected the marshlands, how important the marshlands were to wildlife and water filtration. She spent a great deal of time on damselflies. Not everyone would enjoy that kind of thing."

Emily smiled at the understatement.

"But he appeared to be riveted. The next week he put it to her in practical terms, how he would take care of the section of land your grandfather was going to give her, keep it healthy and producing. He went on about purple loosestrife destroying the natural grasses if it wasn't managed right and how the straw after the crops were cut would make good food for migrating fowl and how to protect the habitat of damselflies he wouldn't drain the marsh. He remembered everything he'd heard her say on those subjects and handed it right back to her so earnestly."

"And that convinced her?"

Eleanor nodded.

"They got married because of purple loosestrife and damselflies?"

"Do you know a better reason?"

Emily laughed. "I suppose not."

They sat quietly until Eleanor said, "Remember, however stiff she might seem your mother feels things deeply. I used to think she was missing a layer of some-

thing, that her emotions burned. That must sound fanci-
ful."

"No, Grandma. It sounds just right."

CHAPTER TEN

THE NEXT MORNING WAS WINDY, with hot drying gusts that bent branches and stirred up gravel on the road. Matthew arrived after breakfast carrying a small cooler that he said contained lunch. He left it in the shade and got to work on the shelves, disappearing into one outbuilding or another, coming out with a single 2x4 or a section of plywood. Sawdust blowing in his eyes, he ripped 1x6 boards from the storehouse dividing wall, sanded them until they looked fresh-cut, then brushed them with a bleach solution for good measure. If mice had ever curled up behind them, no one could tell. The sound of the electric sander drove Julia upstairs, but when it was quiet she went out and happily approved the results.

The wind and sun soon dried the boards. Matthew carried an armload into the living room so he and Julia could decide exactly where the new shelves should go. Emily stayed outside to clean up wood shavings, so she was alone when a patrol car turned into the driveway.

It was Corporal Reed again. He looked at the sawdust on the lawn. "Making bars for the windows?"

Emily wasn't sure how to joke with a police officer. "Shelves for more books. Do you have news?"

"I thought you'd like to know how the investigation is progressing. We checked Jason Willis's fingerprints against those found in the other houses in the area that were broken into recently. They're a match."

"He didn't wear gloves? Isn't that a basic precaution?"

"Nobody said he was smart. We've charged him with seven counts of break and enter with intent. That means even if he didn't get around to taking anything the onus is on him to prove he didn't enter a home intending to do harm. I think he's going to have a little trouble with that."

"And then what happens?"

"His parents tell me he's pleading guilty. He's a youth with no history of violence so he won't get custody. It'll be strict probation, which would include having no contact with you and your mother."

That was fine with her. "Did you ever find his bicycle?"

"We think someone gave him a ride. All of this may be related to an initiation prank."

"You mean a gang?"

"More like some sort of club—dumb kids copying what they see in the movies. Talking about a bicycle was probably an attempt to keep his friends out of it."

Emily walked the corporal back to his car. He turned the key in the ignition, then rolled down his window.

"Where did you say Daniel Rutherford went?"

"I don't know exactly. Ottawa, I think."

"Ottawa. To visit a sick relative, you said?"

"That's right."

He looked as if he was thinking that over. "Okay. Thanks, Ms. Moore." The car rolled partway to the road, then stopped, and Reed poked his head out the window. "Ms. Moore?"

"Yes?"

"Your father—he wasn't from around here, was he?"

The question startled her. "No, he wasn't. He moved here a couple of years before he and my mother got married."

"From?"

Emily's mind drew a blank. She had always thought he came from Winnipeg, the city closest to Three Creeks. She couldn't remember if anyone had actually told her that. "I'm not sure where he lived."

"He came late to farming, didn't he? Do you know what he did previously?"

She shook her head, embarrassed. "I'm afraid I don't know very much about him."

He thanked her again and drove away before she could decide if she wanted to ask why he was interested in her father.

EMILY SUMMARIZED what the corporal had told her, and gave a frustrated shrug. "So there's no bicycle, no real danger, just kids trying to prove something to each other by making us lose sleep."

Matthew thought he heard uncertainty in her voice. "You don't believe it?"

"Do you?"

"Is there any reason not to?"

"No good reason."

"Tell me the bad reason."

That made her smile. Faintly, but it was still a smile. "There isn't a bad one, either. Only a feeling."

He always paid attention to feelings on a job. "Can you attach it to a thought, to something you saw that night or something Willis said?"

Her face changed. She shook her head, but it was clear she'd thought of something she didn't intend to tell him. She wouldn't protect the kid. Her parents? Her uncle?

He put down his hammer. "It's time for a break, isn't it?" Not the break he'd planned, maybe, not with the wind still going strong and rain clouds forming. "Who wants to go for a picnic?"

Julia kept smoothing her hand over the boards. "We ate outside last week."

"Are you sure, Mom?" Emily checked out the window. "It won't rain for hours, if it does at all. We could to go back to the big creek, Matthew. It's a great spot on a windy day."

By the end of the walk through the meadow and the woods Emily was almost her pre-break-in self. They sat on rocks edging the creek, pant legs rolled up, shoes off, feet in the water, listening to the leaves rustle so loudly they sounded like waves.

He began to unpack the cooler. "I've brought Mrs. Bowen's bumbleberry pie, your aunt Edith's macaroni salad and my own tuna *et* Miracle Whip *avec* pickle, lightly peppered and caressed by whole wheat bread. And that's not all…."

He silently put the last of his offerings in front of her.

The smile that had grown bigger with each item grew again. Every time he saw it he wanted to quit his job, like Jack, and become a farmer.

"Pumpkin muffins." She sounded amused.

"I'm afraid so. I had a good look at my uncle's resources and it was this or a sinus-clearing concoction of doubtful antecedents."

"Is that what he keeps locked in the basement? His still?"

Was she serious? "That has such an illegal ring to it."

She picked up half a sandwich, holding it carefully so no filling would fall out. "Mrs. Bowen and I wondered. All the expensive equipment in the main room and then the other door is locked. Did you try it?"

"Try what?"

"The sinus-clearing concoction. Fruit brandy, Daniel says."

He shook his head emphatically. He'd taken one whiff and put the stopper back in the jug. Was she saying Daniel had actually brewed it?

"It's quite good," she went on. "More of a winter thing, though. Makes you warm all over."

"You've had some?"

"Starting by the thimblefull when I was ten. I've graduated to medicine cups. Daniel takes it by the goblet."

"He gave you that stuff when you were a child? It must be a hundred proof!"

Emily shrugged, but she looked pleased to have shocked him. "Good tuna salad."

"Did your mother know?"

"Probably not."

"If I ever have a child, remind me not to turn my back on Daniel!"

She looked at him curiously. "Have you ever come close?"

"To turning my back on Daniel?"

"To having a child."

"No. You?"

"Nowhere near it. So…no ex?"

He wasn't comfortable with the direction the conversation had taken. After he ate half a sandwich she was still waiting curiously so he said, "I suppose I'd characterize any relationships I've had as careful and uncommitted."

He could see right away he'd put her off. He was trying to be honest. Well, to be honest, he was trying to be uninformative.

"That sounds cold, Matthew. Haven't you been in love?"

"Be nice, Emily. I've been pushing a saw all morning. In this heat!" He didn't like the way she looked at him. Almost as if she was evaluating him. She never looked like that. "What about you? Have you been in love?"

"I don't think so. I did at the time."

"Who was the guy?"

She opened the container of macaroni salad. "Hmm, nice, you put pickles in with it." She took some salad before she answered his question. "There were two people who caught my interest, let's put it that way. One more than the other."

"Tell me about the other first."

She shrugged. He liked that. Remembering men with a shrug was good.

"He taught here one year—a temporary job while another teacher was on maternity leave. His next job was miles away so we stopped seeing each other."

"And the one who mattered more?"

"He grew up here. Jack bought his family's house. John Ramsey was his name." For a moment, something clouded her face. "He's coming for a visit soon. Next week, I think."

"High school sweetheart?" Matthew guessed. "What happened?"

"He didn't want to farm. He wanted me to move to the city with him. Of course, I wouldn't do that."

"Why of course?"

She looked at him with a surprised blink. "My mother." She said it as if it didn't need saying.

"You wouldn't move to the city because of your mother?"

"You've seen how she is."

"Lost in her books."

Emily nodded.

"And?"

"*Lost*. Lost in them. She doesn't take care of herself, Matthew."

"I guess this John Ramsey wasn't too happy with your decision."

"He told me to stay in my convent, then, if that was what I wanted."

"He was hurt."

"I understood that." She looked as if it still bothered her. "The other day Mom told me she never liked him."

"She wouldn't, would she? He wanted to take you away."

"That makes her sound selfish. She isn't selfish at all."

"No. But I've watched her enough to know she needs everything to stay in its place."

"*Its* place? Thanks." Emily gave him a quick, tight smile. "The second prospect, the teacher, said I had a martyr complex."

"Do you?"

"No." She didn't take even a second to think about it.

"You haven't given up the life you would have wanted?"

"Haven't we talked about this before?"

"Oh, yeah. Great town, good food. That conversation."

She stood up with a decisive air that let him know the subject was closed. "Do you get seasick?"

"Not usually."

She tucked her wrappers into the cooler and took his hand. "Then come with me."

THEY STOOD at the base of a poplar, watching its branches bend in the wind.

"You're kidding."

She smiled and shook her head. She must have been twelve when she was last buffeted around in a tree with Sue and Liz.

"It's a good day for it," he admitted.

"Perfect." She and her cousins had always come to these trees, but she remembered her father taking her to the oaks beyond the marsh. Not to climb when it was windy. To sit in and eat raisins, to tell stories, to see the end of the property line. He'd point from side to side to side to side and tell her as far as they could see the land belonged to Robbs. She hadn't thought about that for years.

"You first," Matthew said.

"Chicken?"

"Hey. It's so I can cushion your fall."

She jumped to grasp a branch above her head, swung her legs over and pulled herself to her feet. It was like riding a bike. You didn't forget.

As soon as she was off the ground she could feel the tree swaying. She kept climbing until she reached branches that might not hold her weight. Matthew was right behind her. Just when he let go of one branch to reach for another a huge gust shook the tree. Her heart pounded, but he grinned and gave her a thumbs-up sign.

Every time the wind came up the leaves shook so hard she couldn't hear anything else, not even Matthew's voice beside her. It died down, and the tree rocked gently. It blew and the tree swayed like a ship on rough seas. She was exhilarated, but frightened, clinging to the branch even though it didn't feel connected to the ground.

"I always hated this!"

He pointed to the ground, then eased to the next lowest branch and waited for her to follow. Her foot found the crook of the branch where it met the trunk and then she was there, between his body and the tree. They went all the way down like that until they stood in the grass again. They didn't touch, but he was so close she could feel him.

"Okay?"

She nodded.

"That was amazing. Why do you do it, if you hate it?"

His nearness made her body ache. She kept her voice as light as she could. "Because it's amazing."

He let go of the tree and stepped back. She felt it like a pull and almost reached for him.

"I've been thinking about you a lot." The words popped out. She felt her face flush. No doubt a signal to pay attention to, but ignoring it seemed like a better idea. "I know you won't be here much longer. Maybe that doesn't matter." She should just say it. She would, this time. "I'm attracted to you, Matthew."

His eyes were warm. "Country girls are so direct."

"I wish I'd been direct earlier." They could have had a week already.

"Em, you deserve more than a summer fling."

A fling. It was the wrong word. A week with Matthew would matter.

"I think about you, too," he went on, "but I've been doing my best to stop. Maybe I've given you mixed signals because of that. No wonder you were confused. It's not a good idea, Emily."

Cautious and uncommitted. When he'd said that warning bells should have sounded. She picked up the cooler and started walking. Too bad the house wasn't just around the corner. She needed to get into it and shut a door. Tears seemed to be in her future and she wasn't sure how long she could head them off.

"Let me take that." He reached for the cooler. Their hands tangled together while he tried to get hold of it.

She'd kept betting on the warm version of Matthew. Should have gone with the distant one.

Fifteen minutes to home. "Has Daniel called?"

"Not lately."

"I'd really like to talk to him."

"I'm sure he'd like to talk to you."

"Given how simple a thing that would be for him to do I'd say it isn't a priority. I understand he's busy with his aunt. What I don't understand is why won't you give me a number where I can call him."

"I've had trouble reaching him myself. I wait for him to call me."

"Were you always like this?"

"Like what, Emily?"

"Did you choose your job because it suited you, or did you grow into it?"

He looked at her without speaking. What was she supposed to do with a look? Maybe he thought she was an empath. Maybe when he was silent, he thought the two of them were bonding, communicating at a deeper level than mere speech.

"We're not, you know."

His eyebrows gave a questioning twitch. He didn't understand. Nope, no deeper meaning. Just an insurance man's assessing expression. Adding and subtracting, a constant analyzing of value.

"Emily, I take back what I said yesterday. Sometimes you're not transparent. Sometimes I can't figure you out at all."

She nodded, pleased. "Good."

THEY WALKED the rest of the way home in silence. By the time Matthew left for town, after cutting boards to lengths that would fit on the wall around the staircase, the clouds had grown and darkened and the wind held whiffs of ozone.

When he was younger Hamish had raced around the yard when thunder sounded, looking for the herd of whatever creature was making so much noise. Even now it made him restless. He paced, sniffing the air, peering into the distance.

Emily opened the door and whistled. "Come on in, boy." He never did, except on the very coldest days of winter and then only for respite from minus-forty temperatures. Then he was outside again, on the job. He fooled himself as well as any human could.

From the step she could hear him panting. "Come in and protect the ladies, Hamish. We need a fierce dog in here." He ignored her, but the cat streaked through the open door and disappeared under the kitchen table.

A crash of thunder shook the house. In case the power went out Emily hurried to make a huge pot of tea, pouring some into cups for now and the rest into a thermos for later. Sipping without talking, she and her mother watched the rain.

LATE THAT NIGHT Emily sat in bed, knees drawn up. The wind had blown the clouds away, along with some of the past month's heat. There was only a crescent moon so the sky was black and she could see very little outside. Blacker places where trees grew, stars so plentiful the sight of them nearly overwhelmed her. Her throat tightened. This window, this view, this bed. On every sleepless night.

She needed a new bed. That would help her sleep. Uncle Will and Aunt Edith had got her this one when she was nine. It had seemed so grown up then to graduate from her roll-away cot with its thin mattress resting on a woven metal mesh to a flowered twin with box springs. Now it squeaked when she moved and sagged with a permanent imprint of her body.

A new bed—a double—and maybe an armchair. A place of her own to sit with a cup of tea and read. It was exactly what she needed. As soon as her first paycheck came in September she would go into town and take care of it.

With that picture in mind, a dozy feeling stole over her. Her head drooped, touching the cool glass.

She didn't feel as if she slept but she must have because when light flashed across the yard she jerked awake, confused. The security light on the garage had come on. Hamish was there, quiet, watching. Watching a man who stood frozen for a second, less than a second, then ducked into the shadows.

Matthew.

Her mind felt frozen, too. Then it got busy denying that there was anything wrong with Matthew being in her yard at night. Maybe he'd come back for his hammer, maybe he'd been patrolling the place every night since the break-in. Maybe he'd come to throw pebbles at her window and quote Shakespeare.

One remembered question worked its way through the excuses.

Is he a good watchdog?

CHAPTER ELEVEN

EMILY ARRIVED in Pine Point as soon as the library opened. She greeted Mrs. Shelley, the head librarian, and got right into her story before she could reconsider.

"I'm not sure what to do. A friend of mine asked me to look something up for him on microfilm but he forgot to tell me which one to sign out. He's away all day, so I can't call him to ask."

"Do you know which set of microfilm he meant?"

"He was here last week looking at it. Matthew Rutherford? You wouldn't have a record of it, would you?"

Mrs. Shelley turned to a hardcover, ring-bound book. She flipped through the pages, muttering names as she read them. "Here we are. Matthew Rutherford. He borrowed a few boxes. *The Winnipeg Tribune,* January to June, 1979 and the *Pine Point Register,* 1979 and 1981." *The Register* was a weekly paper, so a whole year fit on one spool.

"Could I look at all of them?"

"Of course." Mrs. Shelley smiled wryly. "If your eyes and neck don't give out first."

She took keys from a drawer and led the way to a tall filing cabinet. Emily waited, squirming at how easy it had been to lie successfully to someone she respected. She accepted the boxes of microfilm, set the first spool in place on the viewer and threaded the film into the up-take.

She started with *The Tribune.* Since she had no idea what she was looking for she inched through each day's edition, skimming national and international news, speeding past ads and comics, slowing down for personals, looking for any mention of the name Rutherford.

She stopped when she reached March 11. In the bottom right-hand corner of the front page there was an article about the bush plane Uncle Will had mentioned. Over the next few days short pieces updated the story. The search temporarily suspended due to bad weather, a biography of the pilot, decorated during WWII, years of service in the RCMP. Friends quoted about how resourceful he was, how certain they were he could manage with the survival gear he had on board.

She went on. Grain prices, Camp David peace treaty, Idi Amin overthrown, spring flooding in the Red River valley, increase in the price of oil, Winnipeg Jets in the AVCO Cup finals, protests about the closing of Portage and Main to pedestrians…

After two hours, she sat back from the viewer and held her fingers over her eyes. She had looked at the entire six months, too quickly to read everything. There was no way of knowing what Matthew had wanted to find.

She rewound the film, then started on the 1979 *Register.* She scrolled through photos of prize cattle and visiting politicians and articles about the Agricultural Fair and 4-H Rallies. There was even an advertisement for

Daniel's security business, the one that always made her smile. Punks a Problem?… She could have been reading this year's paper.

The 1981 edition was almost identical. Eyes stinging, she went through the pages, hardly reading anymore. Three Creeks was often mentioned and Daniel was sometimes quoted as the local expert on crime.

Her finger on the advance button paused.

Area Farmer Electrocuted.

A sick feeling went through her. All these years later, and she didn't want to read it.

Just outside Three Creeks this week Graham Moore, 42, died on his property when he stepped into wet ground near a downed hydro wire. His body was discovered when family members went in search of him after he failed to return home for dinner.

William Robb, the man's brother-in-law, said the deceased was a good farmer and a devoted family man.

Moore moved to the area ten years ago. He leaves a wife and eight-year-old daughter.

She looked at the date at the top of the page. Shouldn't it have leapt out at her? Even the year on the box's label, 1981, shouldn't that be etched on her memory? She felt a rush of guilt that it wasn't.

Further in was a brief obituary. Really brief. It didn't give her father's place of birth or list any family other than his wife and daughter. The following week a longer article appeared about the accident and the funeral. It quoted friends and relatives who all thought he was the finest man who ever lived. People tended to talk like that right after someone died. It took a year or two before they remembered the real person.

But she hadn't remembered the real person. He was like a fairy-tale figure. *Once upon a time there was a father.* He had walked into the story and then out again, with so little comment from anyone who was there to see it.

This couldn't be what Matthew had been reading. Could it? He kept asking about her family. At Daniel's door he'd seemed so closed to her until he'd heard her name. But what could her father's death have to do with anything?

She printed the article, went back and printed the obituary and the first article, then went slowly through the rest of the film looking for some other story more likely to explain Matthew's search. She found a short piece about an alarm system Daniel had installed that led to the arrest of a cattle poacher, but nothing else about the Rutherfords and nothing that also accounted for Matthew's presence on her property at night.

She handed in the microfilm, walked to the water fountain to stretch her legs and get a drink, then signed on to use one of the library computers. Her fingers on the keyboard, she stared at the empty search box. It felt wrong to send someone's name into the ether. An intrusion.

Matthew Rutherford, she typed, then hit enter. In seconds, pages of entries containing that name jumped to the screen. There were a lot of Matthew Rutherfords in the world, with various middle initials, addresses and occupations. None of them seemed to be her Matthew Rutherford.

She typed in *Ontario White Pages*. When that came up, she found Ottawa, then again typed his name.

Nothing.

She tried *Rutherford.*

More than twenty listings. Using the little pencil and scraps of paper provided, she wrote down each name and telephone number.

By the time Emily left the library it was midafternoon. She couldn't tell if she was hungry, or queasy from watching too many fuzzy screens of old news. Looking idly around, trying to decide if she should pick up a sandwich or go home, she saw Matthew standing at the end of the block. He was talking to someone. She couldn't see who until the person hidden by his body moved.

Jason Willis.

It was Tuesday. His court day. She'd forgotten.

The boy looked at the sidewalk, every now and then shaking his head. They started walking at a comfortable pace, talking, almost friendly, and stopped outside the courthouse. Matthew clapped a hand on Jason's shoulder, but the boy shook it off. Not so friendly, then.

He didn't leave, though. He stood, his back half turned to Matthew, still listening. An older man came out of the courthouse and joined them. Definitely not friendly. He pushed Jason away from Matthew. The two of them got into a car parked at the curb and drove away.

Emily stepped back into the library's lobby. She waited until Matthew left before going to her car.

AT HOME, she worked through the list of Ottawa phone numbers. She got answering machines, busy signals, children who could barely speak and suspicious-sounding adults who wouldn't say if a Matthew lived at their address, or if a Daniel was visiting, or even if they knew anyone by those names.

Finally, she reached a woman who was willing to talk to her. "From Three Creeks? My goodness, I haven't thought about that little town in years. Oh—" The friendly voice suddenly became concerned. "Oh, dear. Don't tell me something's happened to Daniel."

"No, it's not that at all," Emily said quickly. "He's visiting relatives, but I don't know where. I'm trying to find him or his nephew, Matthew."

"Nephew? I'm sorry, I can't help you there. Daniel isn't visiting any of the family in my neck of the woods. Can I have your number? If I hear anything, I'll call."

As soon as Emily hung up, the telephone rang.

It was Matthew. "Sorry to be so long getting in touch with you today." He sounded relaxed and friendly. "I had to take care of a few things, and then I kept getting a busy signal. Thought I might see you in town. Jason Willis was in court."

"I forgot."

"The judge gave him probation."

"That's what Corporal Reed predicted."

"It doesn't worry you?"

"He's not the scariest guy I've ever come across."

"Now you're sounding worldly."

Emily didn't answer. The country-girl joke was wearing thin.

"If it's a good time for you and Julia I could come now to work on the shelves."

"We've been busy, too." He'd been chatting so comfortably, as if he didn't have secrets to protect. She wanted to ask what he'd been doing in her yard and why he'd been talking to Jason, but a little belated wariness seemed like a good idea. "Mom's busy with book ordering today." Another lie. "I don't want to interrupt her with pounding and sawing. Is that all right?"

"Of course."

"Then you'll have time for your history project. Imagine if Daniel came home and all you'd accomplished was building a new bookcase for my mother!"

"That might be hard to explain," he agreed.

They said goodbye without making arrangements for him to continue the shelves.

Emily took a mug of tea outside and sat on the steps. Hamish ambled over, sniffing hopefully in the direction of her cup. Thanks to the day's slightly cooler temperature he looked livelier than she'd seen him in weeks.

Matthew had asked if she could connect her uncomfortable feeling about the break-in to a thought, to something she'd seen. And she could. All her uneasiness connected to him.

If she removed the Rutherford family history from the

picture, what had Matthew done since arriving in Three Creeks? Toured her house and property, showed interest in Jack's money—*nest egg or fortune*? He'd asked questions about her family, especially about her mother and the books. He'd examined the books as much as Julia would allow. He'd read about her father's death and talked privately to the boy who had broken into the house.

If she also took away friendly curiosity and getting to know each other, she was left with some very strange behavior. She didn't want to leap all the way to the conclusion that Matthew was interested in stealing a rare book, but the idea sat in her mind. She wished she knew if she was being ridiculous.

Well, she was. Either ridiculous and unfair now or ridiculous and naive before.

Okay, then. No leaping, no conclusions. Just wary.

She smiled at the dog. "Hey," she said softly. "You're my role model."

His tail thumped the ground.

"I'm putting off the next step," she told him.

He came closer, wagging his tail more energetically, ready to fall in with any plan.

"Should I just get it over with?" She nodded. "Yes, I think so."

LOTS OF PEOPLE saved things—wedding matches printed with the names of brides and grooms, ticket stubs from special performances—Julia saved everything. Every piece of paper that could say the slightest thing about every single day of her life, as if she needed proof she was here.

Emily didn't like the image of her mother bent over the kitchen table, her attention far away, cutting and filing. The boxes had always made her uneasy. Opening them now felt wrong. Another intrusion.

She read the labels and wondered where to start.

1972. The year her parents married.

1973. The year she was born.

Maybe it was all right to look in that one.

She lifted the lid and found a row of file folders in alphabetical order. One section, set off from the year's other events, was labelled Emily's Birth.

Within that section one file bulged with boxes of unused birth announcements. Not just leftovers. Never opened. Another held her birth certificate and a Baby's Record card from the hospital. Someone had filled out the time and date of her birth, and her weight, length and head circumference.

Several folders were marked, Cards Received. Lots of storks and shades of pink. Every relative and nearly everyone in town had sent congratulations, as well as a few people she didn't know, a Frank and an Andrew and an Ethel. Whoever they were, they'd found out about her, in spite of that box of unsent announcements.

All right, she'd broken the ice snooping, but as far as she could see nothing from the 1973 box connected to Matthew and the microfilm, or Matthew and the midnight visit. She snapped the lid back on, then jumped ahead to 1981.

Of all the folders in the box, one stood out. The label said, Graham's Death.

The wording startled her. The contrast was odd, the

distance of her mother's abrupt manner and the intimacy of her father's first name. No one ever referred to him by name.

She touched the edge of the file and pulled it open without taking it out of the box. Newspaper clippings— the same articles she had printed at the library. An Order of Service from the church.

There was a sound behind her.

"What do you want?" Her mother stood looking at the open box, the exposed papers.

"I'm not sure. Information about Dad. Is it all right?"

Julia's brows pulled together and a flurry of blinking began. "You shouldn't look at that box."

"It's from the year he died."

"You shouldn't look at it."

"I don't mean to upset you."

"Don't look at it!" Julia whirled around and left the room.

Emily stared at the empty doorway. Then she removed the file with the clippings about her father's death, laid it flat on one of the boxes and opened it.

UNCLE WILL HAD been changing the oil filter on his tractor. Emily sat on the seat, high above him, watching as he read the letter she'd found.

"What do you think?"

"I don't think anything." Carefully holding one corner of the paper between black-stained fingertips, he handed it back to her.

She quoted without reading, "'I always wondered what became of him. So many boys in the class went down the wrong road and I'm afraid most eventually came to a bad end.'"

"Sounds like your dad grew up in a tough neighborhood."

"Sounds like? Don't you know?"

"He never talked about himself. We talked about the farm, hockey, things going on around here."

"Mom was upset that I was looking in the box, but the letter was the only thing in it that seemed at all unusual." It began, *You don't know me, but I knew your husband years ago,* and ended by offering condolences.

"Why are you wondering about this now?"

She hesitated. "Matthew seems interested in him."

"Does he?"

"Do you know why he would be?"

Uncle Will didn't answer immediately. What could there be that needed to be considered, rather than spit out in his usual way?

Finally he said, "Your dad and Daniel went way back. I don't know what the connection was."

"It couldn't have been too far back. Dad only moved here a couple of years before I was born." Then his meaning became clear. "They knew each other before Three Creeks?"

He nodded.

"No one ever mentioned that. Daniel has told me so many stories from all the places he's traveled and worked…why wouldn't he tell me any that included my father?"

Will shrugged and lifted his hands. "What can I tell you, sweetie?"

She decided to take the question literally. "Tell me how my dad died."

"Well, now." He looked uncomfortable. "You've heard about that."

"Why was he out in a damp field without rubber boots? How did a hydro line come down? Why didn't he notice and avoid it?"

"Yep." Will nodded, and kept nodding. "Why and how. That's what we always want to know when these things happen. Sometimes they just happen, Emily. There'd been a storm the day before, lots of wind and rain."

"Then he certainly would have worn rubber boots."

"Depends what he wanted to do. Rubber boots are loose, clumpy things. Maybe he figured he'd let his shoes get wet and change them later."

"You found him?"

"I did."

"There was nothing you could do? Mouth-to-mouth?"

"He was long past help, sweetheart. He was a good man and you were the apple of his eye. That's all you need to know."

Emily climbed down from the tractor and gave her uncle a big kiss on the forehead, the spot she always used. "Sorry to bring it all up."

"No, no! Any time. I thought you'd ask one day."

HER NEXT STEP took her into Jason Willis's territory. Just plain old break-and-enter, though. No intent to do harm. Maybe this was how criminals were made. Having good reasons to do the wrong things.

She called Mrs. Bowen. They talked for a while about the last evening's refreshing rain and the difference a few degrees of mercury made. Then Emily said, "I wanted to ask you a favor. It might sound a bit unusual."

"You've piqued my curiosity."

"Next time Matthew's out would you be willing to let me into Daniel's house again?"

She could hear surprise in Mrs. Bowen's silence. After a moment the older woman said, "I don't know whether or not I'd be willing, dear, but it's not a choice I can make. Soon after he arrived Matthew asked me to give him the spare key."

"He did? It seems to me it wasn't his to take."

"I'll admit that's what I thought, too. He said it was unnecessary for me to have one in safekeeping while Daniel's away." After a pause she asked, "Would you be willing to tell me why you want the key?"

Emily had expected the question but she hadn't decided whether to tell Mrs. Bowen the truth. Funny how quickly that became optional once you started. "It isn't important. I wanted to surprise him. Dinner, tablecloth, flowers, the whole thing."

"My, my. This sounds promising, Emily. I'm very glad."

"Please don't mention it to him, Mrs. Bowen."

"Of course not. I won't say a word."

CHAPTER TWELVE

MRS. MARSH DIDN'T play too many games before handing Matthew the mail he'd been waiting for—a brown 4x6 envelope addressed to Daniel Rutherford, with no return address. He hurried from the post office to the house and ripped the envelope open.

Inside was a black-and-white photograph. Two men he recognized, Frank Carruthers and Gerald Easton, coming out of a restaurant in Montreal. No message on the back, no date. For all he knew it had been taken in the seventies, before Frank retired. He checked the envelope for a note. Nothing.

He pulled out his cell phone and hit speed-dial. Not unexpectedly, he got the customer-out-of-service-range message. Over the next couple of hours he continued trying and when the kitchen phone rang he thought for a moment his call was being returned.

"Emily, hi." He needed a second to change gears. "Are you calling about the shelves? I could come over this afternoon."

"Actually, I wouldn't mind an outing. I wondered if I could drop by for tea."

Something was wrong. Her voice sounded stiff.

"Tea? I don't understand how you Robbs can drink the stuff on a hot summer afternoon. This isn't the best place to take a break—the rain hasn't cooled the house down much. Why don't we go for a walk instead, or drive to Pine Point, maybe to the bakery?"

"I'd really like to just come for tea, if that's all right."

"Of course it is."

"Thanks. I'll be there in ten minutes."

He put the picture back in the envelope and started downstairs, taking out his keys as he went. Ten minutes was time enough for a quick check of his e-mail.

A couple of subject lines stood out from those that could wait. One said, Young Lovers. It sounded like spam, except he knew the sender.

He clicked, and read the message.

Nothing to report on the male or the female. The Tercel is registered to a Philip Sawyer. The same Philip Sawyer took out a marriage license this May. Bride's name Mavis Butler. Both clean as a whistle so quit yer peepin'. ;)

Sometimes loitering strangers turned out to be happy people smelling the roses.

He selected the second subject line, *Is this a problem?* The message read, Just to let you know someone called asking questions about you yesterday. Of course I didn't tell her anything. It was a woman called Emily Moore. She said she's from Three Creeks.

"WE COULD SIT in the basement," Emily said lightly, when Matthew apologized again for the heat. She felt sure her suspicions must be blaring out of her. "I wonder why Daniel doesn't build a rec room down there, if it's the only cool part of the house?"

"I wonder why you wanted to visit such an uncomfortable place."

"I needed a break."

"Your mom getting you down?"

"No," she said quickly. "Why do people always think that? I don't get down about my mother."

"You must."

"It's required?"

"I've spent time with the two of you. I can see she's not very good company."

Emily felt a surge of protectiveness, the way she used to in the schoolyard, when kids twirled their fingers beside their heads and said in nasty voices that her mother needed help. "I don't rate the people I love."

"Neither do I. It's not a scorecard. It's about what you need. Sometimes that cat is more responsive to you than Julia is—"

Now she was angry. "I know I'm supposed to be off self-actualizing, but my mother needs help with life. It's an odd world if her own daughter shouldn't be the one to give it."

Mildly he said, "But sainthood isn't necessary."

"We feel differently about it."

"You feel sainthood *is* necessary?"

"That's unfair. And not true. But I'm not talking about that anymore, Matthew. Can we agree not to argue? I came for tea. Tea and company." She tried to smile. "I'd love a snack with it. Do you have something sweet?"

"Mrs. Bowen is my personal baker. I have a couple of her cinnamon buns, some muffins with sticky orange stuff on top and some kind of squares I haven't tried, but they seem to have raspberry jam in them."

"I was thinking of chocolate."

"Oh, well, when a person is craving chocolate nothing else will do the trick. I'll run to the store. Will you make the tea? I'll be back by the time it's steeped."

Emily tried not to show how pleased she was. A trip to Mrs. Marsh's gave her ten or twenty minutes. With any luck there'd be a lineup and Mrs. Marsh would be in a talkative mood.

She put the kettle on and threw a few tea bags into the pot, then, when she was sure Matthew was on his way down the road, she started her search. For what, she didn't know. Anything that would give her an idea if he was in Three Creeks for some other reason than to work on his family history and take care of Daniel's house.

He had told her he slept in the basement, because of the heat. She hurried down, exclaiming when she slipped and banged her leg on the last few steps. She bent over, breathing between clenched teeth until the worst of the pain had passed. Blood trickled from a long, wide scrape.

There was no bed or sleeping bag or clothes in the storage area. She tried the furnace room door and felt over the frame for a key, but Matthew was no more careless than his uncle.

Wincing with each step she climbed back to the kitchen. She tore off a paper towel to hold to her leg, dabbing at the blood so it wouldn't drip on the floor. She crumpled the towel and stuck it in her pocket.

The kettle was on the verge of whistling. She poured the almost boiling water onto the tea bags, then made a quick check of the kitchen drawers before going to the living room to start on Daniel's desk.

The pile of Rutherford family photos wasn't hiding anything. Neither were the pages of notes Matthew had written. She opened a drawer. Bills marked paid, stamps and envelopes, a sheaf of papers stapled together. She unfolded it. A car rental agreement for a gray Honda Accord.

She had already skimmed the top of the page. She read it again. It was an international rental company, but under the name, in smaller letters, was a Winnipeg address.

The car had Ontario plates. Matthew said he'd driven it from Ontario. The long, hot drive was his excuse for being grouchy. The drive from his supposed home where a Rutherford relative had nothing to say about him.

Why would he lie about that? To cover up what?

With unsteady hands she returned the papers to their place and continued to search the drawers. In a back corner of the middle drawer, a single key sat loose.

"What are you looking for, Emily?"

Her heart hit her rib cage with a thud. As she pushed the drawer shut, she closed her fingers around the key.

"Matthew. You startled me."

"I'll bet."

"The tea should be steeped." She tried to keep her voice even. "What did you get for dessert?" If she looked a fraction as guilty as she felt, she was in trouble. She took a step toward the kitchen but Matthew moved into her path, enough to make it clear she wasn't going to leave the room.

"You wanted something from Daniel's desk?"

She had prepared an explanation, just in case. "You've been so stubborn about giving me a number where I can call him. I thought I might find one in his address book. I didn't see it, though."

He leaned past her, opened the drawer next to the one she'd been searching and pulled out a small leather book.

"This address book?"

"Oh, good. There it is."

He held it away from her outstretched hand. "Do you want to try a different story?"

"Matthew, you're acting weird. Daniel wouldn't mind me looking in his desk. Now, let's have the tea before it's cold." Again, she tried to move to the kitchen.

Matthew took hold of her shoulders and backed her into the chair by the desk. He pulled another chair close and sat down in front of her. "I want you to tell me what you were doing."

"Mrs. Bowen saw me come in."

His expression changed. "You're not in danger. I just want to know what's going on. You created a situation that left you alone in the house. I found you searching the desk. What were you looking for? What else did you do?"

He didn't sound like a criminal. But maybe a good

one wouldn't. If he was a criminal, was he really Daniel's nephew? If he wasn't Daniel's nephew, how did he get here and where was Daniel?

"I didn't do anything else," she said. "Well, I made the tea. And you still weren't back, so I decided to see if I could find a number where I could reach Daniel."

"You scraped your leg making tea?"

Emily didn't bother answering.

"You've been different the past couple of days. Guarded."

"You know what? I don't even want tea. I'm going home."

She stood as she spoke, expecting to meet resistance again, but this time he left her alone. She got to the kitchen doorway, and still he didn't stop her. She was surprised to reach the back door, then the driveway, then her car. As she backed out to the road, she saw him watching from the living room window.

WHAT DID SHE KNOW?

Emily took a pad of paper from her desk drawer. She wrote *Daniel*. Joined to the name by short lines she wrote—*where?* and—*aunt?*

Then, *Matthew*, followed by—*nephew?—books?—my father?*

My father—Daniel?—letter?

Jason—thief?—Matthew?

With long lines, she joined *Matthew* to *Daniel*, *Jason* to *Matthew*, *my father* to *Daniel*.

They were all connected, but by what?

Her father had lived in a rough neighborhood, with

friends who came to a bad end. He'd met Daniel, when Daniel was a Mountie. Was it like movies she'd seen? A group of friends, most get into crime, one becomes a cop and brings the rest to justice.

Then why would Matthew be involved? That brought her back to the possibility that he wasn't a Rutherford. That was why Daniel hadn't mentioned him, why Grandma and Aunt Edith didn't recall hearing his name.

Maybe Daniel and her father had arrested Matthew's father years ago and now Matthew had come for revenge. Or to find an incriminating notebook Daniel or her father had kept. And Matthew had hired Jason to help him.

But if any of that was true, any of it... She closed her eyes at the thought of Daniel in trouble.

It didn't feel right. It didn't feel true of Matthew. Black sheep, though. He had mentioned black sheep himself. Was he trying to warn her? What was that, a game? Or conscience?

She looked at the interconnecting lines she had drawn. She couldn't go to the police with something so vague, maybe something so wrong. She needed to know more.

ONE BY ONE she removed the books, leafing through the pages, feeling the shelf under and behind them. The occasional bookmark fell out, but that was all.

"Don't! Don't touch!" Julia's voice was unusually expressive. She hurried over and ran a hand along the books that had been disturbed.

"I put them back exactly the way I found them." Emily hesitated, then asked, "When you go through them, are you looking for something? Something hidden?"

Of course Julia didn't answer. Emily stopped to gather herself. Her mother avoided emotion the way some people avoided the dark, or horror movies. She wouldn't get anywhere with her if she couldn't stay calm.

"Can I ask you about Daniel?"

"Ask what?"

"Do you dislike him?"

Julia heaved a sigh. "Keep away from the books. I mean that." She walked quickly to the kitchen.

Emily followed. "Uncle Will said my father and Daniel knew each other before they lived in Three Creeks. No one in our family has ever mentioned they were friends. Neither did Daniel."

Julia chose a cookbook and flipped it open. "Moussaka. That's something I've never made."

Almost everything was something she had never made.

"Your reaction always puzzles me when I talk about Daniel." Emily had never pushed her mother like this. She could hear herself beginning to speak more quickly, louder. "Even when I was little, if I came home after skating on the creek with him and Sue and Liz, you'd make some huffing sound as if you were saying, 'Oh yeah, you think he's nice because he skates with you.' Are you angry with him, Mom? Did he do something wrong? Something that hurt you or Dad?"

Julia stared at her book, stubbornly silent.

"Please, I don't want to upset you, or pry into something between you and my father. But odd things are going on. I'm trying to understand."

Julia's hand, brushing the page, trembled. "Something is going on?"

It was a little late to be careful. Emily spoke more softly. "Matthew might not have told us the truth about what he's doing here. I think he might be looking for something in our house. Or on our land. I wondered if it might be a book."

Julia had gone very still. She started nodding, slowly and repeatedly.

"I don't want to accuse him if I'm wrong, Mom. So I need information."

The nodding turned into rocking. Julia's whole body went gently back and forth. "They had an argument."

"Daniel and my father?"

"After Frank disappeared. They were loud. Shouting."

Frank. The name sounded familiar.

On the card. *Congratulations on the birth of your daughter. Hope you get some sleep one of these years!*

"Who's Frank?"

Again, silence. Emily tried a different tack. "Did you hear what Dad and Daniel argued about?" She almost missed the slight shake of her mother's head. "You didn't hear?"

A more perceptible shake. "I went upstairs and shut the door. They were too loud. Booming. I put the pillow over my head."

"Okay. Thanks, Mom. Do you mind if I keep looking?"

Julia gave her a fierce, one-second glare.

"All right. Sorry. No more poking around in your stuff."

CHAPTER THIRTEEN

"YOU HAVE LOTS OF PHOTOS from Three Creeks' early days, from both sides of your family, don't you? You can tell Matthew a story to go with each picture?"

"In other words," Martin said, "bore him to death, but keep him here as long as I can."

"But don't let him know it was my idea."

"No problem." He looked at her curiously. "What's going on, Em? You having your naughty adolescent years at last?"

"I'm not doing anything naughty. Why would you think that?"

"Let's just say you couldn't stand beside an empty cookie jar right now and convince me you didn't take any. Sometime you'll tell me what's up?"

"Sometime," she agreed.

"Well, I'll roll out the invitation. Too bad there's no time to get to an engraver. An Evening of Coffee and Local History With Martin Robb. Hey. It sounds good, doesn't it? Maybe I've been in the wrong business all this time."

EMILY DIDN'T WANT anyone to see her car parked and waiting, so she walked from home, crossing the creek and going through woods and grain fields to the meadow at the end of Daniel's street. Her only plan was to try to find out what Matthew was doing and what was behind a door it made no sense to lock.

She hung back until the Accord pulled out of the driveway, and then, with watching neighbors in mind, strolled the rest of the way to the house. Not too slowly, or someone would come outside to visit. Not fast, either. Rushing down the road would be newsworthy.

The key from the desk fit the side door. She stepped inside, pulling it shut behind her, and turned the dead bolt.

So far, so good.

She didn't think exterior and interior locks were the same, but just in case, she went carefully down the stairs to see if the key would also work on the furnace room door.

Not even nearly.

Back up to the desk, then. She checked every inch of it this time. In every book, box and container, under every sheet of paper. She pulled the drawers right out to look at the bottoms and inside the crevices where they fit. Then behind the pictures on the walls, on the undersides of furniture, in the toilet tank and medicine chest, in vases, in cups in the kitchen cupboards. She searched the downstairs bedroom, then the two rooms upstairs.

Nothing. No more keys. Nothing to show Matthew was exactly who he said he was, and nothing to show he wasn't. She stood, hot, thirsty, and out of ideas. Did she have fifteen more minutes or the entire evening? She looked out the living room window. No Accord yet.

All right. Back to the basement. Maybe a key was

hidden closer to the door it opened—she should have thought of that sooner. It could be taped under any of the metal shelves, or in the hollow angle of the units' frames.

No such luck.

She began to check the boxes of equipment. There were too many, and too many bits of machinery with compartments to open and unscrew.

In one box she found a set of screwdrivers. She looked at the furnace room door. No visible hinges to pry off. No visible screws on the knob. Her frustration was growing. She knelt in front of the lock, tempted to bash it until it or the screwdriver broke.

"Daniel?"

He wasn't there, he wouldn't be there after all this time. Matthew wouldn't be keeping him prisoner.

With the thought of Daniel and prisoners in her mind, a memory clicked into place. Daniel owned lock-picking tools. If she could find those—

"Here we are again." The voice came from the stairs. "You should have let me know you were coming. I would have made sure to be home."

Slowly, Emily got to her feet. Matthew stood on the top step. She hadn't heard a thing. Not the car. Not the door. He pulled something out of his pocket.

"Looking for these?"

Keys on a chain.

"You're not cut out for this, Emily."

No, she had noticed that, too. Whatever was going on, she wasn't cut out for it.

"I knew you took the house key from the drawer, so

your cousin's sudden interest in my family history project wasn't very convincing."

He wasn't just back early. He hadn't fallen for the plan at all.

"I didn't think you'd notice the key was gone. It was so far back in the drawer."

Calm, flat conversation. As if they were both trying to figure out what should happen next.

"Would you like to see inside the furnace room?"

She shouldn't. There was a lock, there were bars on the windows, shutters so no one could see in. As stuck as she was now, she would be even more stuck in there. In there was the whole point of the exercise, though.

He started down the stairs.

"Matthew—"

He stopped.

"You're scaring me."

She saw a flash of anger. He reached the bottom of the stairs, unlocked the door, pushed it open. "Go ahead."

She went as far as the doorway. It was a spotless furnace and laundry room, brightly lit, walls painted white, gleaming tile floor. To one side was a cot and a suitcase.

Matthew reached past her to turn on a light over the right side of the room. She saw a wood-and-glass partition, and behind the glass, a desk. On it, a large LCD monitor and a telephone. Thin cupboards, no more than three inches deep, covered most of one wall.

He used another key to open a door in the partition. "Help yourself."

Another lock between her and the outside.

The computer was turned off. Was it Daniel's, or had Matthew brought it? The desk was more like a table, with no drawers to look in. She wondered if Daniel had made the cupboards. They were very simple, plywood painted white.

She tried one of the doors. Finally, something that wasn't locked. When it opened she saw why the cupboards didn't need to be deep. Inside, instead of shelves, there was a corkboard covered with neat rows of maps and yellowed newspaper clippings.

The center doors concealed a whiteboard, a large one, at least six feet across. A horizontal line was drawn from one side to the other. Shorter, vertical marks and handwriting divided it. A timeline.

Along the bottom of the board squares were marked off. She recognized Daniel's handwriting in the first several spaces, notes like *Frank arranges job with Northern Transport, G. invests in new combine, tractor.*

Then a new hand took over. *Value of books, No travel, Minimal Upkeep, No hired man—money an issue? Envy?—Rich b-in-l, cousins who travel. $$$ linen, china, silverware.* Printed in large letters underneath were the words, *SO WHAT?*

Numb, she opened another door. There was her mother, through the kitchen window of their house, reading.

There was Hamish.

And there she was. The day of the picnic, picking raspberries.

SHE LOOKED STRICKEN. He could see her effort to concentrate, to believe her eyes. He wanted to go to her and explain, tell her that he would look after everything, that it would be all right. It wouldn't be all right, though. What he was doing would hurt her. Had hurt her already.

"Who took the pictures of my mother and me?"

"I did."

"Why?"

"Background. It's routine."

Her mouth tightened. She began to look at the other photographs on the corkboard, staring for a long time at one of her father and Daniel with their arms over each other's shoulders in front of the Legion Hall.

"They were friends," she said.

"That's what I'm told."

"Why are they up here?"

He didn't answer. He didn't know if she was ready to hear.

"More background?" She moved to the picture of Frank Carruthers smiling beside his deHavilland Beaver. "That's the pilot Uncle Will was talking about at the barbecue."

"Yes."

"I saw his picture on the microfilm." She shot him a look. "I've been following you, Matthew. Watching you."

She went back to the center panel and began to read the timeline drawn on the whiteboard.

March 8, 1979—Moore leaves transport route. Reports equipment problems.

March 9—Gold bars trucked from Snow Lake mine to Flin Flon airport.

March 10—0900hrs. Carruthers takes off.

1000hrs. Flin Flon airport no contact.
1200hrs. Winnipeg airport no contact
March 13—Moore returns three days late.

She stopped reading. With disbelief and the beginnings of anger she said, "You think my family had something to do with this?"

"I've been looking into the possibility."

Her voice rose. "You've been looking into the possibility?"

For a second he thought she wanted to punch him. He wouldn't have believed she could get this angry.

She hammered the whiteboard with one finger. "Moore leaves transport route, returns late? Who are you saying this is? Some relative?"

"It was your father."

She blinked at him for a few seconds, taking that in. "My father didn't have a route to leave. You've got him mixed up with someone else, someone with a similar name. He was self-employed, a farmer, you know that."

Matthew didn't argue the point.

"This is nuts. You're trying to connect my father to that missing gold. Handy for you that he's dead and can't defend himself. Who are you, anyway? Does Daniel know you're here? Have you even talked to him?"

"Of course. He asked me to come, Emily."

She nodded. "Right. Because he's been jotting down these friendly little observations, too." Her voice was getting louder, tighter. "G. bought a combine. That's sure nefarious. Farmers never buy combines." The corner of her mouth trembled. She put a hand to her face to stop it. "You're what, a cop?"

"Not anymore. I'm a private investigator."

"Not, as you claimed and discussed in detail, an insurance assessor."

"I contract with insurance companies. Also museums, art galleries, mining companies. Anyone who has something of value to recover."

"Anyone? So a gold thief could hire your services?"

"No. Not a gold thief."

"I see. Because you have standards."

He didn't say anything.

"And where is my dear friend Daniel? Obviously not with his poor sick aunt."

"He's up north checking out the Carruthers end."

"The Carruthers end. You've divided the job. He's doing the Carruthers end and you're romancing your dead suspect's daughter. Lovely."

"Emily, that's not it."

She brushed past him and out the door.

EMILY SAT on the steps. Hamish lumbered over from the hedge to put his head on her knee.

"Hey, you sweet old thing." She rubbed behind his ears the way he liked. "Fine old man." The brown eyes looked at her with all the understanding in the world. How did dogs do that? Look so wise and sad and compassionate. She slipped down to the next step to be closer to him.

She couldn't bring herself to ask her mother if her father had ever worked up north. Even if he had, it didn't mean he'd done anything wrong.

She didn't want to think about Matthew. Couldn't stop, though. Somewhere along the line while trying to decide if she liked him she had fallen in love with him. If she could call it that. But who had she fallen in love with? A warm-underneath-it-all, make-no-trouble-for-anyone insurance evaluator or a downright scary private investigator who lied through his teeth with no trouble at all?

Her chest was tight with anger. She hoped it was anger and not undiagnosed heart trouble. Because it sure felt like heart trouble. It hurt.

She took a deep breath. Not to relax, to get oxygen.

It looked as if he really was called Matthew Rutherford. At least he hadn't kidnapped Daniel and locked him in the furnace room.

She swore. She never swore, but she couldn't help it— tears were coming out of her eyes. She never cried. Nearly never. Hated it.

The dog's wet nose touched her cheek.

"Shh. It's all right, boy."

Of course, she was going on the assumption that he'd told her the truth in the basement. Why on earth did she believe him so easily? She was the most gullible person in the world. Hamish was less gullible.

Matthew could say anything. He wasn't very likely to tell her, "Well, as a matter of fact, I'm a crook and a con artist and I killed your dear friend Daniel and took over his house. And of course, now that I've told you this, you're free to go."

Her mother's voice came from behind her, through the screen door. "Are you all right?"

That was the end of Emily's self-control. She put her head in her hands and wept.

It felt like a minute, but it must have been longer. She heard an engine and looked up to see a blurry truck rumbling along the road followed by a dust cloud. It turned into the driveway and rolled slowly to the house.

Susannah awkwardly climbed down from the cab. "Oh, dear." Leaning back, tummy out, she felt her way down to the step and sat beside Emily. "Your mom called and told me to come. 'Right now,' she said, all bossy. What's wrong, Em?"

Susannah's arm came around her shoulders. It felt wonderful because it was Susannah and because she knew, by proxy, it was her mother, too.

"Matthew did something, didn't he? Only men can have this effect. Cry all you like, and after that we'll send Alex to box his ears."

Emily choked on a laugh and then had to lean over her folded arms to contain the ache in her stomach. This couldn't be hugged or laughed away. Not even boxed away. Matthew was a liar, a cheat, and a sneak, and he thought her father was a thief.

CHAPTER FOURTEEN

It was amazing what a fitful night's sleep could do. By morning, a jumble of information and feelings had settled into a pattern that was at least clear enough to examine.

Matthew, she thought, was probably really Matthew, not some unknown crook. And every sneaky thing he had done had hurt him, too. That pleased her and gave him a degree of absolution. All she had to do now was prove he was wrong about her father.

She washed and dressed and headed to town. He let her in as soon as she rang the bell.

"I have some questions."

"Good. I'll do my best to answer them."

She went past him, down the stairs to the basement, where she waited for him to unlock the furnace room door. She tried not to notice his look of concern.

"How's your leg?"

"How's your conscience?"

"Hurting," he said, with a wry look. She tried not to notice that, either. The tired graininess he'd had when they first met was back. If she didn't watch out she was going to start feeling sorry for him.

They went through to the partitioned area, and he unlocked that door, too. Emily sat in the chair by the desk. "This is quite an office. It seems more advanced than Daniel would need." Calm and logical. That was the plan.

"It surprised me, too."

"I didn't think he had a computer. I've seen him use a portable typewriter at the kitchen table."

"He just pretends to be low-tech."

"Neither of you has been entirely honest."

"Because of the job."

"Maybe you could start by giving me a quick review of this whole thing. The plane disappearing. I didn't really listen to the talk at the barbecue."

The room only had one chair. Matthew leaned against the partition. "Twenty-six years ago fifteen bars of gold on their way from a Manitoba mine to a refinery disappeared. Either the plane crashed or someone who prevented it from reaching its destination stole the gold. The company that insured it is my client."

"Someone?"

"Theoretically it could have been hijacked, but the evidence points to Frank Carruthers."

"Fifteen bars doesn't sound like a lot."

"I've heard of smaller thefts and bigger ones. A while after Carruthers disappeared twenty-six million pounds' worth of gold was stolen in England. I don't know offhand what that is in dollars. The thieves melted it down, added pennies and poured new bricks."

"They can do that?"

"They brought in people with the necessary skills,

bought a used smelter from a foundry. The copper in the pennies disguised the gold. The bars were no longer the same quality so they were impossible to identify."

She swiveled the chair back and forth, thinking. "And the fifteen bars. What were they worth?"

"That depends what the market's doing at the time of sale. They weighed a thousand ounces each—that's over sixty pounds. Pure bullion is ninety-nine point nine percent gold. These were eighty-five percent. The refinery they were bound for would have removed the silver and copper that was still in the mix. So, fifteen bars that each hold about eight hundred and fifty ounces of gold…" He looked toward the ceiling and closed one eye while he did the math. "If we found it today it would be worth about five and a half million dollars."

Enough to solve a few problems, Emily thought.

"But in January of 1980 when gold spiked to eight hundred and fifty dollars an ounce it would have been worth nearly eleven million."

Eleven million. Emily could feel barriers going up in her mind. There was too much to think about all at once.

Of all the questions she could ask, one surfaced. "Why do you have Ontario plates on a car rented in Manitoba?"

"Our cover story was that I drove from home to take care of the house, so I arranged the plates to back that up."

"Home?"

"I told you, didn't I? I live in Ottawa."

"I looked you up. Couldn't find a phone number or address or anyone who knew you."

"You were busy while you were avoiding me."

Emily got up and walked away from the desk. His non-answers had been frustrating from the beginning. Now that she knew how much he'd been covering up they were even more so. "I spoke to a Rutherford in Ottawa who knew Daniel. She gave me the impression she'd never heard of you."

"My relatives are protective. Because of the work I do."

That made sense. Everything she had noticed about him was beginning to make sense. The job he wouldn't talk about, the mix of toughness and decency.

She went to look at the corkboard. Most of the clippings were yellowed. "Daniel's been following this from the start?"

"He and Carruthers used to work together. At first Daniel didn't believe Frank stole the shipment. He could have had engine trouble, he could have been lost on the way to Winnipeg. All that bush, all those lakes. Daniel devoted himself to trying to find the plane. In the earliest days, to rescue his friend. Then to recover the body."

Emily felt a twist of sympathy for Daniel. "But he changed his mind?"

"Yeah. That wasn't easy for him."

"And you think my father was involved somehow."

"As the police say, he's a person of interest."

He's. He is. It took millions in stolen gold to hear her father mentioned in the present tense. "And is he? Of interest to the police, I mean?" She was thinking of Corporal Reed's questions on his last visit after the break-in.

"I don't know about now. The old files aren't computerized. It might take a while to find them. In the weeks after Frank disappeared the team investigating tried to get a warrant to search your house and property and to check your parents' bank records. The judge didn't think they had enough evidence."

It was the first encouraging thing Emily had heard. "But you didn't need evidence."

"I didn't need a warrant."

"My father wasn't a thief. I can promise you that." All she had as proof was a feeling that the shadowy figure who had brought Christmas trees through the door couldn't have been dishonest.

Matthew indicated a photograph on the corkboard. "Did you notice this one last night? It was taken north of Flin Flon, in the winter of '78. Your father was working for a transport company, delivering supplies."

The picture showed her father dressed in a parka, standing in front of a tractor. Not a farm tractor with tires, but one with tracks for traveling on snow and ice. The kind Matthew had described. He was bundled up, with a fur hat pulled down to his eyes and frost on a mustache and beard. He was smiling.

"It's him," she acknowledged. "But I know he didn't work up north. He would have been at home with my mother and me, looking after the farm."

"It's not uncommon for farmers to look for other work in the winter."

"Maybe he was visiting there when the picture was taken. I don't remember him being away for long."

"You don't remember much about him. At least that's what you told me."

A burst of anger jolted her. "I told you a lot of things. When you asked."

A telephone rang. Emily looked at the one on the desk, but Matthew pulled a cell phone from his pocket.

"Hi. Yeah, she's here. Not so good. I'll put her on."

He handed her the phone. Without a greeting, a familiar voice said, "What are you getting yourself into, Emily?"

"Daniel?"

"Trying to be a sleuth, are you? Nancy Drew, I suppose."

"I'm a little old for that."

"I agree."

"You've had me worried."

"Here I am, still breathing. But I want you to stay well away from all this."

"Matthew said he's your nephew. Is that true?"

"You're not listening. You're not involved in this, Emily. I won't get into a Q & A about it."

"Where are you? Are you coming home?"

"I can't talk anymore. I'm in the middle of things here. Just wanted to tell you to quit worrying. And…well, that I'm sorry about all this. Now, give me Matt again."

No hello, no goodbye. She held out the phone. Matthew listened, opening the cupboard door that concealed maps.

"I can be ready in an hour. What is it, a six-hour drive? Then why not meet tonight? All right, breakfast, the Cranberry Inn."

He folded the phone and returned it to his pocket. "Sorry. I have to go. Daniel wants to meet."

He locked the furnace room behind them. "Your mother must be unsettled with the shelves sitting there half-built. Will you tell her I'll take care of it when I come back?"

When he came back. She hadn't thought he would.

SHE COULDN'T WAIT at home sipping tea while Matthew went off to prove her father's involvement in a crime. Forgetting to be careful of the toads on Robbs' Road, Emily turned in at Uncle Will and Aunt Edith's house and found them at the lunch table. After a hurried hello to the rest of the family, she told her uncle she wanted to go north with Matthew to see Daniel. She didn't explain why.

He patted his mouth with a paper napkin. "Daniel's up north?"

"Could you look in on Mom while I'm gone?"

"Of course I could. What's Daniel doing up—"

Susannah put an arm around Emily's waist. "Have you and Matthew sorted things out? You're sure you'll be all right with him?"

"It's not really about him. It's Daniel and…and other things."

"Tell you what. Alex and I will sleep over at your place until you get back, in case Aunt Julia's still worried about the break-in. Then she can't refuse to have tea with me!"

"I was going to suggest that myself," Alex said.

Susannah whispered, "You'd better get going. Mom and Dad are brewing questions!"

Emily gave her cousin a hug, and got on her way. At

home she threw pyjamas, a couple of changes of clothes, mosquito repellent, sunscreen and a makeup bag full of assorted necessities into a small suitcase. Then she forced herself to slow down. She needed to take her time explaining this to her mother.

"For how long?" Julia asked.

"That's a bit open-ended. I can let you know each day whether I'll be coming home the next day."

"*About* how long?"

"If I say *about* three days you realize that doesn't mean I'll be back in *exactly* three days?"

Julia nodded, but she didn't look pleased. "You're going north to visit Daniel, you might be two or three or four days, and you're sure Matthew won't poke around looking for anything while you're gone."

Emily had left him out of her explanation. "I was wrong about that. He really is helping his uncle. In fact, he's going north, too. He says he'll finish the shelves when he comes back."

Julia wanted to go over the details again. Emily repeated the plan, listened to her mother's second review of the details, then startled her with a goodbye kiss and hurried back to Daniel's place.

The Accord was gone.

She pulled a highway map out of the glove compartment. Using her thumb as a measure, she checked the mileage north of Three Creeks. Six hours, Matthew had said. Two roads went that far, Highway 6 between the lakes and Highway 10 to the west of Lake Winnipegosis. If he kept to the speed limit there were several towns that distance away.

She drove to the post office and checked the Yellow Pages at the phone booth. Only one of the towns had a Cranberry Inn.

GOING DOWN the wide main street in Swan River three hours later Emily stopped so suddenly the car behind her had to slam on its brakes. The driver honked once, long and angrily, then a second time more briefly. She ignored him. She had seen Matthew's car.

At least she thought it was his…a silver-gray Accord at the curb beside a Pizza Place. She drew into an empty spot a few cars down and hurried into the restaurant. Over a partition in the lobby she saw him, alone at a table for two.

Without a word, she sat in the chair across from his.

"Emily."

Not exactly an exclamation of surprise, but she could see him take a second to adjust. Then he pushed the pizza pan closer to her.

"The mushrooms are great." He signaled a waitress for another cup of coffee. "All right. What's going on?"

"I want to know what you're doing. I need to look out for my dad."

"You think you can somehow protect him from being blamed for a crime that happened a quarter of a century ago?"

"I know it's ridiculous—"

"It isn't ridiculous. It's fruitless."

She couldn't explain any better than she had already tried to do. This was the first time she had been in a position to stand by her father.

"What if I said I didn't want you to come?"

"Matthew, I'm sorry—I don't say this to hurt you— but right now I really don't care what you want."

"Fair enough. You might as well ride with me, then. I want to know what you're doing, too. You'll listen to me from here on in? If I shout 'run' or 'duck' you'll do it?"

He had to be joking. She nodded.

They finished the pizza together, then Matthew stood, leaving some money on the table. "Got your bug spray and your silly hat? This won't be the countryside you're used to, Emily. There'll be a lot more mosquitoes than raspberries where we're going."

If he was trying to dissuade her, it didn't work. "I can use a break from the berries."

THEY GOT PERMISSION to leave her car at a mechanic's garage, and drove together in silence, nearly alone on the two-lane highway. They passed a few slow-moving tractors. In the other lane logging trucks roared by, heading south.

At first the scenery was familiar, mostly farmland— wheat, canola, oats and mowed fields full of big round hay bales. Soon low, blue-gray hills rose to the northwest. Emily checked Matthew's map, already folded to show the area they were traveling. Porcupine Mountains. When they were closer, the blue-gray color changed to green. Spruce covered the hills, cut through here and there by thin bare strips. Logging roads, she supposed.

Whenever she looked to the west she also saw Matthew's profile. There were shadows under his eyes. He had lied to her and insinuated himself into her life, but when she looked at him she wanted to forgive him everything. So she didn't look at him.

After Mafeking, they moved into different terrain. Tamarack—a conifer that changed color each fall and lost its needles—grew lacy and lighter green against towering, sparsely branched jack pine. When they passed a sign that marked the 53rd Parallel, the woods to her right ended to show a body of water so wide she couldn't see the far shore. According to the map it was only a bay that reached out from a much larger lake.

She'd never seen such an isolated place. For miles there were no houses or gas stations, no other vehicles, no help. And she had jumped into a car with a man she no longer trusted.

As soon as she thought it, she knew it wasn't true. In spite of all Matthew's lies, she did trust him. Not to be loyal to her. Not to tell her the truth. What did that leave? She looked at him, concentrating on the road, and couldn't think of an answer.

"You bought jeans."

"Bought them? I've always had them."

"You've never worn them. The whole time you were in Three Creeks."

"I guess I'm hoping the bugs will have trouble biting through them."

"That's the second time you've mentioned bugs."

"You haven't heard about the flies? Little blackflies with great big jaws. Moose hide is tough. When a soft-skinned human comes along they all want to get in on the feast."

"You're exaggerating."

"Not according to Daniel."

The large body of water was behind them. After a bridge that crossed the Overflowing River, Matthew drew up outside a bungalow with a single gas pump out front and an illuminated Open sign in the window. A couple of picnic tables sat in long grass near the river.

"We'll take a break here."

It was a relief to get out of the car. Emily walked quickly to the river, slapping mosquitoes as she went. She could see a campground downstream. A man and a boy were fishing. Two other children walked along the rock bed, watching water rush over their feet.

Matthew had followed her. "Do we need to clear the air?"

"I don't." She'd never liked fighting and she didn't know a pleasant way to talk about deception.

"I fooled you. I gained your trust and used it."

"Since we both know that, what's to be gained by discussing it?"

"We don't need to discuss it. You can yell at me if you like."

"Would that make you feel better?"

After a minute he said, "Getting away from these mosquitoes would make me feel better." He tilted his head toward the coffee shop. "I'm going in."

She considered staying with the bugs or going back to the car, but instead she followed him inside. Calm and logical, she reminded herself.

They ordered tea, with apple pie for Matthew and a butter tart for her. The tart was good enough to ease her anger—wide and deep, with flaky pastry and a rich, creamy butterscotch filling that was liquid enough to drip and thick enough to hold lots of plump raisins and chopped walnut. It was better than her own, better than Aunt Edith's and, although she would never say so out loud, better than her grandmother's.

"You can have another one," Matthew said.

She sat back from the table, embarrassed that her enjoyment had been so obvious.

"Or we could take some with us," he went on. "In case you're hungry later."

She didn't want to take treats in the car, as if they were a couple on holiday. "You know what I thought? That you were going to steal some of my mother's books. That you'd hired Jason to help you."

He looked startled. "Hired him, then turned him in?"

She poured the little bit of tea that was left in her metal pot, very strong now, and barely warm. "When you can't read someone's expression or tone and you can't believe what they're telling you and you can't trust your impressions, I suppose you might come to an incorrect assumption or two."

"Fair enough."

"What were you looking for at my house, anyway? A treasure map? A Swiss bank number?"

"For whatever there might be to find."

She put down her cup with a bang. "The walls. God, you— The shelves." Her voice became loud enough that the waitress and the one other customer turned and stared.

"You were looking for *gold*. In the wall of my *house*.

Asking my mother when the shelves were put in and saying what a fine job my father did building away from the wall like that, how clever he was." She clamped her mouth shut. If she didn't, she really might yell.

"I'm sorry, Emily. Unfortunately, that's my job."

THEY REACHED the Cranberry Inn around seven o'clock that evening. It was in sight of a lake off the highway near Cranberry-Portage, an older motel with a row of cheerful cranberry-red doors opening to the parking lot. Emily bought soup in the adjoining coffee shop and disappeared into her room.

Matthew tried to put her feelings and his aside. He unlocked his briefcase and took out some files—records of the transport company that had employed Graham Moore and transcripts of police interviews from the original investigation after Carruthers' disappearance. He'd already studied the transcripts, but he wanted to be sure he was prepared for whatever his uncle had planned for the next day.

There were interviews with a pilot, a trapper who had known Frank, the mine supervisor, the air traffic controller at the Flin Flon airport and a mechanic who had worked on the plane the day before the flight. They all said they knew Frank, not that well, but that he was a great guy. The bush plane's maintenance was up-to-date. Frank's planned route shouldn't have taken him anywhere near the storm. These things happened, they said. It was a shame.

The transport company's log was difficult to read.

Daniel had faxed it to him yesterday after persuading a secretary to part with it. Weeks' worth of narrow-ruled pages and faint photocopied handwriting listing crew names and delivery routes. The cat trains traveled nearly around the clock to take maximum advantage of the short months of good ice.

He peered closer at the listings for the second week of March, 1979. Was that McNabb? Someone called McNabb had asked for the delivery that Moore had detoured to make? That was the name of the trapper the police had interviewed. Someone must have taken note of the connection before. Probably lost in a storage room somewhere.

The requested cargo was a generator. McNabb wanted it dropped off at an address described by a series of numbers and letters that represented the section, township and range of the property. Matthew pulled out his municipal map and began to trace the coordinates. A knock at the door interrupted him.

Emily stood in the hall, looking deflated. "I've been trying to make a list of things that prove my father's innocence."

"Good. Lists can get ideas flowing."

"Or block them." She held up a small lined notebook. At the top he read *Reasons My Father Isn't Guilty*. Except for the optimistic heading the page was empty.

"Come in." He put away the files and map, then sat on the bed, leaving her the chair. "Did you get hold of your mother?"

"Susannah said Mom's been telling her and Alex all about paleontology. I guess that means she's fine."

"Do you feel all right about leaving her, then?"

"I just feel confused."

She didn't seem as angry as she had earlier, but there was a pale brittleness to her that suggested that could change.

"What do you think you need? Sleep or facts?"

"Let's try facts." She corrected herself. "Your version of the facts."

There wasn't any way to protect her from the truth. Even if she hadn't insisted on coming with him she would have had to hear it eventually. "I don't have any proof that your father isn't guilty. I have some that he might be."

"I'd like to see it."

He decided to lead up to his main evidence gradually. That way she'd see it coming. "The plane was found with no human remains and no cargo. I'm supposing Frank either died from injuries or exposure and someone who came across the wreckage buried him and took the gold, or he was able to leave the site with the gold himself. If so, where did he go, and how? He couldn't just hike out. The gold would be too heavy. It suggests a person waiting on the ground with a method of transportation."

"Maybe someone with a dogsled."

"It's possible."

"You don't need to say it grudgingly. It's a realistic suggestion."

"According to the records of the transport company your father worked for, he took a tractor and sled off the main road to make a delivery around the time of Carruthers' flight. That's unusual. It's dangerous for a cat train to operate with only the driver, but a lot of people were out with the flu and he volunteered. He was away three days longer than expected. He told them the tractor needed repairs."

"Did they believe him?"

"Seems like they did."

"Can't you accept their judgment?"

"You know how fast a cat train goes? Without its usual load, maybe eight miles an hour. A person would need a couple of days to go any distance."

She looked at him the way she often did, as if she had no idea who on earth he was. Sometimes he'd got the feeling she enjoyed the uncertainty. Definitely not now.

He reached into his briefcase and brought out a long rectangle of folded paper. He set it in front of her. "This is a copy of the deed to your farm." He turned the paper over to show her the back.

"Notice in exercising power of sale," she read. "My dad was going to sell the farm?"

"Not your dad. The bank. They had begun to foreclose on your parents' mortgage."

Emily stared at the paper, shaking her head. "My parents wouldn't have had a mortgage. The house and land were a wedding gift."

"Yes, but then your father took out a mortgage on the property. A two-hundred-thousand-dollar mortgage."

"He wouldn't have! He wouldn't risk it."

"He needed money to buy more land and larger equipment and chemicals if he was going to stay competitive. Your relatives must have talked about the seventies. The family farm was on the way out."

Emily nodded. "A lot of people lost their land."

"Your parents weren't immune."

"All right. So he borrowed money."

"Look underneath the notice."

"Disposed of by discharge," she read. "What does that mean?"

"That your father paid off the bank loan."

"Paid off two hundr—" She stopped.

"He did it over a three-year period, starting the year the gold disappeared. I suppose he could have had three astonishingly good crops in a row."

Emily didn't say anything. He could see what she was thinking—that crops never got that good. She looked shaken, but she held her position.

"My father wasn't a criminal, Matthew. He was a wonderful man who took my mother out of herself for a few years. He didn't do this. I know it. And you're right, I hardly remember him, but I know it without remembering him."

If determination could change history she would have done it by now. "I admire your faith in your dad, Emily. It's not my job to hurt him, or you and your mom. It's my job to find the gold."

"That's all?"

He nodded before realizing there was more. For the past couple of weeks his mind had been on fifteen gold bars, his uncle and Emily. On keeping them all safe. But if the gold was gone, sold, his job moved to the next step.

"To find it, or to recover the insurance company's losses. That means if the gold has been converted to assets, I seize the assets."

It didn't sink in right away. "You'd take the farm?"

"Anything bought with the gold."

"You'd take the farm."

"You don't see a problem using the proceeds of a crime to buy things?"

"No proceeds of any crime bought my farm! That land has belonged to my family since the 1880s." She gripped the arms of the chair and pushed herself up, then walked stiffly to the door and out.

She wouldn't forgive him. That was clear. He hadn't realized before this how much he'd been hoping she would.

CHAPTER FIFTEEN

HALF AN HOUR before Daniel was expected Matthew and Emily settled in at a table for four in a corner of the motel's coffee shop.

"He won't come early," Matthew said. Daniel had told him he wanted to check one more thing on his way from Snow Lake to Cranberry-Portage. "We might as well get breakfast."

They both ordered the special—two eggs, hash browns, bacon, toast and coffee. Restaurants in the area were too far apart to risk a light meal.

"Did you sleep?"

"After a while. Matthew?" She stopped while a waitress put their plates in front of them, and then continued, with frequent pauses, as if it was hard to find the right words for what she wanted to say. "I was thinking things over last night. If there's proof, real proof, that my father...that he paid off the mortgage with money he got...illegally—and I'm still confident that he didn't, but if he did—would the people you're working for take payment? Rather than the farm. From me, over time?"

He'd make sure they would. "We can work it out, Emily."

"Because losing the land— The first William bought it all those years ago, thinking of the future. No one in my family has ever—"

"I understand." If he had to, he'd pay the debt himself.

"Okay, good. Thanks." She smiled weakly. "It would take me a while to pay back two hundred thousand. My grandchildren would be paying the insurers' grandchildren."

Eight o'clock came and went with no sign of Daniel. Matthew began to watch the door.

"Are your phone batteries working, Matthew?"

He nodded. "And the phone is switched on."

"Maybe he slept in. Or had car trouble."

"Cellular service isn't widespread up here." If Daniel couldn't call, it meant he wasn't near town.

Matthew got up, reaching for his wallet. Their waitress met him at the cash register. "Did anyone call this morning wanting to leave a message for a customer? It would have been Daniel, for Matt."

"Can't remember anything like that."

He thanked her and led the way outside. "I want you to stay in my room, Emily, in case he gets in touch using a land line. I'm going to look around town, make some calls, check in with the police. I won't be more than a hour."

HE WAS TWO. The whole extra hour Emily paced the motel room checking out the window every time she heard a car in the parking lot. Finally he came through the door, his face set, more with alertness than tension.

"Daniel didn't call," she said right away.

Matthew nodded, as if that was what he'd expected. "He stopped here when he first came north, contacted the local RCMP and tried to pump them for information, then left."

"Pump them? I thought he was working with them?"

"That's what he told me. I would have been up here so fast if I'd known he was on his own—"

"So the police couldn't help?"

"Not much." He picked up his briefcase and overnight bag and made a final check of the room as he talked. "They said they'd ask Highways and Natural Resources staff and lodge owners in the area to keep their eyes open. If there's no word from him by the end of the day, they'll start a search." He glanced at her, then away, opening the door. "I want you to go back to Three Creeks. It isn't safe, Emily. I can't in good conscience take you further."

"I was worried about bears. That's not what you mean."

"I'm talking about serious criminals, Emily. Not people like Frank or your dad."

Odd to be pleased at that. He didn't think her father was a serious criminal. Just a regular one. "What do we do?"

"I put you on a southbound bus."

"And I get off. Then what?"

"Remember in Swan River you said you'd listen to me?"

"If you said 'run' or 'duck.' You're only saying you're worried."

He gave her one of his intense stares. She could see when he reached a decision. "We'll go to Snow Lake.

Daniel stayed there for about a week. He wanted to talk to a trapper who knew Carruthers. Turned out the man died a few years ago, but Daniel spoke to his son. I've arranged to meet him."

THE ROAD TO Snow Lake went west through Grass River Park, past lakes and peat bogs and a dense evergreen forest. Matthew was more concerned than he wanted to admit to Emily. If Daniel was ready to meet he must have found something. Not the gold. He'd sounded too calm for that. But he'd found something, and then he'd disappeared.

An hour into the drive a small car zoomed past them.

"I think that's Mrs. Marsh's honeymoon couple."

Emily said, "Churchill here they come."

"Or not."

"Even if they only get as far as Thompson, they should have a good time. There's supposed to be some beautiful falls near there. And bald eagle nesting grounds."

A few miles outside Snow Lake there was a break in the trees. Water sparkled, looking cold and clear. Rough cabins wound along the lakeshore. A larger building, a combination office and restaurant, stood closer to the road.

Matthew parked near the office door and went inside. A middle-aged woman looked up from doing paperwork. A name plate on the desk said, Doreen Wells, Proprietor.

"You must be Matt. Daniel not with you?" She handed him a key. "It's cabin four."

Not only was it the right place, but he was expected. "How long is it since you saw my uncle?"

"Just yesterday. He left bright and early and said he'd be heading back with you in tow. You didn't run into him?"

"Not yet."

"Well, he'll be along. What's he up to, anyway? Prospecting?" She kept talking, as if she didn't expect an answer. "He's been going out every day on his own, sometimes by car, sometimes by boat, stays away till dark. Friendly as can be, but after a week I still don't know what he's doing."

"That sounds like my uncle."

"He's not fishing, that's for sure. Nobody's luck could be that bad! Even my three-year-old granddaughter's been throwing them back. So I figure prospecting."

She looked at Matthew curiously, giving him a chance to tell her if she was right. He signed the register, thanked her for the key and went to find Emily.

She was on the dock. She didn't turn when he stepped onto it, making it bob on the water.

"It's so peaceful here," she said.

It seemed that way. The water was calm enough to reflect the evergreens around the lake. A duck with a reddish-brown head swam near shore. There were more further out, a mother followed by fuzzy babies, all moving together, changing direction at once, like a single, larger bird.

"Don't get too relaxed. Until we know where Daniel is I want you to assume you can't trust anyone. We're in here blind, Emily."

"You think someone was watching Daniel?"

"Could be. So let's have a look at the cabin and then set things in motion."

"You mean get someone watching us."

"Want to go home?"

She shook her head, but he thought she looked frightened. He should have parked her at the Cranberry-Portage detachment, asked them to lock her up if she wouldn't stay put. However much she wanted to help her father—needed to—she didn't really understand the stakes. To her, it was simple. Nice people populated a pleasant world. If someone was hurt, you helped. If they were lost, you found them. It was a mind-set he barely remembered.

They carried their bags through the screened porch and into the main room, a sitting-cooking-eating area that stretched across the front of the cabin. Two smaller rooms at the back had just enough space for a set of bunk beds each. Between the bedrooms was a tiny bathroom.

Matthew took a quick look around. He was disappointed to find Daniel hadn't left anything behind. Like a map, marking where he'd gone. That would have been nice.

Emily was checking the cupboards. "There's a teapot."

"You can stay and make a hot cup, if you like."

"I'm going with you."

THE COFFEE SHOP adjoined a gas station off the main road into town. Like Doreen Wells, Ross McNabb must have noticed the Rutherford family resemblance. He waved as soon as Matthew and Emily walked in, and called to a waitress to bring two more cups of coffee.

While she poured, a man a few tables away called to her.

"Denise! Hey, good news. I was up in the fire tower last night, saw this little curl of smoke out by the lake. Darned if it didn't come from MacGregor's chimney."

She glanced up from Emily's cup, the pot angled so it wouldn't drip. "Don't you start bugging me about MacGregor."

"Poor guy couldn't stay away."

"You saw somebody's campfire. He never comes south this early." The waitress paid attention to the coffee again, muttering, "The man must be ninety-three."

Ross McNabb gave a snort. "Try sixty."

"Uh-huh, and it's a young sixty. I know. Like I'd live in a shack in the bush skinning rabbits all winter. I don't think so."

McNabb grinned, watching her stalk away. "Nobody avoids the bush like that woman. Don't know why she stays." He smiled again. "Unless it's for MacGregor. It's a pretty spot out there, too, with a nice little lake where she could rub her laundry on the rocks—"

Matthew decided he'd given the man enough time to get comfortable. "Anywhere near your dad's old trapline?"

"My dad's was further north." McNabb changed direction easily, and after a few more questions from Matthew to set the route he seemed happy to talk about his father and Frank Carruthers.

"They had plans, those two." He shook his head,

traces of affection and frustration still apparent. "One day it would be a restaurant serving caribou at an abandoned Hudson's Bay Company post. Another day, a fly-in lodge. That was their favorite idea. Frank the pilot, Dad the guide."

"It sounds realistic, given their skills."

"But not given their bank accounts."

"Did they seem serious about it? Or was it just talk?"

"I was a kid. Who knows? It's the kind of thing people like to dream about, that's for sure."

"Especially a couple of old friends over a beer."

"Yeah, exactly. They were always at it. And they had other ideas. Northern Lights tours. Taking people to Churchill by snowmobile, tucked under buffalo robes— they went as far as looking at machines for that one. Took me with 'em." He smiled briefly. "I went on a lot of rides that day. There was this old Bombardier they really liked. You know those big old things, curved roof, closed in?"

"Little round windows like a ship?"

"That's it. They carry ten or twelve people. It was a museum piece even then. My dad told me later Frank promised to give him one, but he never did."

"Give him one? A present, you mean?"

"He liked talking big like that." McNabb's expression changed. "Once he saw me drooling over this ten-speed in the Eaton's catalog and told me he'd get it for me."

"Not a nice thing to say to a kid if you don't mean it."

"He meant it. For five minutes. Forgot it after six."

"What did your mother think of him?"

McNabb shrugged. "As long as my dad was having fun she was happy. Oh! Then there was the history brain wave. Retracing the fur-traders' route along the Seal and Grass Rivers. They thought for sure city people, teachers and stuff, would go for that."

"Most of their ideas sound workable."

"Given enough money and drive. My dad and Frank, they weren't like that."

"Too easygoing?"

"If you've got customers, you've got timetables, rules."

Having dreams, wanting money. That covered just about everybody. He couldn't call it evidence. Of course, not everybody had access to gold and the opportunity to take it. Frank and Jock did. And so did Graham Moore.

"Your dad lived at his cabin in the bush all winter?"

"Mostly."

"That wouldn't have been an easy life. How did people get supplies in those days?"

"Some guys had dogsleds, others snowmobiles. The train would bring things in, leave 'em on the siding, and it was up to you to get it where it was going."

"Cat trains, too?"

"Not so much. Least I don't think so. Those were more for the big fishing and logging companies. Mines, too."

"Did my uncle say anything about his plans this week?"

"He didn't talk much, except for asking questions. He wanted to know where all the old mines were, cabins, ghost towns, airstrips. You get the picture. Does he figure Frank's been holed up somewhere all this time?

The gold wouldn't be doing him much good then, would it? Anyway, somebody would have seen him." Ross smiled. "Your uncle's an energetic guy, isn't he? I don't know if I'd be able to keep up with him."

TREE ROOTS FORMED natural steps down the hill to the lake, holding in the sandy soil. Through a band of birches Matthew could see water, and floatplanes tethered to a dock. Further down was a small one-story building with Frontier Air Service painted in block letters on one side.

The door was open, and an older man, maybe in his sixties, sat at a desk. He looked up from a clipboard when they approached.

"Rob Jamieson?" Matthew asked.

The man got up, hand outstretched. He glanced at Emily, then ignored her. "What can I do for you?"

"My uncle was here sometime during the past week." Matthew held out a small photo of Daniel. It was the first time he'd needed to show it.

Jamieson's manner became more guarded. "Oh, yeah. Four, five days ago."

"Have you seen him since?"

"What do you mean? Something happen?"

"He was in this area until yesterday morning. Did you talk to him or see him again?"

"I saw him in town once or twice. Picking up a pizza, getting some gas. That's it, I think. Most of the time I'm here or in the air." Jamieson shuffled some papers on his desk. "Why, what's wrong?"

"He was supposed to meet me this morning and he didn't."

"Nobody should go into the bush alone, especially an older person like that. Get chest pain or something, who's going to help?"

"What did the two of you talk about when he was here?"

"We talked about Frank Carruthers. He was the pilot who—well, I guess you've heard about that."

"You knew Frank?"

"Sure. We worked for the same outfit in the '70s, flying people and supplies in and out. The mine always asked for him, though."

"Why was that?"

He hesitated before answering. "Retired cop, bonded. A guy like that would be their first choice. Most people thought he was a real straight arrow."

"Most people? Not you?"

"He probably was as long as he wasn't looking at more gold than he could carry. I always thought he did it."

"Any reason?"

"Because he said he would. Right out."

Matthew's eyebrows went up. "He said he was going to steal a shipment of gold?"

"Not like that. Not like he meant it. But he'd say, 'One of these days I'll keep on going.' You don't take it seriously when people talk that way. But then he disappeared and I figured he did it after all."

"You didn't say that to the police at the time."

"Of course not. But then they found the Beaver and I was sorry for thinking it."

"You thought it was an accident after all? Even though there was no sign of him or the gold?"

"It had to be. The plane's there, busted up. Maybe he tried to walk out—you have to carry snowshoes as part of your survival gear. It was miles from anywhere, though, all bush and muskeg. Even if he wasn't injured—and I don't see that happening—the cold would get him pretty fast."

"And the gold?"

Jamieson shrugged. "People are only human. A trapper comes across the plane, or a bunch of CEOs out on a wilderness adventure—I mean, what would you do?"

MATTHEW FILLED THE TANK with gas, checked the oil and topped up the windshield washer fluid. They bought bottled water and a couple of frozen dinners to heat at the cabin. While he waited for change, Emily saw him reading the Grey Goose Bus schedule.

"You can forget that," she said.

"Just checking. Always have a Plan B, Em."

"As long as putting me on the bus isn't still Plan A."

"That'll be your choice."

Before heading back to the lodge he used a pay phone to call the Cranberry-Portage detachment. His face hardened while he listened. When he hung up he told her, "No one has seen Daniel or his Cutlass. The constable's beginning to sound concerned."

"Good. He'll look harder."

On the drive back to the lodge Matthew seemed deep in thought. They put the frozen dinners in the oven as soon as they got to the cabin, then he pulled a map out of his knapsack and spread it on the table. It wasn't the usual highways map. It was like a painting, showing patterns rather than places. Lakes and rivers were delicate blue against the white of land, like light coming through a pin-pricked lampshade. No wonder there were hardly any roads in the north. How could you even walk on land like that?

Matthew used a pencil to darken some of the lines. "These are winter roads." He circled a large area surrounding Flin Flon and Snow Lake. "These lakes and rivers are part of a system. They all flow northeast, to Hudson Bay." His finger traced the water's course. "But look, every body of water, big or small, has its own system."

She could see what he meant. Small, irregularly shaped lakes were everywhere, with long fingers of water stretching to meet the fingers of other lakes, joined by thin rivers or creeks. They looked like illustrations of the nervous system in school textbooks. There were fingers of land, too, and hundreds of small islands. From what she'd seen so far, forest would cover most of it.

"Are you saying searching for Daniel is hopeless?"

"I'm saying there are transportation routes—road, railway, winter road, water—that indicate which areas matter most to us. Daniel was here for a week, going out by car or boat every day and always coming back by nightfall. That means none of his trips took longer than eighteen hours."

"So we'll pick a direction, do one route each day?"

"We'll superimpose the winter road map on the highways map. We need to keep in mind where the plane went down, where the winter roads are and where Daniel's been exploring. Abandoned mines, cabins, ghost towns, according to what Ross McNabb said. We'll find him."

CHAPTER SIXTEEN

THE FIRST DAY they found nothing but trees, muskeg and mosquitoes. The second day an underground stream that bubbled up through limestone. On the third day, they found Daniel's Cutlass.

They had driven around a No Entry barrier and were following a bumpy road with grass long enough to brush the bottom of the car when Emily noticed a path snaking up the side of a hill through the trees. At first she thought it was a dry streambed—she had seen lots of those in the area—and then she thought it might be a trail used by animals. When they looked closer they realized it was an old logging or mining road, nearly grown in.

They decided to walk up. Matthew parked the Accord as far off the track as he could without getting caught on rocks or protruding roots. They applied an extra dose of bug repellent to their ears, necks and ankles—areas blackflies particularly liked—then Matthew slipped his knapsack over his shoulders and began the climb.

If she hadn't been worried about Daniel, it would have been a pleasant hike. The sun shone, the repellent worked, birds called and the smell of evergreens was in the air. Whenever the path got steep, Matthew took her hand in his with a strong, but gentle grasp that reassured and excited her at the same time. Everything about him felt so good to her. She wanted to trust him.

"Isn't this a bit arduous for Daniel?"

"It depends whether he thought gold was at the other end."

That sounded as if he knew Daniel better than he'd suggested. Emily still wasn't sure if the two men really were related, or if that was part of their cover story. She hadn't asked again because she didn't know if Matthew would tell her the truth. How would she know the difference, anyway?

"You've been detecting all along, haven't you? I mean, visibly detecting. I should have noticed. You were always asking and listening and watching. The insurance evaluator explanation almost made sense."

"Almost?"

"There was that tackle."

"Ah, the tackle."

"The one all guys know how to do. Except they don't."

"I grew up on Daniel's stories, too."

"Did you? He wasn't away from Three Creeks all that much."

"He sent me a long letter every birthday. A novella. Complete with really bad sketches. The continuing adventures of Uncle Daniel."

"So you followed in his footsteps?"

"To the RCMP training academy in Regina. Where I learned to tackle bad guys."

"Not that Jason Willis is much of a bad guy."

"Don't underestimate him. You worry me, Emily. One of these days you'll offer your compassion to the wrong person."

"He's a kid. Kids make mistakes." The conversation had moved into an uncomfortable area. There were plenty of mistakes to go around. "I'm not sure you should have talked to him on Tuesday."

Matthew looked at her in surprise. "You knew about that?"

"It seems like a conflict of interest or something. His parents and the police should deal with him, not the man who caught him."

"I don't see any conflict. I was only encouraging him to be more forthcoming with the facts."

She was about to ask if there were any particular facts he'd hoped to hear when she saw blue metal through the trees. Sky-blue, and glinting in the sun.

They both ran, calling Daniel's name. The Cutlass had gone off the road, tilting where the ground dropped steeply. The driver's door was open. Reddish-brown stains spattered the steering wheel.

She whipped around, looking into the dense bush. "Daniel!"

"He won't be in the woods, Emily." Matthew walked from the rear of the car to the open door. "Looks like it was struck from behind. The impact would have thrown him forward. Must have hit his head." He touched the steering wheel. "Blood's dry."

"A collision, way out here? Where is he, then? The other driver wouldn't have left him. He would have taken him to a doctor."

"You're right. They wouldn't have left him."

She felt sick. He meant on purpose.

Matthew started back the way they'd come. "My cell phone won't work this far from town. We'll have to use the lodge phone to call the police." He gave her a quick, grim smile. "Don't count Daniel out yet, Em. He knows a trick or two."

MATTHEW PUSHED Emily into the woods and went in after her. A black SUV and a Toyota Tercel were parked near the Accord, blocking the road. He would have spent more time being surprised by the Tercel, but two men with rifles were standing near it, scanning the countryside.

He crouched, motioning for Emily to do the same, then pointed, showing her they needed to move further off the path. Northwest, away from both roads. The trees grew close together, the underbrush waist-high and even more dense. Tough going, but good cover.

When they'd gained some breathing room he paused. "Okay?"

She nodded. She looked frightened, but she was doing fine. "Did you see Daniel?"

"No." They could keep six men Daniel's size out of sight in the back of the SUV. "They were using two-way radios. That means there are more of them, most likely within a couple of miles. They'll be watching the roads." He didn't want to take the time to get his map out. "North of here there's a river and a railway track. We'll head that way."

"They had guns, Matthew."

She was taking things in one observation at a time, and not quite putting them together. He kicked himself for agreeing to Daniel's plan in the first place, then for letting Emily come north, above all for not taking these very dangerous people seriously enough.

Some distance away, he saw movement through the trees. They'd started searching.

There was a ridge ahead. "We'll go over that hill." He smiled, trying to encourage her. "As quick and as quiet as you can."

They worked their way through underbrush and poison ivy, ducking under branches, stepping over deadfall. Halfway up the incline Matthew stopped behind a screen of pine boughs and checked the way they'd come. He saw the same sort of movement as before, a flash of something solid between the trees.

Was the movement purposeful? He looked for signs of anyone coming up the side, moving to surround them. Nothing. The only sounds he heard were natural ones. Aspen leaves hissed in the breeze. Far away a crow made a racket. And he heard water.

He signaled to Emily to stay low. At the highest point they stopped again, keeping trees between them and the searchers.

The river was below. Fast-moving, with islands dotted through it. A path ran beside it. Must be part of a hiking trail.

Emily whispered in his ear. "The path? We could run."

Sideways, half sliding between trees, they made for the bottom of the hill. He pulled her into the underbrush, out of sight.

The two men appeared at the top. They saw the path and the river and started down.

"Em? In a minute their view of the water will be blocked." Bits of debris moved with the current. "Can you swim?"

She nodded.

"See how the sticks go around to the side of that island? That's what we'll do, Emily. We go in, we go under and we let the current take us."

She looked at the water doubtfully.

"Ease in, no splashing. Just sink and let it take you."

She headed for the bank. White spruce grew at the water's edge, giving them cover to the last moment.

Two steps and it was over their heads.

THE WATER WAS COLD. The first few inches were warm but deeper down, it was icy. She had to force herself not to fight the current. It bumped her against rocks, pushed her against a buildup of sticks and logs. She walked her hands along the submerged branches, pulling herself closer to the island.

A second current caught her. The cold, the force, nearly shocked her into breathing. She couldn't hold her breath, she couldn't, not for another second—

Matthew was in front of her, pointing up. They rose together, breaking the surface, trying not to make a sound as they filled their lungs with air. They swam for the edge of the island they'd rounded, and this time let the current deposit them against the bank. They were tucked beneath a rock outcropping, bobbing in the water. He pulled her close. She shivered against him, gradually warming.

His mouth next to her ear, he said, "Sound travels across water. We'll talk later."

They waited. His legs kept tangling with hers, his arms helped her stay afloat. She felt every breath he took. She didn't know how she could be so aware of his body right now, how she could need him when Daniel was hurt and someone wanted to hurt them, too.

Ten or twenty minutes passed. Matthew let go of her and worked his way to the corner of the island. He examined the riverbank and the side of the hill, then came back to her.

"I don't see them. We'll go across to the other shore." He gestured with his head. "There, where the rocks jut out."

It was a short swim and the rocks gave them cover when they scrambled out of the water. She couldn't wait to get into the woods. When they were deep in the bush, far from paths and people, where she was sure bears and lynx must live, they stopped and sank to the ground to rest.

"Okay," she said. "What happened? These people have Daniel? That one car, wasn't that—?"

He nodded. "The honeymoon couple. I checked them out. They're not known to the police."

"Why guns, why come after us? We're only looking for Daniel."

"We're bothering them."

"Bothering!"

"We're in their way and they don't need us."

She was still frightened, but angry, too. "Okay, well, they're kind of bothering me. So what do I do about that?"

He smiled. "You sit tight."

"Great." She started wringing water from her hems and sleeves. "Do you have a gun?"

"Sorry."

"But you're an investigator."

He made an apologetic face. "It doesn't usually involve so much running and plunging into icy rapids. Usually it's more about checking into criminal records."

She wasn't sure she believed him. He was too comfortable with all this for it to be unfamiliar. She leaned to the side and twisted the ends of her hair, letting water drip on the ground. "You think these people have been looking for the gold too, and they attacked Daniel? To stop him finding it?"

"They may be hoping he can help them find it."

"So they need him."

"I hope so."

She could see he was afraid for his uncle, but more than that, he was focused and determined. She found comfort in that.

As far as he could tell no one had followed them across the river. The two men must have gone down the hiking path instead, or given up and returned to the SUV. If these were Easton's people they had a reputation for being ruthless, but only if it paid them to be. There was no percentage in a long search through acres of bush. Stuck out here he and Emily would be seen as a minimal problem, easily managed by keeping guards on the transportation routes.

Uncomfortable in wet shoes and clothes that only

dried where the sun touched, they walked until midafternoon, then stopped for lunch. Most of what he'd carried in the knapsack was soaked, either temporarily
unusable or ruined. They sipped bottled juice, conserv-
ing it, and shared one of two sandwiches kept dry in a
plastic container with a tight-fitting lid.

Close to dusk, they came across a worn-down cabin.

"What do you think about this as a home for the
night?"

"Think there's porridge waiting on the table?"

He smiled. If they tried to put in a few more miles
before dark they risked not finding other shelter, and
Emily looked ready to drop. Plenty of blackflies had
ignored the repellent they kept reapplying and from
her limp he guessed the wet shoes were giving her
blisters.

He unhooked the latch and pushed the door open.
There was one room, with a rusted potbellied stove, a
table and chair and a wooden platform that must have
been the base of a single bed.

"It's not too bad," Emily said.

"No dustier than my apartment."

"More spidery, I'll bet. No cupboard, bare or otherwise."

Hours ago they'd eaten a chocolate bar that hadn't
fared too badly in the water. He poured all the juice they
had left into one bottle and put it on the table for her,
then returned the empty one to his pack.

"I'll see what I can find."

"You're not leaving? We still have some food,
don't we?"

"A sandwich and trail mix. Enough if we get back to town early tomorrow. See what you can do with the place while I'm gone, Em—"

"Do with it?" She sounded half amused, half annoyed.

"Sure. Kill the mice—"

"Right."

"Stuff leaves or something in the cracks between the boards. We don't want too many mosquitoes sleeping with us."

She looked doubtfully at the darkening woods. "Okay. Maybe I'll get us a bearskin for the night, too."

"Now you're talking."

A few steps into the trees and he couldn't see her anymore. He'd noticed an elevated area to the north. If the height meant Precambrian granite there was a good chance of finding a snack.

Soon he was climbing rocks, rounded, sharp, cracked and flaking, smoothly weathered and dotted with low-growing blueberry plants. Slipping on lichens and listening for bears, he reached the top and looked out over the woods. He could see the river and the top of another hill, scarred Shield rocks, and far away, narrow as a rope, a road.

Nothing moved. No trouble for them and no help for Daniel.

HE WAS BACK almost before she had time to worry, with the juice bottle full of water and his shirt pockets stuffed with blueberries. They sat side-by-side on the platform sharing the berries and the last sandwich. When the food was gone he held out the bottle of water.

"Are you sure it's okay to drink?" she asked.

"It tastes great."

"But is it safe?"

"People with guns chased us into the woods today. You're worried about the water?"

Her schoolteacher tone surfaced for the first time in days. "Those are two different kinds of problems."

"And dehydration's a third kind."

She still hesitated.

"It's supposed to be very clean. The peat moss around here filters the water."

Emily finally accepted the bottle. After a careful, testing sip she took a long, grateful drink, then settled back against the wall.

"Can I ask you something?"

"Of course."

"Maybe it doesn't matter now, but it's been on my mind. I keep wondering…if everything was a lie."

"Emily—"

"I mean, was it all a cover, like the license plates? How much of who you seemed to be was true? Because I liked who you seemed to be."

Matthew didn't answer right away. He pulled his feet up on the bench and leaned his elbows on his knees. "My reason for being in Three Creeks was a lie. I tried not to add to that. I tried to keep you out of it. Not hard enough, obviously. Daniel will be furious." He stopped, as if he had forgotten that Daniel might not be anything anymore, and added gruffly, "He told me to look out for you. So you wouldn't get hurt."

"I don't think that was possible."

"When he called me I was in the Bahamas. I'd fol-lowed someone there. A young mother traveling with a five-year-old. Pretty and kind, great with the kid. I heard giggles all the time. They were having fun."

Emily could feel his tension. The story bothered him.

"She had one of those big straw purses that people take to the beach. In it she had sunscreen, jelly beans, crayons and a box of pose-able plastic toys. And in the box of toys she happened to have a set of stolen ivo-ries—tiny, intricate carvings that disappeared from a private collection in Toronto. So you see, it's not all scary men with guns. Sometimes it's pleasant people doing bad things."

Emily gave his arm a pat, and he put a hand over hers.

"I'm trying to explain that I can't go around trusting people just because they don't look mean. It was dif-ferent with you. I was sure of you from the first. I tried not to be because it meant I was doing a poor job. But I hated lying to you."

"You had good reasons. I've had a bit of experience with that lately."

"Can you understand the job I took on? Forgive it?"

"Yes."

He gave a short, disbelieving laugh. "Just like that?"

"That's how it works. Otherwise you'd have to call it something else. Grudge-holding, maybe."

She pushed away from the platform. It wasn't that she needed to get away from him. She needed to move, see the sky, remind herself they weren't rabbits chased by hounds into some hole in the ground.

"What if they're waiting outside, Matthew?"

"They wouldn't bother waiting."

"So if they haven't jumped on us, they're not going to?"

"That's what I figure."

The air was getting cool, but they couldn't risk a fire. A new stab of fear for Daniel gouged at her. He didn't have a Matthew with him, or a safe place to hide.

"Can we reach the lodge tomorrow?" she asked.

"I think so. Depends if our feet hold up."

Then they'd still have to notify the police, organize a search. It could be days before they found him.

When the moon came up, it somehow made things simple. There it was, always, day or night, whether they could see it or not. Lives came and went, centuries, good people and bad, and there it was. She could believe they were alone in the world, that the woods held no danger, that the logs of the cabin walls cut a hole in the universe just for them.

She touched the top button of her shirt and held it, then with slow deliberation slipped it out of the button-hole. Five more, and she slid the shirt down her arms.

"Em?"

She turned to face him. She answered by reaching behind her back and finding the clasp of her bra. He stayed in the shadows while she removed it, then her slacks and finally her underpants, the hopeful pink lace no one ever saw.

"Em." He moved into the middle of the room where the moon's light was strongest.

Shame, regret, hope and fear. She let them all go. How could it hurt if for one night there was nothing but her body and his?

SHE REACHED FOR HIM again during the night and a third time near dawn. It must have been the cabin, the cabin's personality, because when they left it soon after sunrise her confidence seemed to leave her, too.

"Are we pretending nothing happened, Emily?"

"If you don't mind."

It had been too soon—making love. Whatever was between them, it wasn't built on solid ground.

They walked in silence. They had to go southeast to get back to the lodge. Surrounded by towering trees he couldn't get a sight line—no horizon, no landmark. In case the people who'd come after them were close enough to notice he didn't want to climb another hill in broad daylight. All he could do was keep the sun in front of them in the morning and behind them in the afternoon.

He let his mind go blank, only busy keeping an eye out for trouble. After a while, with all that room to spare, a memory popped in. *He never comes south this early...* The waitress pouring coffee when they met with Ross McNabb had said that. He'd hardly paid attention to the time. He'd been too busy planning how to part McNabb from incriminating information about his father.

Never comes south this early. Never was pretty definite.

Smoke from a chimney on a cabin that should be empty. What were the chances? He stopped and pulled out the map. By the lake, the man teasing the waitress had said. A lake near town. That narrowed it down to about twenty. He checked the list of symbols on the side of the map. If any of the lakes, small and close to town, were also in sight of a fire tower...

He needed the municipal map for that. He opened it and right away saw his own handwriting. The section, township and range coordinates of Jock McNabb's property in 1979.

Okay. Back up. Smoke from a chimney. That's all the man in the coffee shop knew for sure. He'd seen smoke. The rest of what he'd said was noise to bug the waitress. Forget a cabin by a lake. McNabb's place wasn't beside a lake and it wasn't near town, but a couple of miles away, there was a tower.

He stuck the map inside his shirt for easy access and started walking.

"Matthew? Haven't we veered a bit north?"

"Change of plan."

"Is the lodge still in the plan?"

"We're taking a detour." He glanced behind him. She looked tired and strained. "It shouldn't be much further. Do you need a rest?"

She pulled herself straighter. "I'm fine."

Two hours later they stopped at the edge of a clearing. If this was the right cabin there was no smoke coming from the chimney now. Matthew stood waiting, watching for movement.

He turned to Emily. "It looks quiet, but if I don't come out in ten minutes you'll need to keep going on your own."

"Matthew—"

He had to make it very clear. She couldn't refuse to

leave this time. "Go southeast. Keep the water on your right. If you come across roads, stay off them. Don't approach anyone. Just get to a phone. Call the RCMP, and that's it, Emily. You're done. Agreed?"

She nodded. "But you'll be careful?"

"Always."

A window faced them. Keeping behind a narrow rim of trees he circled to the back of the cabin. As he'd hoped, the north wall was solid, unbroken by a door or window. He crossed the open ground quickly, then made his way to the cabin's east side. Again, one window. Single-pane glass. No voices or sounds of activity came through it. One more look at the surrounding woods, then he swept around to the front and tried the door. It opened.

He pushed it wider. A bare wood floor…shelves holding tins and dishes, a freestanding counter. Woodstove. Finally, the door was open all the way. A table and two chairs stood in the middle of the room and a folding cot covered by a plaid blanket was pushed against the east wall. Nobody was home.

He stepped inside and closed the door. There was a coffeepot on the stove. Cold, but there were used grounds in the filter. Still damp. No closet, no bathroom.

He went still, listening. Had he heard a noise?

There it was again. A sort of thud. Muted. At first he thought the sound was outside, but then he heard it a third time. It came from under the bed.

He lifted the cot—nothing. He pushed it out of the way and got to his knees, feeling the joins between the floorboards. One was loose, the nails removed. He pulled, and it came up easily.

Something was wedged under the floor. Cloth. When he pulled the next board, anger flooded through him. Legs. One by one, faster, the boards came up. Chest and shoulders. The last boards and then a sack from the man's head and a rag from his mouth. Daniel. God. There were bruises and dried blood, but his eyes were open.

He made a rough, throat-clearing sound. "Hey, Matt."

His hands and feet were fastened with twist ties. Matthew cut through them with a couple of passes of the knife he got from his backpack. "Can you move? Can you sit up?"

"Sure." Daniel flexed his fingers, then stretched his arms. "In a minute." He managed to bend his knees, but when he tried to sit up, he flinched.

"What hurts?"

"I think it was the boot in my ribs."

"All right, easy does it. Can you get your arm around my neck?" With most of his uncle's weight on his shoulders, Matthew slowly straightened, raising him to his feet.

"Daniel?" Emily stood in the doorway.

"You brought her?"

"She doesn't listen."

"He didn't bring me. I came." She stared at the hole in the floor, the relief on her face mixing with horror. "Oh, Daniel."

"All's well, sweetheart."

"Your eye—"

"How about if we get out of here? I don't want you

around when those weasels come back." He glanced at Matthew. "They're always a little testy at the end of the day."

IT WAS SLOW GOING. Emily didn't feel tired anymore and her bites didn't bother her. How could anyone treat an old man so badly?

Daniel needed to lean on Matthew, but he got stronger as they went. He said it always helped to have a little circulation to the feet. Every time he said something like that, something offhand, low-key, her eyes moistened and the path ahead blurred.

They kept to the trees near the river so they could look for abandoned canoes or rowboats. It wasn't unheard of for adventuring cottagers to forget one. Just unlikely. They got a scare when a motorboat went by, once with its throttle open and another time at trolling speed.

They rested often, but never for long. Each time he caught his breath Daniel told them bits of the story, then stopped to save his energy for the next quarter mile.

He knew where Frank Carruthers had gone after the plane went down. He told them that right away. Since Easton's thugs had taken him he'd managed to string them along—

Matthew interrupted. "Easton? You know that for sure?"

"They talked openly about it. Right in front of me."

Emily knew what that meant—at least she knew what it meant in movies. Her anger grew. So did her confidence that her father had nothing to do with the disappearance of the gold. Prairie farmers didn't mix with sadistic people who hurt old men. "Who's Easton?"

"Gerald Easton," Matthew said. "He's had years in the business and he's never been caught. Not so much as a speeding ticket or an overdue library book. But we know he's head of a theft ring that deals mostly in gems." He turned back to Daniel. "Your contact finally sent the photo. Carruthers and Easton leaving a restaurant. There was no date given. It's still not a speeding ticket, but it's a connection."

Daniel continued his story. On his way to meet Matthew he'd stopped to look for Jock McNabb's old cabin. Might have been a mistake, because he'd ended up with a monster of an SUV on his tail. It tried to ram him, run him into the ditch. Poor old Cutlass hadn't worked so hard in a long time. He took off, found himself on some little mountain-biking path of a road, all rocks and uphill…well, they caught up with him there.

For the next few days he'd followed the example of the *Arabian Nights,* he said with a smile, feeding his captors pieces of a theory he'd abandoned earlier in his search for the gold, making them believe he was coming up with the ideas day by day, and sending them to look for clues he had already discounted himself. He told Emily he'd pretended to be a weak old man incapable of resistance. "Maybe they didn't buy it, though, since they kept me tied to a chair when they were around and stowed under the floor when they went out."

Another engine came near. A floatplane this time.

"Single engine turbo-prop," Daniel said.

Matthew went to the edge of the trees to get a better look. "Frontier. It's one of Jamieson's. What do you think?"

Daniel began to shrug, then grimaced and stopped. "Wave him down." He gave Emily an encouraging half smile. "If it turns out he's one of them, Emily can overpower him."

At the moment, she almost thought she could.

CHAPTER SEVENTEEN

JAMIESON FLEW THEM to Flin Flon, passing over the rough terrain that had swallowed them up for the past two days. He told them Doreen Wells had come to his dock that morning, concerned that three of her lodge guests had disappeared within days of each other. She'd sent one of her sons out on the hiking trails and the other in a boat. Neither of them had found a trace of Daniel or his nephew and friend. So Jamieson had taken to the air. Their thanks soon had him frowning and silent, and after Emily's grateful hug when they landed, he taxied back down the runway as if he couldn't escape quickly enough.

Daniel refused a doctor's offer of a hospital bed and gave the RCMP a detailed statement before taking a couple of painkillers and stretching out in his hotel room, holding an ice pack over his eye and cheekbone.

Showered and fed, Matthew and Emily sat with him. They all agreed to take a break from discussing the gold and anything connected to it. Instead, Emily told Daniel about the wedding. That led to Daniel's absence, Matthew's arrival in Three Creeks and jumped from there to Jason Willis.

"So, what is he?" Emily asked. "A misguided kid mixed up in a prank or a misguided kid mixed up with some really dangerous people? Is he safe?"

Matthew answered her last question first. "If he keeps his mouth shut he'll be fine. A misguided kid, sure. With no record, so no alarm bells going off if he was caught."

"But they couldn't have sent him to look for gold."

"Maybe they did. Or information."

"About?"

"Safe-deposit boxes. Bank accounts."

"Why all the other break-ins? Uncle Will's place is just down the road so I can see them sending Jason there accidentally—"

"Or intentionally," Matthew said. "He's a relative, a next-door neighbor by rural standards. He could have agreed to hang onto some gold for your dad."

Emily let that pass. "For this long?"

"It's not easy to unload stolen gold if you don't have the right contacts. The other break-and-enters, along the creek road and near Pine Point, puzzled me more. I checked if anyone in those houses was associated with your father or Carruthers. Most of them knew your dad—through farming, the Legion, curling, hockey—but so did everyone else in the area."

"Was their research that bad, then?"

"Smokescreen," Daniel suggested.

"Could be," Matthew said. "If so, it was risky and in-efficient. A lot of time and energy expended to make it look as if the search they really cared about was part of a wider pattern."

"It just made us get better locks."

Daniel moved the ice pack to a bruise on his shoulder. "The kid could have been a decoy."

"To distract me from the real investigation?" Matthew nodded. "Or he could have been a catalyst."

"Bit of a blunt instrument as a catalyst," Daniel said, "but they were in a hurry. I like it, Matt. Produce a thief and see who runs where. Old Will trundles out to make sure his supply of ingots is still down the well. Julia digs up the roses—"

"Daniel!" None of this made sense to Emily. It was horrible to think of the honeymoon couple sending Jason into houses and waiting to see what happened. "You mean they were there that night? Watching? These people of Easton's were watching my house?"

"Now, now," Daniel said. "That was a while ago, wasn't it? Water under the bridge. First you bring her on a job, Matt, then you scare the poor girl."

"Mom's alone—" Emily headed to the door.

Matthew followed. "You can't get to your mom right now. It's the middle of the night, we don't have transportation. Anyway, I've got someone keeping an eye on her."

"You didn't tell me you had another partner, nephew."

"Signed one up on the spot. Alex Blake."

"Alex?" Emily exclaimed. How many more people were going to be put at risk because of the gold? "I wish you hadn't involved him. Susannah is weeks from having a baby—"

"He jumped at the chance." Matthew looked at Daniel. "Did I tell you about Blake? It came up when I got a criminal record check done—"

"On Alex?" Emily said indignantly.

"He works with the RCMP and Interpol to track down fossil poachers. No training, but they say you'd never know it."

A few summers ago Alex had helped catch poachers who hit a fossil bed Susannah discovered, but no one had told Emily it was a regular thing. She was beginning to wonder if she really knew anybody.

MATTHEW HADN'T SPOKEN to Emily alone since he went to search the cabin where he found Daniel. He tried calling her room and got a busy signal. Checking in at home, he supposed. He waited ten minutes, then went down the hall and knocked on her door. As soon as he saw her he knew he didn't want to leave her alone for the night.

"Hey." She looked pale, subdued. "Come in. I was just thinking this room was too big for one."

"Did you reach your mother?"

"She's fine. Alex says not to worry."

"Think you can manage it?"

She smiled, just barely. "Nope."

"You're exhausted."

"Hands up anybody who isn't."

One after another, things he could say popped into his mind. He discarded all of them. *Sorry I lied. Sorry I tricked you. Sorry I think your father was a thief. Sorry I didn't put up a big fight last night when I knew very well it was circumstances that brought us together.*

"You look so worried, Matthew. It's all right, all of it. Really."

"You're being kind."

"No. I—" She stopped. He had decided that was all she was going to say when she added, "I love you." Then she closed her eyes and began to cry. Silently, tears streaming.

He loved her, too. At least he thought he did. With guilt and sympathy on his side and fear and anger and loneliness on hers, how could either of them be sure? But the first thing you did when you thought you loved someone was try not to hurt them.

So he held her, hoping to give comfort. She reached to kiss him. "Shh," he said, against her lips. They were wet with tears. He didn't have a hanky, so he tried to dry them with his hand. "You need sleep, Em."

"I need you."

His body reacted predictably. Rain or shine, that was one thing you could depend on. He could feel tension and fatigue in her body. Red, raised bites were all over her. By the corner of her eye, on her scalp where her hair parted, on the soft skin above her collarbone. He kissed each one and looked for more, telling himself he would stop in a minute and tuck her into bed to sleep.

So many bites. A big, sore-looking welt on her shoulder and a whole row on the back of her neck. When he kissed those he heard a quick intake of breath, then a faint throaty sound that made it hard to remember what he was supposed to be doing. Nurturing. Comforting. But he kept remembering how she'd felt last night, soft and warm and welcoming.

She turned in his arms, hands under his shirt, pulling at him, under his waistband, tugging his belt, fingers on his skin, a hesitant touch of her tongue, teeth light on his chin. She kept surprising him, gentle Emily.

SHE SLEPT, her head on his shoulder. His arm began to get pins and needles but he didn't move. Finally she woke, sleepily scratching the bites on her neck before she noticed him. She smiled. "Nice to see you."

"Nice to see you, too. Unfortunately—"

"No, hush, we're not having anything unfortunate."

"Unfortunately," he repeated, "I think I should go back to my room. If Daniel needs anything that's where he'll call."

"Not yet. Soon." She rolled onto him, grasping the sheet on either side to anchor herself. "Think you can escape?"

He made several halfhearted attempts to rise, pounding the mattress the way frustrated wrestlers pound the mat.

"You got me."

"Good."

THE NEXT MORNING Daniel claimed to feel as good as new. Maybe he did—the investigation was finally rolling. RCMP detachments from Cranberry-Portage, Flin Flon and Snow Lake were all involved, preparing to check the Cutlass and the trapper's cabin for evidence left behind, and to search the bush and canvass every lodge, motel and campground for miles around for anyone fitting the kidnappers' descriptions.

He asked Matthew to coordinate with the police

while he had breakfast with Emily. To save time, he wanted to use a helicopter to retrace the path he'd taken since coming north.

He shook out the paper napkin and put it over his lap. "Matt says you were about ready to call in a search party for me a couple of weeks ago." He smiled. "Before there was even any trouble."

Emily wasn't going to accept that fussing label now, if that's the way he was thinking. Not after all that had happened. "You disappeared without a word."

"What do you mean, without a word? I left a note with Liz and Jack's gift."

"You did?" What kind of note? she wanted to ask. One about a sick aunt, or one that said her father had been implicated in a major crime? "It must have got lost in the shuffle."

Daniel pushed his coffee mug over to her. "How about a refill? Go ahead, Em. You must have questions."

"They can wait."

"They're popping out of you, like penny firecrackers. All these silent little explosions. But I can tell."

Emily looked into her tea, amused and embarrassed. It was exactly how she felt, sitting here with him. But how could she, after all he'd been through?

"Why do you think I sent Matt on an errand? I'm not the kind of man who idles over a room-service breakfast."

She smiled at his tone. "Grandma said the Rutherfords are always good in a pinch."

"That was nice of her."

"And it's true."

"And that's nice of you. She's nice and you're nice and I'm good in a pinch. Now that we've got that all straightened out, go ahead. Let me have it."

She took a breath, and slowly exhaled. Some tension left her body, making her more aware of sadness. "You knew my father."

"Yes, I did."

"Before, I mean. Before he moved to Three Creeks."

"I knew him really well. And I liked him, Emily."

Her stomach went tight. "Anyway" was implied. Daniel had liked her father anyway. Even though. In spite of everything.

He shifted his position and winced. "Your dad came to us when he was still a kid. Late fifties, '58, I think. He'd got into a situation he didn't like and he wanted to do something about it."

"Us?"

"His local police station first. He got bounced around from there to an RCMP detachment and finally to Frank and me. We were in Special Branch at the time—mostly involved with counterespionage—but we had a case that overlapped with Criminal Intelligence. So we met with your dad and the three of us were a good fit."

Emily let all that settle in her mind for a minute. "What kind of situation was he in?"

"What do you know about him, Emily?"

"Not much. I found a letter that mentioned boys taking the wrong path. Coming to a bad end, it said."

"Where'd you see that?"

"Mom had it in a file labeled, Graham's Death."

Daniel winced again, sympathetically this time.

"Must have been from a teacher or a social worker. Your dad was one of those kids you hear about, growing up in one foster home after another."

"My dad?" she repeated. "Where was his family?"

"Frank and I looked. We never found his parents. An aunt took care of him the first few years, died of cancer, and there wasn't anybody else. So he got into the system."

"How old was he?"

"Five, the first place they sent him. Mad as hell, according to the report I read. The family wouldn't keep him."

Keep him. "They couldn't manage a five-year-old?"

"Apparently not."

"A frightened five-year-old."

"He wouldn't settle down. Over the years the social workers kept moving him. Pretty soon he was looking to other kids for a family. Children do that. They start following each other's example, trying for approval, looking for a place to belong."

"He got into trouble?"

"He and his friends found their way to the edge of a crime family operating in their neighborhood in Montreal." Daniel looked at her, apparently wanting to see how she was before he went on. "The kids started doing little favors, nothing much, delivering an envelope, taking a message, making a little money in the process. It seems harmless at first."

"Like Jason."

"Maybe." Daniel drank some coffee. "When Graham and his friends started to get in deeper, he saw what was going on. He tried to persuade the others to back out of it with him. They weren't having any of that. They thought they had a good thing going. Steady money, steady meals, a sense of purpose. I've seen it over and over. Kids who felt like nothing start to feel important. So, as I said, your dad came to us."

Daniel stopped. When he spoke again he sounded less sure of himself. "And we told him to stay where he was."

Emily stared at him.

"We told him the best way he could help his friends or himself was to help us. Work with us."

"You said he was a kid!"

"Nineteen, maybe. I don't remember exactly. Look, Emily, Graham grew up fast. He was tough. He wanted to do the right thing."

She wished she was tough. Then maybe she wouldn't be trying not to cry all the time. "So what happened?"

"He became what we called a long-term source. He worked with them, kept us informed, we went after the guys at the top. Thanks to your dad, several shipments of heroin didn't hit the streets, a couple of murders didn't happen, an off-shore shell bank got closed down."

"He was good at it?"

"Very good."

What a dark world he'd lived in. It must have taken courage to go to the police. It would have been a last resort. Maybe he thought they would arrest him, but was willing to risk it. Maybe he thought they'd protect him.

"That went on for fourteen years. Then Frank and I retired. We didn't want to leave Graham hanging there. By then we were friends. I told him I was going to check out this little town where I grew up, a place so far off the map no one would ever look for him. So he came with me and he met your mom and that's that."

"Did they look for him? Is that what happened?"

Daniel shook his head. "I can't say for sure. I don't think so. His cover was never blown."

"Matthew thinks he helped Frank take the gold."

"Don't be angry with Matt. He thinks that's what happened because I told him it did."

"But you said my father wanted to do the right thing. Why would he turn around and break the law?"

"It happens. Guys like him live with it so long they can go either way."

She wouldn't cry again. It was ridiculous. Absolutely no more. She drank some tea and waited until she thought her voice would be steady. "What about Frank? He was like you. Why would he become what he fought against?"

Daniel shrugged. "He liked a challenge. He had the contacts to do it."

"So did you."

"He had access."

"You're not saying that's all that separated you and Frank? That he had access to the gold?"

"I think he felt unappreciated. A little bitter, maybe. All the dots connect, sweetheart, with both of them." He smiled sadly. "I don't like it, either."

DANIEL YELLED over the roar of the engines and the whir of the propeller, but Emily could hardly hear him.

"Look down there!"

She had been looking, ever since the RCMP helicopter had taken off so dizzyingly from the Flin Flon airport. Trees, water, rock. Bare and beautiful and wild.

He jabbed a pointing finger at the ground. An eddy of soil began to form, a miniature whirlwind over stone.

Matthew shouted, "I see it!"

The pilot, an RCMP constable introduced only as George, nodded. Then, through parted branches, Emily saw it, too. The cockpit and wings of a small plane.

"You see?" Daniel bellowed. "He didn't crash. He rammed it up and into the trees."

"Why is it still sitting there?" It was found weeks ago. Daniel didn't hear the question so Emily leaned closer to him and called louder. "Are you going to move it?" Where, she wasn't sure, but she felt an urge to tidy up and show some sort of respect.

"Too expensive from way out here. No need."

He gestured to George. The helicopter rose and turned, going southeast. The forest that started by the lakeshore went on for miles.

"This is it," Daniel called. "The winter road."

All they could see in summer was a wide gap in the trees, long and straight. Where bush gave way to muskeg, Emily thought she could still see a road-sized impression where the ground had been packed down. Had her father really driven one of those cat trains way out here, in danger from frostbite and breaking ice?

Muskeg became pockets of water connected by streams, streams widened into a river, the river emptied into another lake where seagulls dipped to the water and flapped away. Then the helicopter was over woods again, and that same broad strip of cut trees. They followed it until Daniel tapped the pilot's shoulder, motioning to him to land.

"Now look, Daniel," George said, when the engines were quiet, "you've got to be careful about getting ahead of the evidence."

Daniel, gritting his teeth and bracing one arm against his ribs as he got to the ground, didn't answer.

"Our crash investigators noticed the same things you did," George went on. "It's true the damage to the plane isn't consistent with an impact from any height, but the storm could have forced him down. Maybe he was trying to take off again and didn't have room. Who knows?"

Daniel acknowledged all that with a brief nod. He looked at Matthew and Emily. "It's a little walk in."

He didn't say what *it* might be, and no one asked. The ground was spongy underfoot, wet in places. It reminded Emily of the marshy field at home.

"Here we are."

They were standing in front of a ramshackle caboose. There was a small window on one end, a door on the other, more windows on one side. The rest was weathered plywood.

"You think this is where he came?" Matthew asked.

"For a while. They ran these things at the end of cat trains, a place for the men to sleep and eat. The winter road passes by fifty feet from here. Guess somebody dropped the caboose one year and left it. A company that went out of business, maybe."

Moving stiffly, Daniel led them up rotted plank steps

onto a porch in the same condition, and then inside. Under their weight the floor creaked. The whole structure tilted as if it had hit a bump in the road. Matthew reached for Emily.

"Don't worry," Daniel said. "This thing has a few hours of life in it yet. I slept here a couple of nights."

It was like a little house. There was a wood-burning stove, a table, and several bunks. The mattresses were still in place, but full of holes. Some creatures or other had been helping themselves to the stuffing.

Daniel pointed to a duffel bag lying under a ground-level cot. "That's Frank's."

"You're kidding," Matthew said. "After all this time?"

"Shelter's a matter of life and death out here. You leave a port in the storm as you find it."

George peered inside the bag, moving items as he identified them. "Hatchet. First-aid kit. Tarp. Fishing net and snare wire. A paperback, an aerosol can." He read the label on the can. "Ether."

"An anesthetic?" Matthew asked.

"It's for starting engines in cold weather," Emily said. "I've seen my uncle use it."

"How do we know all this belonged to Carruthers?"

"It's typical survival gear," Daniel said. "Except for the ether. Look, the orange tarp is still there. If Frank had wanted to be found he would've spread it over the wreckage."

George zipped up the bag. "These things could belong to anybody. Or someone could have taken them from the Beaver."

"This is one of the pieces. They all fit together."

"You got more pieces?" George said. "Feel free to share."

Daniel eased himself onto the bench beside the table, one arm pressed against his ribs. "Take a look around, see what you can figure out. I'll give you a hint. Go right to the end of the field before you start. West."

"If you know something just tell me. I don't have time for games."

"I do," Emily said, "if it'll get me out of this creaky place." Couldn't he see Daniel needed rest?

She left the caboose, and Matthew and George followed. The three of them started walking.

"What is it your uncle thinks we'll see?" George asked Matthew. "Gold? Or the mansion Carruthers built with it?"

"Give him a break."

"It's all instinct or wishful thinking or something. He doesn't have evidence. Not real evidence."

"He knows the people involved, understands their motivation. After twenty-six years that might be the best we can do."

When they reached the end of the field Emily looked into the bush ahead of her, then turned and looked back at the caboose. Trees, grasses, rocks. More trees, more grasses, more rocks. She slapped her neck. And more blackflies.

George grumbled, "I know he's your uncle and he was a fine cop in his day, but this is really pissing me off."

"There." Matthew pointed to the other side of the field. "Maybe twenty feet south of the caboose, going east—do you see that swath of trees that's shorter than the rest?"

George and Emily looked.

"Kind of curving," George said.

Matthew nodded. "We've got a twelve-foot band of twenty-year-old trees in the middle of a hundred-year-old forest."

George smiled. "An old winter road. Turning off the main branch. Wonder where it goes?"

"I'll bet my uncle can tell us."

They took to the air again. The line of young trees wound deeper into the bush until it met the Grey Lake mining road, grown in, too. They flew over the lake, deep and clear, and landed near an abandoned town on the other side.

"We're going to visit Frank's house," Daniel said, leading them along a dirt path.

George muttered, "Here we go again."

"There used to be gold mines here. The last one closed near the start of the Second World War. I'm told some people stuck around for twenty years after that."

Above them, a huge bird soared. A bald eagle, Emily realized, with a sense of wonder. A wall of rock rose beside them, split into pillars that looked constructed, more like a neolithic ruin than a chunk of Precambrian shield worn down by nature.

They passed buildings with roofs and walls fallen in, tattered shacks, furniture and tools sitting as if someone had just put them down, except the furniture was falling to pieces and the tools were rusted. Emily almost expected to hear voices, doors opening and closing, bells on bicycles, but there was only the sound of water lapping against the shore and the buzzing of bees.

"This one," Daniel said, walking faster toward one particular wreck of a cabin. Inside was mostly dirt and moss, and grass coming through the floor. Smiling, he held his hand out to what Emily thought was a potbellied stove.

"Well," Matthew said. "Would you look at that. A forge."

GEORGE POINTED OUT there was no conclusive evidence that Frank Carruthers had anything to do with the forge. Yes, it could be used to resmelt gold bars before smuggling them out of the country for resale to people who wouldn't look too closely at things like refiner's stamps. But an old forge wasn't a surprise in what used to be a mining town.

"And that's why he chose the location," Daniel said.

"That's why you *think* he chose it."

"Granted. I appreciate your skepticism, George. Keeps me on my toes." They each picked a boulder to sit on and Daniel opened a bag of sandwiches to pass around. "Puzzle piece one—an experienced pilot disappears without trace in spite of having a radio he can use to call for help. Two, he's carrying triple the number of gold bars as usual."

Matthew interrupted. "And he's been heard to say he might fly off with his cargo one day."

"Three," Daniel went on, "when the Beaver was found the level of damage wasn't consistent with a crash. Four, he's not in the wreck. Neither's the gold and neither's his survival gear. Five, a winter road passes not too far from the so-called crash site and not too far from a cat train caboose."

George started to nod. "And survival gear's found in the caboose. *And* at the end of another winter road is an abandoned cabin with a forge."

With an apologetic glance at Emily, Daniel said, "I've lost track of how many puzzle pieces that is, but let's call this one six. A cat train driver is gone from his crew and his route for a few days before and after the aircraft disappears."

Emily couldn't sit listening. She paced away from the boulders, clutching her sandwich half. Daniel's thirst to solve this thing seemed stronger than his feelings for his two old friends. Or for her.

She heard Matthew say, "Do I give this a number? Seven? McNabb and Carruthers were friends. McNabb's son remembers them talking, making beer-soaked plans. Money-making schemes. Carruthers told Jock he'd get him a snowmobile one day. He was prone to talking big like that, but Ross remembers going for rides at the dealers'. So it went past talk."

"You're thinking it was a real shopping trip?"

"They buy the snowmobile, Jock keeps it at his cabin until Frank needs it—"

The ether, Emily thought, for starting cold engines.

"—and when Frank is done with it he gives it to his friend, as agreed," Matthew continued. "So maybe Graham's out of it after all. Frank could have used a snow-mobile all the way from the airplane to this ghost town."

"He's not going to ride all those miles on a winter road on a snowmobile," Daniel said. "He'll be seen. Anyway, Ross told me the same story, but he said his dad never got the snowmobile."

"Read all about it," George said. "Crook goes back on word."

"Here's where the snowmobile comes in," Daniel said. "Frank uses it to get from the wreckage to the main winter road. A cat train picks him up there, along with the snowmobile, so he can stay out of sight. The cat train takes him as far as the caboose and leaves. After all, Frank doesn't want anyone to know exactly where he is while he's smelting. Not Jock, not Graham. This lit-tle forge? It's going to take a while. What if they're picked up and talk to the cops? So the snowmobile is important on the last leg of the trip."

Emily turned around. "Where is he, then? Some tropic isle, like my Uncle Will always thought?"

"That's the question," Matthew agreed. "Did he use the forge and ride out of here to sell his newly smelted gold?"

"I kind of hope so," Daniel said.

George looked at the sky. "Oh, brother. After all this?"

Matthew pulled out his map. The abandoned town at Grey Lake was accessible by plane, boat in the warmer months, snowmobile in winter. On every side of the lake were miles of bug- and bear-infested bush and muskeg. It was hard to get to, but if you could, it was a very good place to hide.

"In the middle of March, when Carruthers' plane went down—aren't winter roads nearly finished by then?"

"Unless it's been a really long, cold winter," George said.

"So the blizzards that delayed Frank's flight a couple of times would have made the roads last longer?"

"Could be the opposite. Too much snow can insulate the ice, soften it."

For the first time, Matthew began to feel sorry for Frank Carruthers. "And the Grass River runs through Grey Lake, doesn't it? The current would thin the ice even more. Take a heavy Bombardier snowmobile filled with nine hundred pounds of gold..."

Daniel muttered something under his breath.

"What's that?" George asked.

"Impulsive. Frank. I always had to make him slow down and think."

THEY HAD CHOSEN two possible routes over the lake from the winter road on the opposite shore. One to the old town's main boat dock, the other ending near the cabin with the forge. For the past hour, George had been diving to check under the first route; Matthew the second. This wasn't a southern mud-bottom lake. It was as clear as drinking water. If Carruthers had gone through the ice they should have found something by now.

Matthew sat on a slab of granite to let the sun warm him. A breeze rustled the trees. Not enough to move the jack pines, but he could see the changing shade pattern on the water as the aspen and tamarack nodded.

He stared. One of the shadows didn't move. He stretched out on his stomach to look closer.

It wasn't a shadow. Could be a stone. Twenty feet down, maybe.

George was by the dock warming up, too. Matthew waved and pointed at the water in front of him. Pulling on his shoes, George called to Daniel and they both started over to him, going at Daniel's pace. Emily stayed where she was, stiff, arms protectively around her middle.

Matthew decided not to wait. First he did a surface dive to check for hidden rocks. The rock wall seemed to go straight all the way down. He climbed out and back up the hill. He took several deep breaths, held it, leapt.

He struck the water and went deep, pulling with his arms, getting closer to the thing that wasn't a shadow. His ears soon began to feel the pressure. He could feel the current where the river flowed, stronger than expected.

Not a rock, either. Something resting on a rock.

He touched it. Metal. Long, thin. A runner.

He reached the lake bed. Wood? Collapsed, covered with sand and something green. He tugged at a piece. It came apart like wet cardboard. Underneath he saw scattered rectangles, like a bunch of sandy shoe boxes. He rubbed silt from one. It gleamed.

His chest was bursting. He turned and began to reach upward. The water warmed, sunlight glistened. He broke the surface of the water and breathed.

THE NEXT DAY police divers started recovering what was left of Frank Carruthers and his haul of gold. Matthew and Daniel wanted to be there, so Emily went, too. She didn't stay near shore with the others—that clear a view of what the divers brought to the surface was more than she wanted. Glad of a breeze that kept bugs away, she walked back and forth on a path that had once connected the little town to the beach. She tried to influence whatever it was that had already happened by hoping, hoping as hard as she could, that the police would find something to erase their suspicion of her father.

Matthew left the group by the water and started along the path to join her. They'd had no time alone since the night in Flin Flon. The breeze had tangled her hair, and she found herself afraid that he would take one look and wonder why he'd ever wanted to be close to her. She pressed her hands on top of her head, holding her hair flat.

"How's the recovery going?"

"It's a bit grim. I think Daniel's saying some kind of goodbye." He took her hands and pulled them away from her head. "There! The natural look. Windswept."

"A while ago Martin told me I looked like Einstein. You know those posters that exaggerate that mane of his—"

"Martin's an idiot." Matthew checked his pocket. He found an elastic curled up in a pile of paper clips, matches and loose change. "That any use to you?"

"Thanks." She pulled her hair into a ponytail and twisted the elastic around and around.

"I have to admit I don't think of aging physicists when I look at your hair."

"No?"

"I think of it draping across your face while you

sleep. Hiding you from me. Until I brush it the other way, behind your ear and over the pillow. And there you are. My beautiful Emily."

She was too surprised to say anything.

"I found some gold." He held out a rough, dull stone and tilted it so that here and there metallic flecks caught the light. "Will you marry me, Emily?"

She ignored a pang and managed a small laugh. She didn't know if he meant it. "If it fits."

He put the stone in the palm of her hand and closed her fingers around it. "Perfect fit."

He did mean it.

"You'd like Ottawa. You can see the Peace Tower from my living room window. In winter, you can skate on the canal. And Stratford's not far."

"You know I can't."

"Your mother?"

"She can't go to Ottawa. Not at her age."

"With time, she'd adjust."

"She grew up in my grandmother's house and moved a mile down the road when she got married. That's her world. I can't make her unhappy, Matthew. She has so little." It was almost word for word what she'd said to John when she was eighteen.

"She's gone further than you have, Emily. And she has more. A child. A home of her own."

"I can't abandon her."

He touched her cheek. "That's one of the things I love about you. Too bad for me. But I think you're doing the right thing, staying in Three Creeks. Don't let anyone tell you you're not."

A throat-clearing sound came from behind him. "Sorry," Daniel said. "Didn't mean to intrude."

Matthew moved away from Emily. "That's all right. We were just talking."

"The divers seem to have found everything." Daniel looked at Emily so kindly it frightened her. "They can't account for one gold bar."

CHAPTER EIGHTEEN

IN SWAN RIVER she picked up her own car. The quiet was welcome. No plans, no theories, no male voices. She didn't want to think about anything more complicated than the speed limit.

But it was a three-hour drive. Matthew and Daniel and her father were in her mind the whole time. It would take a while to sort out what she'd learned about the three of them. Three very important men in her life and they were all like icebergs—mostly out of sight.

On the way from Snow Lake to Swan River she had asked Daniel and Matthew to explain why a man who had made such an effort to resist crime would suddenly embrace it when he had the most to lose. His wife and child, his home. His freedom would have been worth a lot to him right then.

"Yes, exactly," Daniel had said. "Graham had a lot that was worth protecting when he made his choice."

Wrong choice, Dad.

She didn't remember him as the conflicted person Daniel saw. She remembered him holding her hand, the two of them wearing black rubber boots with orange soles and orange trim at the top so they could wade in the marshy field in spring. When the snow first melted it was more than just marshy. It was a huge pond. He'd lifted her so she could see the flooded field from higher up.

"It's our Hudson Bay," he'd said, and later he had shown her a map of Canada, pointing out the big, round inland sea with James Bay reaching down from it. Their field really was shaped like that. So then she had started saying, "Let's go to Hudson Bay," and he had never said no. He had never said he was too busy.

That was the main thing she remembered about him now. It was actually quite a lot to remember. All those days and all those walks.

If he had worn his rubber boots the day he died, he wouldn't have died. If it had been wet or mushy, he would have wanted his boots. And it *was* wet because if it had been dry the ground wouldn't have conducted electricity from the downed hydro wire.

That had been going around and around in her head without progress. Progress was impossible if you couldn't let yourself think.

But turning down the Three Creeks road, she remembered something. Uncle Will saying that wearing boots on a wet day depended on what you wanted to do. And at last she thought she knew what her father had done that day.

THE DOG AND CAT were their usual selves—Hamish thumped his tail and the cat rubbed against her leg, maybe a little more emphatically than usual, as if it had missed her—but Emily's mother was different. She waited in the doorway.

"You're back."

"Hi, Mom." It was a relief to see her, safe and apparently content. "How are you doing?"

"Martin brought the check."

It was less than half what her cousins owed for rent, but enough to pay the hydro and phone bills and still have a bit left over. She smiled at her mother. "I believe I see an Egyptian book in your future."

Julia must have, too. The catalogs were out. She hovered near the table, clearly eager to turn her attention to them.

"John Ramsey's been and gone."

"I forgot all about him." Mrs. Marsh would rib her about avoiding him again.

"He came to see you. I told him you were traveling with a man. A tall man who knows how to build."

"Mom!"

"It was true."

"Well, thanks. I appreciate it."

Soon Julia was intent on her book order. Closing the door before the cat could follow, Emily went outside and through the back yard to the meadow. She kept going in the direction she had taken Matthew when she had showed him the big creek, but this time she turned north, to the marsh.

Going to the place where her father had died always felt uncomfortable. She hadn't been anywhere near the accident when it happened, so it wasn't bad memories. It wasn't even all that personal. It was more like the dread people felt passing one of those crosses on the side of the highway. The cross said an awful thing had happened right there, that someone had suffered in that spot, that someone else remembered them with pain.

A different sort of grass grew here, with sharp, thin blades and sharp, pointy tips. She passed the middle of the field, where the water sometimes splashed over the tops of her boots when she was small, and reached the edge. Willows grew here, scrubby, short ones that hid a maze of paths, some made by cattle or deer, some natural gaps.

She parted the branches and ducked under, picking up a few scratches until she found the first path. To follow it, she still had to walk bent over, taking care that twigs didn't poke her eyes. Chipping sparrows, dainty with little rust-colored caps, fluttered out of her way, disappearing deeper into the bush.

She came out the other side of the willows, and there was the oak. It looked different than her memory of it, the first climbing branch she couldn't reach when she was six, now so low.

She clasped her hands around it, swung her feet over, and pulled herself onto it as if it was a horse. Hands against the main trunk for balance, she stood, got one foot on the next branch, reached for hand holds, pulled again. It was so easy, not a challenge, not an adventure at all.

High on the main trunk, twelve feet up, was a fist-sized hole. When she was six she had pictured elves living there. Her father had agreed it was possible. More likely it was chipmunks or owls, he'd said.

Thinking of teeth, claws or sharp, curving beaks, she tried to look inside. She turned her face away and pounded on the trunk. Nothing burst out, or attacked, so she put her hand in the hollow and felt around in the dark, her hand jumping when it touched something that wasn't tree.

Plastic, like a bag. She tugged at it gently. Something hard inside plastic. Not heavy. She pulled it into the light.

A freezer bag secured with black electrical tape. The something hard was wrapped in cloth, part of a blue striped flannelette sheet.

She tucked the package into her waistband and climbed down before opening it. On firm ground, the tree at her back, she pulled off the tape, opened the bag and unwound the cloth.

It was a book, bound in green leather.

Dissertation sur la nature et la propagation du feu. Something about the nature of fire.

Gabrielle-Emilie le Tonnelier de Bretueil Du Châtelet.

She stared, disbelieving. Carefully, touching only the edge, she opened the cover.

Paris, 1744.

Oh, Dad. What did you do?

MATTHEW WAITED for her near the barn.

"Your mother said you went into the woods. Didn't get enough of it up north?"

"I didn't think she noticed."

"What are you hiding?"

"Not a gold brick."

He held out one hand. "May I see?"

"I think he did it."

"What changed your mind?"

"I don't want you to think I cry all the time." Her voice wobbled.

"I don't think that."

"It was the boots. Uncle Will said there was a storm. A hydro line was down. So why would my father walk in a marshy spot after heavy rain without boots? On the way home it hit me…this tree we used to climb. It had a small hollow way up off the ground. You can't climb a tree in rubber boots, right?"

"And you looked. What did you find?"

"I was afraid it would be gold. Or money from selling it."

"And instead?"

She held out the package. Matthew took it, testing its weight, then he unwrapped it as carefully as she had.

"1744? That's a first edition. A first edition of du Châtelet." He sniffed the pages. "No mildew. That's lucky. It's not the recommended way to store rare books." He looked at Emily. "I'm not sure I understand what this means. Your father bought the book for your mother but didn't give it to her? Or he took it from your mother's library and hid it in a tree…why?"

Emily shrugged. "Why not a safe-deposit box? Why not in the storehouse? Mom never goes out there. Did he think I wouldn't climb that tree again?"

"The police can get a warrant to search a safe-deposit box. They'd never find it in a single tree among all those trees. They would in the storehouse. So would I."

"I've been trying to figure out what to do." She usually made a point of keeping things calm for her mother. "I guess I'll give it to her."

Julia stroked the book, turning it over, from front to back to front to back. "I knew it was too much."

"What was too much, Mom?"

"He couldn't sleep. He said he was going to lose the land. It was different if *he* lost it. I gave him the book to sell. 1744. Du Châtelet's book about the nature of fire. I thought that should be worth a lot."

"You gave it to him to sell?"

"For three years every fall after harvest he took a payment to the bank. After three years he brought me the mortgage papers. All paid. He said he was sorry. He said he would never, never risk the land again."

"He pretty much had to," Emily said. "Nearly everybody took the same risk. Expanded, or sold and left."

"Come." Julia hurried from the kitchen and through the living room to the front bedroom. Emily followed, with Matthew close behind. "Not him."

"Yes, him." Matthew deserved to know what was going on. Beyond that, she wanted him near her.

Julia scowled, but then she opened one of the archives boxes. It was the one with the file about Graham's death. Handful by handful, she removed the folders. When the box was empty she dug her fingers down the sides and pulled out a hard piece of plastic. It looked as if it had been cut from another box and pressed over the bottom of this one.

She moved out of the way so Emily and Matthew

could see. There were more files inside, lying flat. They were all labeled. *Money*.

"Mom?"

Julia flipped one open.

Money.

Wads of bills, hundred-dollar bills, the old kind, shades of brown and green with a picture of Sir Robert Borden, no raised dots to help the blind, no shiny holographic square to outwit counterfeiters.

"Is it real?" Emily asked.

"He thought we should keep it here. For emergencies. For the farm." Julia looked toward Matthew, then away. "Will they arrest me?"

"No. For sure not. Did you know where Graham got the money?"

"I knew it was too much to get from selling my book. Then Daniel came and they argued. They stopped being friends. It was after the plane went down. I'm not stupid."

"They won't arrest you," Matthew repeated. He looked from Julia to Emily. "We may never find definitive proof that the money came from the sale of the missing gold brick. Will we agree to assume that it does, that the brick was Graham's payment for helping Frank?"

Both women nodded.

"I think Frank had arranged for Easton to handle the whole shipment. Then only one bar turned up."

Emily thought of Daniel's bruised face. "He must have felt like the gold was already his. No wonder he was so aggressive."

"Julia, you'll have to return what's left of the money," Matthew said. "It'll be minus the two hundred thousand Graham paid to the bank and minus whatever he paid to have the brick smuggled and sold. There'll be a lot to make up."

Julia held her book out to Emily, offering it.

"Keep it, Mom. After twenty-six years in a hollow tree, that book deserves its place on your shelf. I think Dad wanted you to have it back one day. After a perfect summer and a perfect fall when the crops were wonderful and prices were good. So you wouldn't be hurt by any of it."

THE AUGUST LONG WEEKEND, with the Fair that had seemed so far away, came and went, and Susannah and Alex left for Alberta. Aunt Edith couldn't believe it.

Emily sat beside her on the kitchen steps. "You thought Susannah would have the baby here?"

"Why not? They stayed this long. I tried to make it nice for them."

"You made it very nice."

"I don't want to be silly." Aunt Edith's mouth trembled. "I know it's wrong, but I want my children near me, and my grandchildren."

"It isn't wrong."

"Keeping on about it is."

Emily couldn't deny that.

Aunt Edith's voice cracked. "It isn't just the dinosaurs, I realize that. It isn't Alex's fault, either. Susannah simply doesn't want to stay close to home. I'd understand if she wanted city life, but she still lives in the country."

"Not everyone's a homebody."

"Like you. Your mother is so fortunate. It isn't even as if she was a good mother. She hardly raised you at all. The rest of us raised you! But here you are, the two of you, companions, part of each other's daily lives."

Edith broke off, staring at her niece. "Emily? Oh, dear. You're upset. It's your father, I suppose, and that business with the gold." She put an arm around Emily's shoulders and squeezed. "So he was a criminal. The main thing is, he saved the farm."

SOON AFTER, new bookshelves complete, Matthew was gone, too. The night before Emily needed to pull out a blanket for the first time since April. When she got up Daniel called to say Matthew had left for the airport.

He hadn't said goodbye. Well, he had in a way. He had hammered the last nail into the last bleached and painted board from the storehouse and said, "There you go," to Julia and "See you," to Emily.

She kept thinking of his last touch, that light, re-membering touch to her cheek when they stood near Grey Lake waiting for the divers. She knew she had touched things the same way. Irish crystal goblets that made rainbows on the wall, dolls that spoke, pink-and-white lady's slippers in a field. She touched them like that and then left them in their place. No. Not quite the same way. His touch had promised a whole life. And she had said no.

Emily closed her eyes and hunched over, arms around her middle, around the sudden jolting empty ache inside.

ON THE LAST DAY of August Emily leaned a birth announcement against the teapot on the top shelf of the hutch cupboard. "It's an unusual name. Cassiopeia."

Julia was bent over her brand-new copy of *Sinuhe,* her nose inches from the text as if it was in its original hieroglyphics and nearly impossible to decipher. "Cassiopeia is a constellation. Or a Greek heroine."

Susannah had always liked sky-watching, so the constellation was the most likely inspiration. "Maybe their second child will be called Big Dipper."

A huffing sound came from Julia. She was amused.

"I wish we'd thought of Cassiopeia for the cat before Susannah and Alex used it. Don't you think it would be a good cat name?"

"The cat has a name."

"It does? Since when?"

"Since it got here."

"And neither of you told me." Emily waited, but her mother had leaned closer to *Sinuhe* and didn't reply. "Is it a secret?" With an impatient sound, Julia picked up her book and left the room.

Emily looked at the cat. "Is your name Rapunzel?" It stared unblinkingly. She lifted it, gently tapping its paw to remind it not to embed its claws in her shirt, and carried it to the window so they could both see outside. "There's a yellowy tint to the poplars. Fall's coming."

When she'd taken a walk that morning she'd come across the first of the fringed gentians. They were a September flower. In a few days Liz and Jack would be home.

School would start and life would be exactly as it had always been.

Emily liked the beginning of the school year. New books, sharp pencils, children who were, however briefly, glad to be back. Then there would be a blur of harvest and Thanksgiving, Halloween and Christmas.

She loved all those holidays, but thinking about them, her mood sagged. The New Year would come next, with hopes and resolutions, and the whole thing would start all over again. Not looking forward to that was ungrateful. Wasn't it what everyone wanted? Year after year of good health and loving family and as little upheaval as possible.

AT LUNCH TIME on the first day of school she sat at her desk and closed her eyes, breathing in the quiet. Even when the grade ones swarmed all over talking in what they believed to be their indoor voices, Emily found the library peaceful. When she was alone, it felt almost like a church. Quiet, cool and holding something more than she could understand.

"Hi, Miss Robb!"

It was Stephen Cook, wearing what seemed to be his one and only shirt, an oversize Edmonton Oilers jersey.

"You grew this summer, Stephen! That shirt is going to fit you one day soon." She added, "You always call me Miss Robb. That's not my name, you know."

"I forgot."

"It's Moore."

"Oh, right." He looked at her leerily, as if she was a stranger. "I'm supposed to read a book."

"Already, on your first day? That's not fair."

Stephen smiled sheepishly. "About anything I want, the teacher said."

Hoping to expand his horizons a little from the steady diet of NHL biographies he had read the year before, Emily handed him an older book, *Scrubs on Skates* by Scott Young. Cautiously interested, he signed it out and disappeared down the hall.

The grade one class had been in the library just before lunch, always a wild time of day, between hunger and eagerness to get out to the playground. The books were a mess, *M*s shelved with *A*s and half of them upside down or spines toward the wall. She needed to clean things up before the grade twos came in at one-thirty and did the same thing. On her knees reshelving, Emily started to laugh. Give her some gray hair and she'd look exactly like her mother.

"Books are no laughing matter, Ms. Moore."

Emily sat back on her heels without turning around, *Little Tim and the Brave Sea Captain* on her lap.

"Such a mess," he said, his voice soft, and now right beside her ear. He reached past her to turn *The Runaway Pony* right-side up. "That's no way to treat a book."

This time she would say yes. If he asked. If he didn't, she would ask him. Her mother would understand what he meant to her. She'd try her best to adjust. They would help her.

Emily blinked to clear her vision. Matthew was holding something in front of her. She took the small, rectangular card and read the centered lines.

Rutherford Investigations
Insurance Fraud, Theft, Lost Articles Recovered
Three Creeks, Manitoba

"Matthew." He couldn't.

"I'd need to do a lot of traveling, but this would be my base. It's going to be a family business."

"Matthew—"

"How long have we known each other?"

"Not counting while you've been away?" He had arrived during the first week of July and left in the middle of August. "It's either a very long time, or five weeks."

He smiled. "With any reasonable definition of love I don't see how it can happen at first sight. But there sure can be something at first sight. There was a click. We clicked into place."

Emily nodded. Even the first week when so much of what he'd said was a lie, she had trusted him, and not, after all, because she was gullible. It was because she could. Hamish might not have thought so, but his joints were beginning to ache and his outlook on the world was increasingly grouchy. Poor old thing.

"So I think we belong together," he said. "We don't need to date and see how things go. We can spend the next fifty years learning all the interesting details."

She blinked back tears. Since they'd met, she had got tears in her eyes more often than during the whole rest of her life. "I'll go with you to Ottawa, though. I was going to tell you that."

He waved the business card. "It's all arranged. Daniel and I have done the paperwork, my apartment's sublet, my gear's in a moving truck right now, somewhere on the Trans-Canada."

"You were sure of yourself."

"I took a leap."

"You mean you evaluated the situation, did a risk analysis and then leapt?"

"Just leapt, Em."

"And all this has been going on in secret! I guess that's why Daniel's been winking at me every time I see him."

"He's been winking?"

"Actual, full-fledged winking."

She moved closer, much too close for two people in a school library. "Are you sure, Matthew? Can you really work from here?"

He brushed his lips over her forehead. "You want me to evaluate? All right. Here's the situation. Three Creeks has a bit of untouched forest here and there, it's got relatively unpolluted creeks with not particularly tasty fish, and it has this very beautiful, kind and brave woman—"

She leaned her head against him and muttered against his neck, "My grandmother? Yes, she's wonderful. I don't know if you should pull up roots for her, though."

Matthew laughed. "So, you'll marry me?"

"Absolutely. Anytime, anywhere. Richer, poorer. Sickness, health. Forsaking all others."

"You know the words."

"Well, I was just at a wedding a couple of months ago."

"You didn't mention the part about forever."

"Oh, of course forever."

He kissed her then, although the bell had rung, and the books were still out of place.

If you enjoyed what you just read,
then we've got an offer you can't resist!

Take 2 bestselling
love stories FREE!

Plus get a FREE surprise gift!

Clip this page and mail it to Harlequin Reader Service®

IN U.S.A.
3010 Walden Ave.
P.O. Box 1867
Buffalo, N.Y. 14240-1867

IN CANADA
P.O. Box 609
Fort Erie, Ontario
L2A 5X3

YES! Please send me 2 free Harlequin Superromance® novels and my free surprise gift. After receiving them, if I don't wish to receive anymore, I can return the shipping statement marked cancel. If I don't cancel, I will receive 6 brand-new novels every month, before they're available in stores. In the U.S.A., bill me at the bargain price of $4.69 plus 25¢ shipping and handling per book and applicable sales tax, if any*. In Canada, bill me at the bargain price of $5.24 plus 25¢ shipping and handling per book and applicable taxes**. That's the complete price, and a savings of at least 10% off the cover prices—what a great deal! I understand that accepting the 2 free books and gift places me under no obligation ever to buy any books. I can always return a shipment and cancel at any time. Even if I never buy another book from Harlequin, the 2 free books and gift are mine to keep forever.

135 HDN DZ7W
336 HDN DZ7X

Name	(PLEASE PRINT)
Address	Apt.#
City	State/Prov.	Zip/Postal Code

Not valid to current Harlequin Superromance® subscribers.

Want to try two free books from another series?
Call 1-800-873-8635 or visit www.morefreebooks.com.

* Terms and prices subject to change without notice. Sales tax applicable in N.Y.
** Canadian residents will be charged applicable provincial taxes and GST.
All orders subject to approval. Offer limited to one per household.
® are registered trademarks owned and used by the trademark owner and or its licensee.

SUP04R   ©2004 Harlequin Enterprises Limited

HARLEQUIN® *Super*ROMANCE®

**A powerful new story from a
RITA® Award-nominated author!**

A Year and a Day
by Inglath Cooper

**Harlequin Superromance #1310
On sale November 2005**

Audrey Colby's life is the envy of most. She's
married to a handsome, successful man, she
has a sweet little boy and they live in a lovely
home in an affluent neighborhood. But
everything is not always as it seems. Only
Nicholas Wakefiled has seen the danger
Audrey's in. Instead of helping, though,
he complicates things even more....

Available wherever Harlequin books are sold.

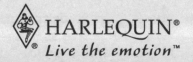

HARLEQUIN®
Live the emotion™

HARLEQUIN *Super*ROMANCE®

Critically acclaimed author

Tara Taylor Quinn

brings you

The Promise of Christmas

Harlequin Superromance #1309
On sale November 2005

In this deeply emotional story, a woman
unexpectedly becomes the guardian of her
brother's child. Shortly before Christmas,
Leslie Sanderson finds herself coping with
grief, with lingering and fearful memories and
with unforseen motherhood. She also
rediscovers a man from her past who could
help her move toward the promise
of a new future....

Available wherever Harlequin books are sold.

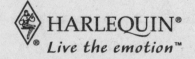

HARLEQUIN®
Live the emotion™